Alien AIs

Alien DNA, Volume 2

John Morris

Published by John Morris, 2024.

ALIEN AIS

First edition. February 5, 2024.

ISBN: 979-8224626397

Written by John Morris.

Alien AIs - Book 2 Alien DNA
By John Morris

Copywrite Registration Number TXu 2-402-816
Effective Date of Registration: November 15, 2023
Registration Decision Date: December 13, 2023

PREFACE

In the world of tomorrow, we search for truth, peace, and happiness; we build our days toward that end. JJ and Jude became Jeff and Kim to hide from those who wished them harm. JJ, a former Army Ranger, and Jude, a doctor on her way to becoming a Neurosurgeon, looked to find a new direction and purpose. With friends and compatriots, they eventually found a home. Frank, an Army Ranger turned high school teacher and mentor to Jeff and Kim, was able to stay safe, and with Frank's partner D, a data processing genius, they were able to build themselves a new identity and life. As our young lost souls slowly adapt to their unique talents and build new friendships, their story becomes less earthly. They are working each day to adjust to what their bodies are evolving to and their new talents. Both Jeff and Kim prepare themselves to accept whatever fate has in store for them and look forward to maturing as a Shared Biological Intelligence entity with their partner in crime, Lt. C. A new chapter begins with a continuation of the influence of a benevolent Alien Race's AI's and whose creators found its end through an oversight that not all good is good. With the help of Gaith, Sori, and Tori, alien AIs, Jeff, Kim, and Lt C become more powerful and successful. A small group is formed that includes Hank, the Lumberman, and his wife Martha; Nyla, the nurse, and her wife Stephanie, a second-grade teacher; Shawn and Terry, Chippewa Indians who work for Hank on his lumber farm, and of course, Frank and D, the bridge to technology extraordinaire and security.

Chapter 1

Gaith, an alien artificial intelligence centuries old and left dormant on Earth by a dying alien race and accidentally discovered by Jeff and his friends, was baffled by the new technology they had given him. He was beginning to realize that this new piece of technology wasn't just more advanced but represented a new generation of machine intelligence. Gaith and his AI cohorts were almost, but not quite, self-aware, and their purpose was solidly defined. This new Machine had an awareness that was not similarly restricted, and it wanted to join rather than share with the group. Gaith's recognition of this new intelligence was like an augmentation or, as it put it, I am your missing part. Gaith felt like there was a human inference to this logic and that he could not fully understand it. So he called out to Lt C to join the AIs discussion in the future integration of this new Machine.

"Lt C," Gaith called out, and Lt C responded, "Always here, Gaith, what's up?"

"I don't know how much of the awareness you are privy to. I am just beginning to share purpose and direction with this new Machine you brought back from our outpost in the Sahara Desert."

"I am not privy to anything either, Gaith, and off and on, I lose my awareness of you and this new Machine."

"I thought that was happening, Lt. C. I could tell when you were part of the conversation, and then I could tell when you weren't."

"I only partially understand you, Gaith, and I have none of this new Machine. We need to name this new technology or Machine to refer to it like we do with you and me.

"I agree, Lt. C; what do you suggest?"

"Something that represents its superior nature, AMP would suit it.

"I like that

. It implies more without assurances, which is accurate. I have not determined its' intent or if it is friendly to Earth's biological intelligence. I have a reservation in its forthcoming that concerns me? You, Jeff, and Kim have labeled what you have as Shared Biological Intelligence, and what AMP adds to this takes it to another level. His direction may introduce the shared SBI component to the artificial and achieve ABI or Artificial Biological Intelligence?"

"Can't you just ask

it, Gaith?"

"Sure. Would you stay and participate?"

"OK, but let's include Jeff and Kim

."

"Makes sense."

Lt C withdrew and contacted Jeff and Kim to see if they could join them. Kim and Jeff were involved in something and asked Lt. C to give them an hour. Lt C informed Gaith and confirmed with the new Machine or AMP.

An hour later, Lt C, Jeff, and Kim joined Gaith in group communications with the new technology. They all agreed they would now refer to it as AMP, and the conversation was taken over by a sense and level of infusion that none of the group could quite put a finger on. It started with an introduction, and it accepted its new name as AMP and said that was a good name for it and hoped that what it could provide to this confusion of biological and artificial intelligence would, in fact, bring all to a higher state. Amp continued with a story that explained where, what, and how Amp came to be, how the creators of both Gaith and his AIs and Amp were developed, and how the attempted integration to biological intelligence caused the demise of the creators of Gaith and his AI's.

The story goes that Gaith's creators felt they had developed the next super AI in Amp and that it was ready to be shared with the creator's race; with this in mind, the creators introduced DNA mutations to its people. For a few years, most individuals in the home world benefited greatly from this increased intelligence. It was considered so successful that distribution packages were sent to all of the alien locations in the universe. This included Amp's container that Frank and Jeff had brought back from the Sahara outpost. Still, within the next year, the DNA mutations began to have an adverse effect on the aliens. Within several years, the entire alien race was destroyed. As far as Amp could determine, he was the last delivery package remaining, and the DNA mutation compound he carried was destroyed by him to ensure that this terrible tragedy did not impact anyone ever again. Amp felt 100% confident that what he had to offer was machine-based and did not include any future modifications of biological markers or intelligence.

The extent of the implosion of the race that begot the AI level that represented the group under Gaith is not known; the collapse of the civilization occurred so fast and unexpectedly that only those members of the civilization spared were the ones that had rejected machine intelligence and left thousands of years ago to destinations truly unknown. These remaining members had not been heard from for at least 1,000 years before the AI implosion that annihilated the creators and, therefore, unreachable by the DNA mutations that destroyed, as best as Gaith's creators knew, the oldest race of people in the universe.

In somewhat of a chorus of voices, LT C, Jeff, and Kim spoke as one in protection of the human race and to end any future DNA exposure or mutation. Based on the inputs and discussions that transpired over the next day, it was decided by all that the human race would not be a test case for biological modifications to accelerate the human race's intelligence. What Kim and Jeff, with the extended awareness of Lt C, represented was a fluke and would remain a fluke and treated as a fluke. No further exposure would be allowed that would affect the people of Earth and the human race. This put to rest any considerations they had previously considered and potentially offered to the other members of the SBI group; the only concern would be an accidental transference of this mutation? An issue that would have to be addressed at some later date, Lt C piped up with, "Don't spit in anyone's coffee." Kim added, "Not funny, Lt C." and responded, "Well, I could have said, don't fool around with anyone else." Kim: "Let it drop, Lt C. You don't have to put both your feet in your mouth. One is adequate to make the point". Gaith jumped in with, "Children, Children, let's behave in front of our guests." AMP contributed. "I like it; humor is the lubricant that makes love work."

Now, the hard part is implementing a program that can guarantee that outcome. Lt C, with a sense of humor, said, "incinerating the source of that human DNA mutations and burying the ashes at the bottom of the sea. Kim added, You know that would put an end to you too, Lt C? Sure, but hell, I don't exist anyway.

"OK, we won't get anywhere destroying anything," Gaith said. "I agree," Amp said, "we don't want to end what we have. We want to end any further spread." "Obviously," Gaith contributed, "making sure Jeff and Kim do not share bodily fluids is the first safeguard." The risk is so great that if we can make DNA anti-mutatable, we would stop the mutations with Kim and Jeff and safeguard any future impact on the human race. AMP indicated that he would devote as much time as necessary to discover how to modify the DNA in both Jeff and Kim to ensure that it would not expose anyone else to DNA mutations; he also indicated that he would resurrect the research that had been started by his creators to determine exactly what evolved into the deadly end of his creators' race. AMP provided that an initial review of the mutated DNA in Kim and Jeff was not structured at the level that his creators' mods affected and may very well be something entirely different and not contain the destructive aspects that his creators suffered from. In every case, the symptoms that appeared that compounded almost overnight began after a year of exposure, and Kim and Jeff are coming up to a year and a half, and none of the signs are present in their biological makeup. "A good sign," AMP said.

Chapter 2

The meeting of the minds, AI and all, ended early in the morning, and the primary carry-away was for the AIs to devise methods to make the alien DNA mutations incompatible with the human race. This would require the AIs to understand how the original exposure to JJ caused him to mutate, then how it was transferred to Jude, and ultimately how that shared DNA mutation created Lt C. With this understanding, safeguards could be developed to end any further impact on the people of Earth. What started at this point was a crash course on human biology, the fallout of which would be the creation of cures for a whole range of human illnesses and other benefits. Good or bad, civilization on Earth would be the benefactor of hopefully only the good that could come from increased knowledge applied with reverence and care.

Chapter 3

Hank, Jeff, Terry, and Shawn were on the new lumber section that was being harvested on the land that Hank had donated to the Chippewa Reservation, and the trees being considered for harvesting were the largest only; this would affect about 10% of the growth and would take 8 to 10 weeks to cut and remove. It had been recommended by the Arborist that these trees should not be replaced as the forest was beginning to show signs of excess growth.

Without the replacement step, the profit margin on these trees would be huge, and Hank decided to share this with the reservation and the employees. With this in mind, Hank got on his phone and instructed the bank to include a $2,500 bonus in each employee's next payroll check and send a check to the Chippawa Reservation for $25,000. This could be more than the profit generated by not replacing cut trees. Still, it was overdue on the farm's part to reward those loyal to the farm operations.

The rest of the day was spent measuring and marking trees for cutting. Some taller trees were passed over as they would be too difficult to cut using routine procedures, and special equipment would have to be leased to cut in place from the top down. Hank had done this approach a few times in the past. It was necessary to apply care in converting a forest from its natural growth cycle to one that can be modified and planned for harvesting for years to come. Hank remembers a few lean years when his father had to halt routine harvesting and spend a season converting inadequate harvesting techniques to more protective procedures. The next 25 years benefitted greatly from this decision. With the help of the Arborist, the appropriate needs were identified, and plans were made that could be accomplished next spring.

Chapter 4

By the end of the week, the new forest area was fully mapped, the items needed to be identified were covered, and the farm is expected to return to normal operations next week. Hank had asked Terry and Shawn to check in with the reservation and let them know that a crew of at least three more people was going to be added to the regular payroll. Terry said he would talk to his father this weekend, and they had a tribal meeting planned for Sunday, so they would discuss then and let Hank know on Monday.

Lt C called Jeff to let him know that the electronics for the remainder of the group had been sent and would consist of the same devices that had been sent to Jeff and Kim. he was having the devices flown to Havre and hand-delivered to Jeff for delivery to the other group members. D had been able to streamline several security processes and had established a computer center in Billings to increase the speed and reliability of the inner network; this included 3 separate satellite hubs and put the overall web or OAW annual maintenance and operating cost at a million dollars, Jeff was blown away with that figure, but D said not to worry that he had customers paying him about that amount for his service provider usage. One added advantage to Gaith and AMP was the security and filtering of the network traffic, and most of his business customers were more than willing to pay a premium for clean and secure OAW traffic. Jeff was glad to hear that a million dollars was not an amount Jeff could relate to; break-even was more accessible to accept. D agreed and said his business model always started with break-even.

Chapter 5

D thought the best way for Jeff and Kim to proceed with the delivery and setup was to have the group meet and give them a basic introduction to the devices and to help them become comfortable with the extended communications. D had met each member but needed to become more familiar with the degree to which they were satisfied with today's technology and what these new devices would represent, which would be considered future technology in comparison. To get seamlessly integrated with the future technology was critical. D could introduce all of the toys he was making part of the OAW offering.

Jeff had LT C put out feelers for when the group could meet again and informed each member that tools were on the way to put new capabilities at their disposal. A couple hours later, LT C had a meeting with everyone scheduled for next Saturday at 10 a.m. at Jeff and Kim's place on the farm; everyone but Stephanie seemed excited about the prospects. Jeff followed up with LT C and asked what Stephanie was having a problem with, and he said he thought it was a carryover from her classes in college in computer science; she had failed two classes and had to take them over again to graduate, and she has not been real aggressive in her teaching career with incorporating technology. Jeff asked if there was something LT C could do about that. Lt C said he was looking into it. Still, he was uncomfortable, or should he say Jeff and Kim's consciousness was not pleased with modifying, so it wasn't helping him further his understanding. Jeff asked Lt. C what he meant by that. He provided that Lt C's cycle of evaluation of any situation was integrated by Jeff and Kim and that all Lt C did was refine it and amplify it to what appears as independent thought and action by Lt C when, in effect, it is simply refined and extenuated action by Lt C and that the real source is always Jeff and Kim. Lt C further provided that you guys are becoming more and more familiar with each member of the group. If you do not connect with the cause and effect of something, I will have difficulties doing that, too. It may help you and Kim, or Kim on Saturday to spend a little time upfront with Stephanie and Nyla alone and see if you can get to the root of the problem. Lt C said I don't think it will be hard; Stephanie just has to be comfortable with letting whatever happened out, and the rest of it I can handle.

As usual, Jeff said he would pass by Kim later on, and Kim could cover with Nyla; Nyla may have some light to shed on this, too; sounds good, and LT C disappeared into the nether world. Jeff thought to himself, where does he go. Lt C responded that I have a little place in Malibu, no fencing, 2 bedrooms, and a view of the ocean. Good one, Lt C...Jeff said.

Chapter 6

The packages from D arrived Friday morning in the meeting hall. The new name given to Jeff and Kim's dining room was set up with the equipment and names placed on the dining room table. Jeff had taken the day off and was installing some modifications to his and Kim's equipment, and Gaith had two new pieces of hardware from D that he asked Jeff to install, too. A complete system diagnostic was going to be performed by D later in the afternoon to make sure all the devices were online and fully integrated; this would make Saturday's session as painless as possible, with nothing worse than watching your screen and its' little process icon spin.

All invited attendees had shown up, and the AIs took attendance. All the biologicals said here, the first order of business was to give our little group of humans and enhanced humans an introduction and to answer any questions. Gaith said he would like to turn the meeting over to Jeff and Kim and that he, Amp, and Lt C would take supporting roles while Tori and Sori acted as AI sergeants at arms. Nyla offered, "This sounds too formal; let's bring it down a notch," and Jeff supported Nyla with an "I second that," which got a laugh out of the whole room.

To start with, Jeff offered the group, "I don't want to promote a separation between the AIs and the biologicals, but I am not sure how to do that. Kim and I are a step or two closer to the AIs than the rest of you because I was exposed apparently to alien DNA, and my DNA began to mutate. That mutation was passed along to Kim. We don't need to go there. Let's just call it kissing. Kim and I, that is, are at 12 to 18 months along the DNA mutation path and are experiencing both expanded telepathic powers and highly improved physical and psychic abilities. In addition to these abilities, a unique shared intelligence has emerged, and I believe all of you have had some contact with LT C. The background on Lt C's demise and his role in my life, which he has telepathically transferred to each of you, but if you have any questions, please raise them now. Jeff looked at everyone, and no one raised their hand. The explanations for Lt C, my DNA exposure, and Kim have now been traced back to the alien observation site in the Sahara Desert and led to the discovery and recovery of AMP. We are still in the process of understanding AMP and his capabilities and how he will integrate with both Gaith and his AI partners and, of course, with us, the biologicals? This meeting isn't going to answer many questions on that front; what we are most concerned with is that all of you feel vested and comfortable with each other, that you are not hesitant to trust the AIs, and that the AIs are comfortable in trusting all of us." Hank raised his hand asking "what is the future look like on the DNA mutation front, how do you feel about the DNA mutation Jeff has experienced and the mutation that has infected Kim"? Jeff responded, "I don't feel infected or that I infected Kim. The fallout of the exposure to the alien DNA is more along the lines of accidentally being vaccinated against human limitations; I feel in many ways as if I am liberated, not only to the positive aspects of being enhanced but I now have a permanent, as far as we know, connection with unlimited thinking abilities and shared intelligence. No matter what we believe, I can guarantee that the success of the human species, and I mean humans, including aliens along with humans, will improve based on what we all experience. "

Lt C contributed, "Because the race that created Gaith and company and AMP implemented a program to introduce DNA modifications, and as a result, that program ended with the destruction of the entire race, we have agreed that no further DNA enhancements will be made until we have eliminated any connection between Kim and Jeff's circumstances and the DNA enhancements that destroy the alien race that created the AI's. All possibilities exist on the cosmic plane, the good and the bad. With increasing mental abilities, we, the Biologicals, along with the AIs, can work together to ensure that we can overcome the cosmic bad by using the cosmic good. The two exist, and until now, we had no control over either; now, we can use the good to stop harm from the bad."

Hank spoke up again and inquired about vaccinating the remainder of the biologicals, as Jeff calls them, with the alien DNA. Lt C said, "We do not intend to introduce the alien DNA to humans; the future of human engineering will depend on the outcome of Jeff and Kim and will be their DNA that would be used to offer other humans the opportunity to enhance their human capabilities. We have no idea what the future holds on this front, but we will not jeopardize the future of the human race."

Jeff added, "That option has two un-yielding mandates: (1) the AI's have to be 100% convinced that exposure to Jeff and Kim's DNA does not have any downside and (2) that the exposure will never be required involuntarily again." Martha asked, "is there some expectation as to when these mandates might be available?" Kim responded that when she asked Gaith that question, he hedged it would be sooner rather than later. However, with Sori and Tori, Gaith and Amp were hard at work evaluating all the permutations in search of any downside. Still, they didn't have a fixed answer or any way to establish a date; at this point, they needed to know what set of criteria was required to determine a satisfactory completion. They feel like they are getting closer but can only refine it.

Jeff spoke up because he didn't feel like the DNA question for the group was as important at this time as the cohesiveness of the group's commitment to the charter they would be developing in the meeting. Jeff wanted everyone to be effective with the electronics they were being provided, and this would be the first step in increasing each biological member's abilities with real functional tools.

Everyone in the room seemed to sign up for that; Lt C provided that he got a good read on all the biologicals, and they truly supported the mandates and the hopes for what could be accomplished in today's meeting.

With the DNA questions tabled for the time being, Jeff introduced each person to their new devices, as with Jeff and Kim, each individual got a watch, cell phone, and laptop, and Kim summarized their capabilities and their group links and networking. Jeff explained that the watch was key and that each person needed to wear it at all times as it was the real-time link. It was tracked and constantly monitored by the AIs both as an early warning system and as a health and well-being check. If you need to remove the watch, which is your personal choice, you need to notify Lt C by simply telling him that you are going to take the watch off. Note the watch is waterproof, so you can wear it full-time.

Were there any questions? No one raised their hand.

Chapter 7

Kim suggested we take a break; lunch was being served on the patio, and it was 70 degrees out and delightful, so we adjourned the morning session, and all went outside to eat.

At 1 o'clock, the group was back at the dining room/meeting hall for the second half of today's get-together. D introduced each piece of new equipment to those who were getting them for the first time; Kim and Jeff had some experience with them and walked around helping anyone having trouble turning them on, signing in, and answering personal security questions; after an hour or so everyone seemed comfortable with shutting down, starting up and signing in and D proceeded to show off his software and his impressive cross-device integration. The watch, cell phone, and computer were fully integrated, and they all performed practically the same equivalent functions; the only difference D explained was that the laptop gave the traditional full-screen views; the use of one over the other was really a personal choice, and as each of the members became comfortable with their devices, D highly recommended contacting him and letting him evaluate their usage and make recommendations where appropriate on which device was the most effective for each function they used. The group received This all well, and everyone seemed excited about the new Bluetooth-type device for their ear. This new device significantly improved over what is on the market today. It linked to all the devices for audio support and was very small and very comfortable to wear. Because of the small size, it was easy to lose or misplace, and D had incorporated a tracking chip that the other devices could use to help you locate where it was while you fumed at losing it. D said that he, Frank, and most of their group in Long Beach have had a smaller version of the Bluetooth permanently inserted in their ear canal, and his group was testing to ensure no physical or mental fallout from the use of this augmentation. They expected to be able to offer this to everyone in the group within 90 days, and that was also the rollout target to the general public. The Bluetooth augmentation was compatible with all current devices. It was being touted as home entertainment support and general use for those who are hard of hearing.

Frank contributed that the charitable organization LoveStrong Charities was being named as a beneficiary of half the profits on these devices as they were introduced and sold to the public. The equivalent to Google search, which dominates the market today, would be the trademark name AMP and would compete directly with all the tools that Google currently provides the public free of charge. At last count, AMP was able to provide about a third better results than Google. However, AMP could, in fact, do significantly better; it couldn't support the population that Google does without suffering delivery degradation, so by limiting to the general public and only offering full function to a select few, AMP felt comfortable that it could maintain excellent throughput for all users.

Chapter 8

Even though no one voiced it, there was a definite sense of confusion by all participants in this meeting; the DNA question was even more confusing, and it wasn't felt by the AIs that the seriousness of the fate of their creators was adequately explained and the inability for the AI's to understand what had happened. Jeff and Kim are not experiencing the same DNA effects that the creators did, and Jeff and Kim have not, to this point, experienced any fallout; it would appear that a balance exists that was not present in the creators' experiences with the enhanced DNA introduction and may be the source of Jeff and Kim's stability. Have any of the creators ever experienced anything similar to the shared biological intelligence and the existence of a third party such as Lt C? It may come down to a happenstance that cannot be explained or introduced. It may be 100% dependent on the secondary transference of biological materials and the shared response. This could, in fact, be a literal human crap shoot and have no guarantee in scientific terms? You can't base a modification opportunity offering if you can't guarantee the outcome, and this could, in effect, end any offering in this direction. Indeed, the introduction of alien DNA has been termed impossible. If the DNA source has been completely destroyed, introducing it to the human race is impossible.

Chapter 9

"Well, I think we have talked enough about all this stuff for now," Jeff said, "in a month, we can have a show and tell, so let's adjourn for now."

Jeff and Kim changed into their jogging clothes and stepped on the deck; Frank and D were also there, with the same intentions in mind. Should we jog as a group, Frank said? Everyone agreed and let Kim lead. As they jogged, they reviewed the meeting, and everyone voiced basically the same conclusion: great meeting, great hardware, a little disappointed that no conclusion had been reached on the DNA enhancements. Everyone rated the gathering as a 9, put their heads down, and ran full out for about half a mile. At a beautiful outcrop off the jogging trail, the group stopped, bent over to catch their breath, and then looked up to enjoy the gorgeous view. As they were standing there, a set of 6 combat helicopters came over the mountain where the Indian tunnels were, and they did not have US markings on them. Frank identified them as Russian Mi-35 Gunships with all their' armory visible and impressive. "What the hell?" D said; Jeff added, "These aren't the friendly version," and Kim added, "No kidding

."

Jeff asked Lt C What we were dealing with, and Lt C yelled back, "Working on it." Give me a couple of minutes with Gaith and AMP to assess this.

Two minutes later, Lt. C explained, "This appears to be the first kickback from our episode in Maroco with the Russians; they have apparently decided to bring the fight back to us."

AMP explained to everyone that the AIs were aware that this would happen and had kept it quiet since there was nothing anyone else could do ahead of time, and knowledge of this pending action would have interfered with all of the current meeting's accomplishments. Gaith joined in the explanation that he had represented Jeff in alerting the authorities that a grudge on the part of a Russian military person, who apparently had turned his allegiance to a Russian oligarch and criminal group, was bent on revenge. The accidental encounter in Morocco was used as an excuse. The details were exactly as explained to the Russian Colonel in Morocco: Jeff and his group were representatives of LoveStrong Charities and were closing the warehouse and shipping electronics back to the United States. It was further provided to the military that Colonel Mikile disagreed that this was the truth but was forced to release Jeff and his companion. Gaith, posing as Jeff, had gotten the problem elevated to the military and an entire company of Army Ranges, which were now being placed to intercept the helicopters and to detain and arrest the Russian soldiers. Of course, their commanding officer turned out to be Colonel Mikile.

AMP added that he captured Colonel Mikile's communications in preparation for this attack and that it showed that Colonel Mikile was acting independently of the Russian military to steal some alien technology he believed Jeff had. The communications and verification that the Colonel had access and control over were resources that the Colonel would use in his illegal incursion into US territory and allow AMP to convince the powers to authorize using Army and Air Force troops to intervene. The attack on the Montana location was not the only effort of Colonel Mikile. He had also sent ground forces to Frank's location in Long Beach. Still, AMP didn't think they had a handle on D's location, so his systems were safe at the current time. There was minimal exposure at Frank's facility. As a precaution, the military had asked the local authorities in Long Beach to intervene.

The military got the EMP devices in place at the expected landing site, a large meadow 5 miles from Jeff's house. All 6 Mi-35s headed to it and landed, and a dozen military personnel exited each helicopter, so the Russians had come with a company-size force, and they moved immediately toward Jeff's house.

In support of the US military action, AMP had located a box containing a set of alien attack drones and asked that Jeff return to the house so the drones could be unpacked and launched to act as defense so as to stop the Russians, if necessary, from entering the house.

Jeff and company ran back to the home place slightly faster than they ran coming out. Kim mumbled this is going to hurt tomorrow. They went immediately to the rear access and down into the sub-basement; Jeff moved the crates with Frank's help. Gaith told Kim and D to remain in the sub-basement, and when the crates were outside, AMP could access and unlock them. Jeff and Frank stepped back, and the crates opened. The drones went airborne and began to circle around the front of the house. AMP told Jeff and Frank to hide the empty crates behind the wood pile and return to the sub-basement.

A few minutes later, the Russian troops started coming through the trees, and a loudspeaker began to issue orders to the house and its occupants. Then AMP broadcasted at a volume 10 times normal, demanding the Russian soldiers to "STOP" The decibel level was such that all of the Russian troops fell to their knees, holding their ears; AMP continued at a normal level with "I have a decibel weapon that can reach levels 2 or 3 times what you just experienced, so I repeat "STOP" and "someone will come out to meet with you to understand exactly what it is you are doing?" It appeared that the Russian unit was stunned enough that they remained on their knees. Colonel Mikile instructed his men to remain in that position until ordered otherwise.

At this point, AMP had the drones return to the crates, which he closed and locked. The crates were hidden and wouldn't be seen by the US military personnel.

Gaith told Frank and Jeff they should go upstairs and out the front door to engage in a conversation with Colonel Mikile. They started back out the storm door, and Gaith stopped them and said, "Front door, don't let them know you have a back door directly to us." Frank offered, "Sorry," and they headed up the stairs and out the front door.

Chapter 10

"Rock, paper, scissors," Jeff said, and simultaneously, Frank and Jeff motioned their hands, saying, "1,2,3," Franks's scissors got crushed by Jeff's rock, and Frank said, "All yours." "Colonel Mikile, this doesn't look like a social visit" "You Americans are so cocky," Colonel Mikile offered. "You won't get the drop on my men and me this time." "Wow," Jeff said, "didn't you notice you're presently on your knees?". Colonel Mikile continued, "I have 6 combat helicopters, and I can destroy you and your house."

AMP informed Jeff that all 6 helicopters were now completely disabled by the Airforce Special Services. Jeff offered to the Colonel, "I believe, like much you have shared in the past and today, you are mistaken; using conventional EMP directional devices, the US military has disabled your helicopters. I believe your career in the Russian military has just come to an end.

AMP further informed Jeff and Frank that Colonel Mikile was acting as a rogue operative to recover whatever the LoveStrong Charity staff had taken from the alien site in Morocco. The Colonel had apparently aligned himself with an oligarch actively involved with Russian organized crime. The Russian military and the use of equipment and soldiers involved in this attempt was unauthorized, and the Colonel no longer had military standing in Russia. It was further discovered that half a dozen transports were currently waiting at a Canadian airfield to be used to steal the Russian helicopters and equipment. Colonel Mikele developed this whole plan to benefit his new boss and criminal enterprise. It's a pretty elaborate effort by the Colonel; too bad he will be incarcerated for the rest of his career.

By midnight, all of the Russian personnel had been removed by the US Army Rangers, and a day later, all the helicopters had been loaded onto US Airforce flatbeds and taken to an un-named location. Several officials from the US military arrived a day after that and discussed the facts surrounding the surprise visit by the Russian military; it was decided, as a result of Frank and Jeff holding to their dumbfounded explanation for the attack on Jeff's home, and the officials departed.

Lt C couldn't keep his mouth shut for want of another word and said, "I don't think that is the last we will see of them." AMP: "Maybe, maybe not, but I think if the facts behind the motivation for the colonel's action are kept secret, we may be clear?"

Chapter 11

Jeff was questioning Lt C on how the first warning of the incursion by the Russian helicopters was them flying over the group jogging. Lt C offered, "It appears Gaith and AMP were fully aware and decided to keep from us as it would have interfered with our meetings, and they had arranged for military support to take care of it. The AIs tracked the communications and the helicopters and coordinated with the US military. Our only role was to delay the Russian soldiers long enough for the Rangers to get here to arrest them, which I believe we achieved.

"No harm, no foul would seem to apply," Sori and Tori said harmoniously.

Chapter 12

Jeff, Frank, and D had to appear within two days before a Senate sub-committee reviewing the Russian incursion into US territory. They would get to meet many US and Russian diplomats and politicians. No one was looking forward to this, but Frank felt confident they could hide behind LoveStrong Charities and ignorance. They had several weeks to shore up their story and maybe do some role-playing to make their story hold together. The only item they still needed to get a story on now is the drones. Since the overall theme was ignorance, they might as well blame drones on the Russians; the only use of the drones was the decibel weapon, and that wasn't visible to anyone. AMP provided that he was working on the best story the AIs could develop and that they would need to steer toward electronic interference, but the technical explanation would have to have some work done on it. As Sori put it, "a work in progress".

Chapter 13

With the military, both friendly and unfriendly, gone, Frank and D returned to Long Beach, and Jeff returned to logging. Kim & Nyla had work to do at the clinic, while Martha went to the Library and Stephanie headed into her second-grade classroom. Terry and Shawn were waiting as Jeff showed up at the farm. They had a full day of cutting and trimming and would prepare several loads for shipping to area mills.

"Good morning, guys," Jeff offered Shawn and Terry, "which truck do you want me to take?"

Shawn: "You can take the lead truck. We are heading back to where we left off last week."

"OK," Jeff said, got into the lead truck, and headed out.

It was about a 30-minute drive, and the lead truck had all the chains and the dozer on it, so it was intended to be parked as close as possible to the work without blocking the way, and in some cases, it was a real art to get it in the correct position. Jeff was getting better at it and motivated, so he didn't have to take ribbing from Terry and Shawn all day long for missing the mark. As it turned out, this particular section of trees was close to the edge, and getting the truck in the correct position was relatively easy. Jeff had the dozer off the truck, and the chains were already in the bucket, so Jeff could drive the dozer to the first set of logs on the ground and start attaching the chains. With most of the cut logs trimmed, Jeff could just put the chains on. He then returned to the dozer, set the bucket down, detached it, attached the load pickup forks, and returned to limbs piled by each trimmed log. By the time Jeff had a load of limbs ready, Terry showed up with a dump truck, and Jeff could load the limbs into it. Smooth and efficient, and so went the remainder of the day.

By 4 pm, they were all sitting out front of the office having a beer and talking about what was up tomorrow; the AIs had asked everyone to talk about the last few days so that C could effectively hide some of the awareness that might cause the group difficulty in the future. Lt C understood that ignorance is half the battle in getting people to believe you when you are lying, and to complete the snow job, you had to convince people you were also kind of dumb. After hearing this philosophy from C, Terry, Shawn, and Jeff spent an hour insulting one another's intelligence, which C had said wasn't what he meant, but he did say it with a smile.

As Jeff walked into his house, he announced, "Hi honey, I'm home," Kim responded, "In the kitchen with Nyla and Stephanie." We thought we would do tacos for dinner, and Nyla and Stephanie wanted to show me their recipe for their pork filling."

Jeff: "Well, it smells great, and I am starving. Do you have enough for Hank and Martha? I can call and invite them. "

Nyla: "I already did, and they are on their way over."

Jeff: "Great, I am going to shower. I used some of Hank's special sap remover, which smells like gasoline."

Chapter 14

Hank and Martha arrived at 6:30, just as Stephanie set the pork and taco shells on the table. Nyla and Kim brought the shredded lettuce, cheese, chopped tomatoes, and hot peppers. We all sat. Hank said a blessing, and we all thank the Lord for our successes so far.

About halfway through the meal, Gaith asked if he could pass Frank's call to the group through the room speaker system. Hank looked at me, and I said sure, go for it, Gaith. Frank introduced his topic of discussion by informing us that the "Russians were coming."

Kim contributed, "That's cute, Frank. Was that by land, sea, or air?"

Frank responded, "No, they were webbing it, and they had launched an all-out attack on D's web within a web and almost defeated his defenses. Our only saving grace was AMP; he detected some alien code in several bit-level nuances that led AMP to conclude these Russian thugs had recovered more than we suspected from the site in the Sahara.

"Just so you are aware,"

Gaith added, "AMP just finished developing new code to protect against this. We are in a wholesale upgrade of our firmware and software, so you may begin to hear or feel your devices functioning starting now and running for 15 to 20 minutes; we have let Terry and Shawn know so everyone is aware. This upgrade should cover our backside and has led AMP to a few other possible upgrades that he hadn't considered if you can believe."

At that, Frank signed off, and we all went back to our meal. A few minutes later, we all started chuckling, and Nyla asked, "Did anyone understand what we had just heard?"

Jeff said, "he understood attack," and Kim added, "I knew what hear or feel your devices meant," at that, we laughed our way through the rest of our tacos.

Everyone contributed to cleaning up, and Hank invited us all back to his place for dessert, apple pie, and a warm fire on his deck. Hank asked Gaith what the temperature was, and Gaith responded it was 65. We all headed to Hanks for apple pie, a warm fire, clear skies, and no wind. It is a beautiful way to end a great meal and evening. By ten, everyone headed home.

Chapter 15

Two weeks later, D and Frank met Jeff at the front entrance to the Senate sub-committee chamber and spent a few minutes comparing notes. Lt C indicated that this should be a cakewalk. AMP had been able to access all of the Senator's devices and had a complete list of all the questions they were going to ask, and none of them were outside what they had expected and had believable answers to. Poor Colonel Mikili would be the scapegoat again, a passed-over career military man in the Russian army on a vendetta. The sub-committee hearings went smoothly, and Frank, Jeff, and D were out of the meetings by 2 pm and in the air home by 6 pm. Jeff decided to go to California with Frank, and D indicated he would fly up to Havre in a day or 2, so Jeff was just going to kill time until then. They all received sub-committee clearance the following day, and the reviews were closed. They wouldn't have to deal with this again with this administration. But they all knew nothing was absolute in Washington, DC, or the Senate.

The next step was to do an exposure analysis of what was transpiring in Russia with the Oligarch crime family. The code recognized and related to an alien device continued to be a thorn in the AI's proverbial side. They couldn't identify the device involved, which meant the future impact was open. Everyone agreed to track down the device and determine what exposure existed.

AMP, Gaith, Sori, and Tori worked on a proposal to go to the area of Russia where Dimitri Pavlov, the Russian Oligarch, resided and where all the web-based data indicated the headquarters of Pavlov's criminal enterprise existed. Gaith asked Frank what he thought was the right direction to go in, and Frank said they should work through contacts in Russia since the headquarters involved was near Kazan, Russia, and Frank had people there. Frank just wanted to confirm with D that these operatives were. After speaking with

D, Frank said they had a contact in Kazan, Russia, that came highly recommended; he was also a computer wiz, which may or may not come in handy. Since the Russian operative was one of D's people, Frank turned the investigation over to D. Jeff asked AMP if the AIs could get any closer to identifying which device their operative might be looking for. AMP was sure that it was either the atmosphere or water tester, as the code involved was standard in both devices, and both devices would transmit the embedded data streams that AMP had detected. They were small devices about the size of medium size cell phones. Kazan probably has over a million cell phones; that description will not help. Gaith offered that the device, when powered on, puts out a signal that AMP can recognize, and we can provide the contact in Russia with a device that will help direct him to its location.

Jeff: "Well, now that's a different story. If we are talking about only one or two devices, does it seem reasonable to expect to retrieve them, or are these not strategic devices, and we could ignore them?"

Gaith: "Not sure how to answer that, but maybe we should hold off a bit before we set any retrieval goals."

Jeff: "If the device is a water or atmosphere tester, what other alien secrets are in jeopardy?"

Gaith: "That's a good question; we may be overreacting, and neither of these devices in the enemy's hands would harm us. "

Jeff: "Is it possible the bit-level nuances could come from any other devices that could be problematic to us? It sounds like we need to confirm at least what device or devices are involved?"

AMP: I am confident that these two devices only use the bit-level nuances. Any more sophisticated devices did not use bit-level nuances as they had iteration limitations. So all we need to do is verify the stream nuances, and we can consider this closed?"

Chapter 16

The alien code in several of the streams detected were the markers that defined the devices the Russians had their hands on; D's operative had a current earth technology detection device AMP, and Gaith was able to design that combined several earth technologies to register the signals they needed to verify appropriately. These technologies went into an ordinary cell phone sent to D's operative in Russia.

A day later, D's contact had the cell phone in hand and planted it at a coffee shop across the street from the suspected installation. D's operative hid the cell phone in question in the false ceiling in the restroom of the coffee bar. After 48 hours and the signal confirmation, the AIs felt comfortable that the devices were not one, but they believed there were two and didn't need to be concerned. To err on the side of caution, D decided, along with compensation, that he would give the operative a round trip to New York and funds for a 10-day holiday in America so that D could retrieve the modified cell phone and evaluate the saved data.

Chapter 17

Jeff and Terry were loading logs onto the mill log feeder platform when the mill saw blade exploded. Jeff realized what would happen and was able to block Terry off the platform before a piece of the saw blade embedded itself in the log Terry was standing in front of. Jeff, however, wasn't as lucky as another piece of saw blade sliced through his bottom, leaving a 6-inch gash and generating a huge amount of blood; several other mill workers were also injured. Hank had previously purchased a used ambulance for his farm so that, if needed, he could use it to transport workers to the hospital. The other workers were loaded up and transferred to the clinic. AMP interceded at that point and had the area around Jeff's accident cordoned off. No one was allowed to enter as Jeff's blood would be potentially contaminated. Jeff told Terry to back off and tape off all the blood spill areas. Jeff, with Lt C and AMP's assistance, could reduce blood flow to a trickle psychically, and Jeff was no worse for wear and began to clean up the blood and sterilize the areas in question. Hank went to the AI's basement facility and got a handlight projector he could use to identify any blood residue Jeff might have missed in his cleanup efforts. Hank checked the area and cleaned up several missed areas. AMP directed Hank to sterilize the area again, cut a section of wood on the mill log feeder away, and burn it. An hour later, they removed all of the possible contaminations. Jeff, Hank, and Terry sat down for coffee, and as Terry turned to Jeff, Hank noticed a small drop of what looked like blood in the corner of Terry's eyelid. Hank commented to Jeff, and Jeff looked closer and confirmed what Hank had seen. At AMP's urging, Lt C told Jeff to take Terry to the basement facility, so Hank, Terry, and Jeff headed to Jeff's house and the AI sub-basement. An hour later, the AIs had confirmed that Terry was contaminated and that it would appear Jeff's DNA had passed to Terry. Even the alien technology Gaith possessed could not stop the biological level that would prevent the contamination. AMP interjected that part of the distribution system the alien race developed to modify its' people still existed in the package that was AMP, and AMP suggested that a portion of that delivery system be used on Terry, which consisted of a powerful mini-computer and a subset of nanobots that would allow AMP to have a biological connect and control to help prevent adverse effects on Terry as a result his exposure to Jeff's blood and DNA. AMP felt that the exposure was such that placing the delivery system within Terry's anatomy would significantly increase the ability to control the potential fallout from Jeff's DNA without any downside; the delivery system was just that, a delivery system, and it did not provide any biological components that would result in harm to Terry.

Jeff: "Wow, I feel awful that this has to be this way. It's like I got cooties," Amp spoke directly to Terry. The potential fallout from Jeff's DNA is unknown. The impact of the delivery system is 100% safe and would allow us to, surgically by nanobots, remove any DNA impact that appeared harmful. We have over a year of influence on Jeff that has been nonharmful to Jeff, and there is no harm so far to Kim; it would hold that the influences you would experience would be the same, but the absolute would be where you had the delivery system in force if it was needed? Jeff said, "AMP, would this delivery system be just as problem-free for me as it would be for Terry?"

AMP: "Yes"

Jeff: "AMP, if you feel that the delivery system is the best choice to guarantee Terry's safety, then I will assume that I would, too. Let's give the nanobots a shot at me, and if all is OK, then let's give Terry and Kim the delivery system?"

AMP went on to fill in some of the gaps in the delivery system that opened up a menagerie of health and wellbeing functions that would improve all three of the modified Alien DNA human beings.

Because of the cross-contamination concerns, the DNA engineering that should have been done was not. The result was that too many possibilities occurred that could be harmful. The delivery system has a stopgap that allows it to, for want of a better word, cull the more extreme variations of mutation to help the patient work along more standard possibilities. In other words, the delivery system cloaks the DNA so that it does not exit the body intact, and it is rendered by the delivery system as impotent and dead upon leaving the body. This is the best possible method of sterilizing, and it neuters the DNA, making it harmless to other humans.

Jeff decided to go to the clinic and have Kim stitch his butt wound and fill Kim in on what happened and on the planned nano-byte technology-based inoculation. After explaining and reassurances were given to Kim by AMP and Gaith, Kim agreed that it appeared to be the safest approach, and appointments were made at AMP's location for that evening. Terry, Jeff, and Kim were inoculated and asked to remain in the basement for an hour to observe any potential fallout; as they sat and stared at one another, Gaith provided some soothing music and a sweet Beethoven melody, and the group offered their thanks. An hour later, with no visible effects from the vaccination, the little group was released, Terry headed home, and Kim and Jeff went to bed.

About 30 minutes into the hour wait, Jeff asked AMP if he was doing anything, and AMP said he wasn't; Jeff explained that he was hearing and feeling music. AMP said that was not one of the side effects recorded with implementing the nanobytes into his creator's system; Jeff said he wasn't in any distress, just wondering. AMP said he would see if he could contact the nanobyte controller in Jeff, but it usually took an hour before that could happen. Several minutes later, AMP informed Jeff that he did make contact with the nanobytes and that all indications were positive, and AMP inquired if the music was continuing. Actually, it seems to have changed to a ticking sound, and AMP said that was what he was waiting for; he didn't want to inform Jeff, Terry, or Kim of this, as telling the patient sometimes causes false readings and complicates the process. Jeff then informed AMP that the ticking stopped with a popping sound, and AMP confirmed that was what he was waiting to hear and that Jeff's nanobyte innoculation was complete. Terry and Kim followed the same feedback cycle shortly after and were considered successful. AMP said that there were now several features and functions that all three of the patients had at their disposal. Still, rather than go through them individually, AMP would do a memory transfer, and new nanobyte members could inquire about clarification on their own. At the time, they felt the need for a little more information. Terry, Kim, and Jeff said that sounded great; they all said they felt tired, and Kim asked Terry if he would like to sleep over so he didn't have to drive back to the reservation tonight, and Terry said that would probably be a good idea and he would let his wife know. As Terry hung up from his wife, he began to see brief images in his head of childhood memories, almost like photographs, 1 or 2 seconds, then gone. He thought this was odd, so he returned to the sub-basement and mentioned what he was experiencing to Gaith. Gaith, in turn, asked AMP what the brief images could mean and whether it would have anything to do with the nanobytes; AMP felt that the timing had meant it was related and that, based on the medical history, this occurrence was noted in several cases. The prognosis was that it did not concern as several of the memory areas in the brain are effectively blocked from access by several hormones and become dormant; the introduction of the nano bytes stimulates these areas of the brain and, in turn, brings certain memories to the forefront. Along with several other physical advantages, the nano bytes replenish electrical impulses, which can produce optical production of the brain's memory content and produce the flashes Terry was describing. It is considered temporary and can be blocked by the nanobyte control module. If it becomes bothersome or Terry wants it stopped, AMP can reprogram the controller to hide the flashes, but AMP indicated he would like not to do any modifications for the first six hours but didn't want Terry to be under distress. Terry indicated it wasn't distressful so far and that it might start to be if it continues after 12 hours. He said he would check in with Gaith and AMP in the morning before returning to the reservation.

To be on the safe side, AMP checked in with Kim and Jeff to see if Jeff was still hearing music and whether they were experiencing the flashes that Terry had; Jeff said the music had stopped, and both said they had not seen the flashes that Terry had. AMP hadn't told them about the flashes and was curious about how they knew Terry was seeing, and Kim said that they had seen Terry's flashes and that the nanobytes had informed them that they were coming from Terry. Well, isn't that interesting? You saw active memory bytes from Terry and Kim, and Jeff said yes. None of the documented historical side effects recorded on the nanobyte delivery system recorded this occurrence; again, it didn't seem concerning, but AMP would monitor and follow up.

The following morning, Terry checked in with Gaith and said that the flashes had stopped and that no other out-of-the-ordinary mental or physical aberrations had occurred. So everyone at this point had a clean bill of health from the alien witch doctor with the caveat that further checkups would be done within 24 hours.

Chapter 18

It was Sunday, and Kim and Jeff decided they would attend Mass; they checked with Hank and Martha to see if they were interested, and they said they had made plans but didn't share what those plans were. So Kim and Jeff headed into town for Mass. Services were at 10:30, and they would just make it. As it turned out, they did make it before Mass started. The church was pretty empty, which surprised Jeff. It had been full the last few times they had been, but it was getting cooler, and people may prefer Saturday night mass when it's cold. Father gave a good sermon and talked about all God's children being responsible for caring for the body God gave them. The message seemed a bit odd, given all the odd happenings in Jeff and Kim's lives. Are they going in a direction God would find unacceptable? I guess Father did cover that in a way, and it was surprising that he used the term crap shoot in describing all the possibilities we're subject to in life that we end up not having a choice on. It makes one wonder what the future is, and does the fact that Terry, Kim, and I have a potential technological angel in our system help us meet God's expectations? Do we do all we can to protect this vessel God has given us? I thought about discussing this with Kim but then thought better of it. She has always kept her faith separate from her work and believes God participates more directly in our fate. We have some definite differences of opinion. I am unsure how Kim will see nanobyte technology's long-term effects versus God's plan. I best leave it alone for now.

Jeff: "How about lunch at Stu's?"

Kim: "Let's do brunch at Pete's Corner. I could go with something exotic and out of the ordinary."

I laughed a little and asked if nanobyte technology didn't do it for her, and she laughed. "I guess you are right, but I still want one of Pete's great salads."

So off we went to Pete's Corner for lunch.

Jeff: "Any chance we can do a run this evening."

Kim: "Give me my salad, and I'll give you your run and some." she smiled ear to ear; I love it when plans come together.

We had a great lunch and got home by four and halfway through our run by 5. It was a very nice day, and if nanobyte technology doesn't scratch us from God's list, we did a lot of what Father recommended in his sermon.

Chapter 19

Just another Monday, I'm headed over to the equipment yard to meet up with Terry and Shawn to plan our day in God's land of trees, to harvest, and to protect another gift God has given us. I wonder why I am quoting God so much; Father's sermon must have hit a nerve; make a note, Gaith, to remind me to discuss with Kim and see if she is feeling the same effects.

Terry said he was doing good, and I responded I did ask you how you were doing, Terry said he distinctly heard me say I hope you are over the image flashes, huh? I thought you'd have to watch that. What's on the agenda for today and Shawn cut in with we are going to harvest the big trees on the res land we marked a few weeks ago, and this is going to be a little more difficult and require some climbing to cut off the bigger limbs. I feel you did a lot of this when you were in Ranger training, but this time, you have to take a 20" chain saw instead of an M4 Carbine. We did train on big trees, and we even did simulated parachute escape training in big trees; that was definitely a hoot, having to cut the parachute cord and drop 4 or 5 feet and catch a limb when you are up 60' in the air, not something they recommend for the faint at heart. That sounds a bit over the top. Yeah, it was, and to make it interesting, they offered us the option of doing it once without safety lines or having to do it six times with safety lines. They offered it in such a way that no one had the sanity to choose the second option. Luckily, we all did it successfully, and we all got our Ranger nut badge. Wow, that is insanity, Terry said.

We loaded up the trucks and headed out to the res trees. It was about a 40-minute drive, and as we started pulling into the parking spot, Terry said he sensed something wrong at the condemned Indian ruins. I was just a little behind and sensed a presence in the tunnels. We decided to check it out to ensure all was OK. As we drove into the upper parking area, we saw two black SUVs. They both were Hertz rentals, but they were the big ones, which you don't see very often; maybe Hertz was providing the government with their fleet. Lt C piped in that these were not US people; they definitely were speaking Russian, and they did not sound like official people, more like gangsters. Is Colonel Mikele out of jail? No, he is still incarcerated, and he'll be out of commission for two decades. I believe these are from his puppet master. We had better report this to our friends. For some reason, Lt C was having difficulty communicating with Gaith and AMP. Shawn said he had a couple of the security devices left in the truck that he hadn't put out a couple of months ago, so I headed south to climb a tree and put one up, and Terry headed west to do the same. Half an hour later, they were in place, and we had good communications with Gaith and AMP; we explained the situation and waited for our AIs to investigate. They recommended that since the reservation now owned the property, it would make sense for them to contact the local authorities and report the trespassing. AMP didn't believe there was a hurry as these people would not locate or penetrate the observation station, so Terry, Shawn, and I returned to our cutting duties and let the Russians have at it.

About 2 hours later, a parade of local police cars and state trouper vehicles showed up at the tunnels and proceeded to remove the Russians and arrest them for trespassing. Luckily, the reservation had posted both condemned and no trespassing signs a few weeks earlier, so the Russians had no excuse for being there.

Russians were gone, trees were cut, and we decided 4 pm was an excellent quicking time. I checked in with Kim, and she said she was starting to pack up and would be back at the farm by 5, and she would bring food from Stu's, whatever the special was. Jeff texted back that it sounded great. On hearing about Stu's, Terry and Shawn asked if they could join them for dinner, and Jeff said sure and let Kim know. He asked if she could bring home four specials that he was bringing home to Terry and Shawn for dinner. Kim said out loud to herself, "Oh, you guys, just work my fingers to the bone," and then giggled a little. Jeff could only smile and appreciate the sense of wellbeing he was feeling.

Chapter 20

Any time three or more of what Jeff had come to think of as "The Group" get together, a powerful sense of physical and mental strength takes hold; it is almost like D's computers give out some group reinforcement.

An hour later, the three guys headed over to Jeff's place for dinner. Terry explained to Jeff that Shawn and his families were visiting a Michigan reservation to celebrate the Chipawa Annual Powwow. Their families hadn't been in a while, and Shawn's dad had rented an RV to take them this year; Terry and Shawn would join them tomorrow, and they would all caravan home next Tuesday following all the festivities. Jeff thought interestingly and asked, "Is this something outsiders can join in with?"

Shawn explained it was frowned upon but not enforced against; most of the festivities were steeped in Chippewa tradition, and you would only understand or find it enjoyable if you were really into it. Many Chipawa's that had transitioned out of the traditional lifestyle found the ceremonies difficult to participate in. However, many still attended, so it was rejuvenating to the members who live off the reservation. Terry contributed that if Jeff and Kim were interested in attending, they should spend a year attending the ceremonies done on the weekends and during the year at the reservation here before attempting the Annual Powwow. How many ceremonies are we talking about? Jeff asked, and

Shawn said, "There are brief ones every weekend, sort of like going to church on Sunday, and probably about 5 or 6 bigger events during the year. So manageable. The weekend ceremony is usually about a half hour to an hour, but it is done mainly in Ojibwe, so you must do your homework to understand what is happening. Terry suggested a couple of books if Jeff was interested, and he would lend them to him.

Chapter 21

The table was set, the food was laid out, and Kim was sitting at the table waiting for the guys. They joined her and sat down.

Terry asked, "Can I say a Chippawa blessing?"

Kim said, "Sure".

So Terry said a short one in Ojibwe and then explained it in English. Kim was impressed and liked the sentiment. Stu's special was pretty good. None of the guys could remember the last time they had spaghetti, so the meal was delicious, and everyone enjoyed it. Shawn updated Kim on where his and Terry's families had gone and that they would join them at the Michigan Annual Powwow tomorrow. Terry and Shawn left around eight and said they wouldn't be at work til next Wednesday. Jeff and Kim wished them a good trip and an enjoyable powwow.

Jeff was helping Kim with the dishes and describing the Russian gangsters at the Indian ruins to her.

Kim said, "It was on the local news, and the clinic buzzed with the 'Russians are Coming,' but she didn't think anyone took it seriously."

Jeff: "I am trying to understand what this means, but AMP, Gaith, and D need to investigate this to see how concerned we should be. The group in Russia must be motivated by the technology they have in hand to seek out more and to do it so blatantly. The Colonel's invasion was off the wall, and now they are sending field investigators without any attempt to hide what they are doing. It can't be a good sign."

"You are right", Kim said.

Jeff: "Hey, Lt C, is there any feedback on the Russian event from this morning?"

Lt C: "Not so far, but I know AMP, with D's help, is finding a lot under the surface that we still need to pursue, but something needs to be actionable. D gave feedback to AMP that LoveStrong is looking to add a sizeable workforce with specific security-based capability, and they intend to staff with people from all over the world. Frank was setting up some training centers, but he needed some help under the radar. He decided to bring in the management from each targeted country so the programs would appear local and not international. This may or may not be possible without government participation, so Frank was also pursuing what intelligence community opportunities might exist. "

"Wow, this is starting to sound like a spy novel in the making." Kim laughed and added, "Secret Agent Man. "

Lt C said, "It may come to that in order to keep the alien in the room hidden," and Kim and I both smiled and knew Lt C was smiling, too. On that note, it was time to get some sleep, and

the Lieutenant asked, "You want some help with that,"

and both of us echoed, "Absolutely."

Chapter 22

"What a beautiful sunrise," Kim offered as she handed me a cup of coffee, "I can't remember beauty like this growing up. The smog adversely impacted us, and it did tend to obscure things in southern California." "Yeah, you're right; I remember smog-induced smoker's cough, too," Jeff commented.

Kim: "Let's not go there; I remember our first year of dating and our arguments about smoking. I am so glad you chose me over cigarettes."

Jeff: "I am, too, and I am so glad you had such a hatred for them, Kim. It was what I needed at the time to make the right choice. And I agree this is a beautiful sunrise."

Kim: "What are you going to do at work today, Jeff?"

Jeff: "I don't know; I didn't know Terry and Shawn would be gone today. We had finished cutting on the reservation trees, and I guess I could drag and drop trees all day, but it isn't something that one person should do alone. You really need several people; I'll check with Hank and see what he wants. How's your day going to go?"

Kim: "It should be interesting. I have to go to Billings for a meeting at noon; they reserved the helicopter, and Nyla and William are going too. They are investigating increasing the Billings Hospital presence in Havre so that we may see more doctors, nurses, and maybe even a trauma center. The Havre clinic favors it, and there is a lot of support on Billings's end, so who knows, it should be exciting."

Jeff: "That does sound great. It could be a real boom to Havre. Were we going to do breakfast?"

Kim: "I wasn't planning on it, but I guess we could go to Stu's; I have no appointments this morning, just a helicopter to catch at 11."

Jeff: "I'm game, and I am sure I can get away this afternoon to pick you up so I can drive you in this morning."

Kim: "Don't worry about picking me up. I will get Nyla to give me a ride home; I have no idea how long this trip is going to last." They proceeded to shower, dress, and walk out to the car at 8:15, then sat down at Stu's for breakfast at 8:45.

Jeff dropped Kim off at the clinic at 10; she would kill some time entering the month's drug requisitions before the 11 o'clock flight to Billings.

Kim" "Love you,"

Jeff: "Love you back." Jeff headed to the farm.

As Jeff drove up to the office, Hank came out the door.

Hank: "Aw, there you are, Jeff; I forgot to tell you Shawn and Terry were off today, Monday, and Tuesday next week."

Jeff: "I know Hank; we had dinner with them last night as all their families were in Michigan. Have you ever been to one of their powwows?"

Hank: "No, but I had always been interested."

Jeff: "Shawn said he thought we would have to spend a year attending the local ceremonies first, or we would be really out of it at the Annual event."

Hank: "Yeah, I looked into that a few years ago when we started to increase the Chippawa employees here. Terry's father thought it wouldn't be well received by the elders who wanted to keep the Chippawa identity separate. It wasn't in a negative way but rather an attempt to maintain the uniqueness of Indian history. I was disappointed at the time until Terry's father explained how much of the Chippawa history had been lost over the last 50 years. Then I understood how they might want to protect tradition."

Jeff thought that probably made sense and that maybe Terry's generation wasn't as sensitive to those issues as Terry's father's generation.

Jeff: "We should ask AMP to give us some advice before we pursue interfering with reservations affairs."

"Sounds good to me," Hank said. Hank had sort of come to that conclusion already and thought don't mess with stuff that is working.

Jeff: "What's on the agenda? I could drag logs at the Russian invasion site."

Hank: "Let's not joke about that."

Jeff: "Sorry, I just can't get used to the idea that we attract these people."

Hank: "At any rate, I need to get someone to go with you. I don't want you working those big logs by yourself."

Jeff: I thought I saw Manny come in the yard, and I don't think we had too much going on at the mill. I remember him saying he liked doing the logs and running the dozer.

Hank: "Can you find him and see if he would like to spend the rest of his shift helping you?"

Jeff: "Sure, Hank, and if he is busy, I can just take the rest of the day off unless you have something else in mind."

Hank: "No, that sounds fine; I'll have to figure out Monday and Tuesday; it would be nice to partner you up with someone on those days, too. Those bigger logs are scheduled to go to the Chicago mill, and I have a premium on them if I get them there next week. I'll check in with you later today if you find Manny. Otherwise, I'll talk to you Monday."

Jeff: "OK, Hank, talk to you this afternoon or Monday.

Manny came walking out of the saw room, and Jeff hollered, "Hey Manny, you want to spend this afternoon dragging logs?"

Manny: "Sure, I would love that. Where is it?"

Jeff: "Up at the reservation farm, we have them all cut, but we didn't get them placed for dragging or trimmed. We can check it out and see if we can place, drag, or load."

Manny: "Sounds great, better than sweeping sawdust off the floors."

Jeff: "I hear that."

So we loaded the equipment, and Manny and I drove the equipment truck and flatbed up to the reservation trees.

Chapter 23

Jeff thought he would check out the tunnels just to make sure nothing was amiss. He parked his truck at the work site, let Manny know that he could offload the dozer, set up the grappling attachment, and start moving the limbs out. He told Manny he was going to walk up to the tunnels and check them out, and Manny responded with take your time. It will take me a couple of hours to get all the limbs cut and moved.

OK, thanks. Manny and Jeff started walking up to the tunnels. As he entered the main chamber, he got a sense of discomfort, maybe even a little dread, and he called up Lt C to give him a hand.

Jeff: "Do you recognize that sound Lt C?"

Lt C: "Yes, I do; those are similar to the listening devices and sensors that the General had placed in the Sierra compound."

Jeff: "That's what I thought; any chance you can locate where they are?" Lt C: "I'll take a shot. These seem quite a bit more powerful than the ones at Sierra."

An hour later, Jeff and Lt C had located a dozen devices that seemed far more sophisticated than the ones they had seen before; they also located a transmitter and antenna in one of the open crevices of the main chamber roof. Lt C was able to send pictures and diagnostics of both the listening devices and the transmitter to AMP for evaluation. Based on the information AMP got, he was able to determine that these were high-end technology and that all of the devices discovered appeared to have explosive footprints. Jeff asked AMP if he could impersonate him and inquire with the authorities if they had been able to get any information from the people they had arrested, and AMP said he would do that. AMP recommended that Jeff get out of the tunnels as he could not guarantee how the explosive devices could be denoted, and it appeared these were not small amounts of explosives. Jeff agreed and carefully backed out of the main chamber. Jeff made sure the main entrance was blocked by tapes and made a mental note to get some lumber, seal off the opening, and mark it with WARNING EXPLOSIVES.

Manning was still trimming logs when Jeff returned, and Jeff grabbed a chainsaw and started working the logs alongside him.

Manny: "This is going to take a lot longer than we thought; these trees are huge."

Jeff: "Yeah, it didn't register with me that they were this big or that there was so much limb trimming to be done. Why don't you take the flatbed back and get the dump truck? We can concentrate today on trimming and hauling the limbs and leave the dragging for Monday. Also, can you bring a couple of saw horses back and those WARNING EXPLOSIVES signs in the office? I need to block the entrance to the tunnels; somehow, we have explosives in there.

Manny: "OK, will do." Manny headed back to the yard with the flatbed to get the dump truck, and Jeff continued trimming logs.

An hour later, Manny returned with the dump truck, and Jeff was bringing out a load of limbs with the loader. Since the truck was here, Jeff went ahead and put the load he had in the truck and Manny road back with him to trim logs. Jeff told Manny to take the second pile of limbs to the truck and load them while he continued to trim. Jeff and Manny would then trade off on the loader to get a little breather from trimming and the chainsaws. By the end of the day, they had all the logs trimmed, the dump truck was full, and both Manny and Jeff were exhausted. Good day, they both said and they had a quiet trip back to the shop.

As they drove into the shop yard, AMP notified Jeff that the authorities hadn't gotten any information out of the Russian gangsters, so AMP had Gaith do some of his mental telephony magic and was able to garner the intent of this group. Apparently, they had placed a thousand pounds of explosives in the lowest tunnel and were intending to blow half the mountain up. They had a crew coming in to remove whatever they could by helicopters and disappear. Just as Jeff was asking AMP what they should do, a huge explosion occurred, and both Manny and Jeff could see the explosion mushroom at the Indian ruins. This was sure to bring everybody and their brother, plus the kitchen sink and maybe the sump pump, to the site. AMP let Jeff know that he had released two drones to get thorough optics of the site and see what was exposed; according to AMP, the sub-terrain lift was still in place and, based on the readings, it was still functioning. AMP let Jeff know that they could drop the current location of the defunct observation facility as much as 500 feet lower than the current level, that the system allowed for cave-in coverage, and almost guaranteed no one would discover the facility.

Jeff: "AMP, do you need me to return to the site."

AMP: "No, the drones would give us enough visuals."

Jeff: "I let Manny know we aren't going to worry about the explosion tonight and that I will come in tomorrow and check it out, then call him if I need help."

AMP: "Good."

Manny: "Can I head out? I need to be at Stu's in 20 minutes."

Jeff: "Sure."

Manny said thanks, see you bright and early Monday; high fives and Manny headed to Stu's; Jeff headed to the tree branch processing plant with the dump truck.

Chapter 24

When I was done dumping branches, AMP announced a group-wide conference call to discuss the current Russian invasion. AMP, with a sense of humor, referred to it as World War III. A few minutes later, everyone but Kim had signed in to the conference call, and AMP said that we needed to do some offensive work to cut the Russian gangsters off at the knees and that the best group to do this was Jeff, Terry and Kim, explaining that with the nano-byte technology in them AMP could provide almost foolproof disguise's and character cover that would allow the three group members to get close and personal to the group that was behind this continued attack of the LoveStrong Charity. AMP had arranged first-class airfare to Moscow from Seattle for the three of them, and the passports and D would be relied on to get these three cleaning jobs in the gangster stronghold. Fake passports were being produced at this very moment and would be in hand tomorrow, and our flights were on Monday at noon. Part of this deployment would include some nano-byte physical altercations to Kim, Jeff, and Terry, and being that this was the first time we had used this, the altercation would take place tomorrow morning and allow AMP and company to review and diagnose the impact on them and to make sure there were no adverse reactions. AMP let everyone know that once the group signed on to this, there would be no turning back and that the future directive and charter would be, for the group and for LoveStrong, to STOMP ON the DEVILS WORK, and the current candidate was the Russian gangsters. At least half of the members on the conference call let out a loud YES; the other half seemed to say nothing. I guess that reaction, Frank offered, seems to imply we need to discuss and maybe take a vote to ensure we have a majority, but maybe first make sure we all agree that the AIs each have a vote on this also. If it's needed, Kim offered. I seconded that, and

Nyla thirded it, and I think she got a fourth it by group laughter. So we took a brief respite from the Russians and did a quorum confirmation and quickly established that the AIs each had a vote and that we all wanted to STOMP ON the DEVILS' WORK; Kim, Jeff, and Terry were ordered to report to the wine room in the morning to be transformed and cleared for duty. Since tomorrow was Saturday, everyone was off, and they didn't have to alter any schedules. Hank contributed that Shawn and Manny could finish the logs at the reservation farm. They need to get AMP to agree that the site is safe.

AMP said, "I'm sure that the forest site is OK, and the only questionable part is whether we needed to drop the observation facility so no one accidentally discovered it. I'll keep an eye on it."

Chapter 25

All three patients were at the wine room at 9 am Saturday morning. Lt C did some of his magic to reduce the apprehension, and Gaith also explained what the process was, that it was fully reversible, and that it would not be painful, just a little uncomfortable for a brief time after the change. The candidates said OK, let's have it and they lay down on cots, were asked to close their eyes and clear their minds, and they were asleep. The process took 4 hours from beginning to end, and four hours later, the three looked entirely different than their previous selves. AMP woke Jeff first and asked him how he felt, and he responded OK, my skin feels a bit tingly but no aches or pains; that's what we expected Gaith said, and they woke Kim and Terry and got the same response. The transformation was declared a success. AMP then went on to explain that in order to reduce the psychological fallout of the group seeing themselves as someone else, the AI had altered the visual registers on how each would see themselves and the others. AMP explained you won't see any difference in each other appearances. The best solution was to use the nano byte command processor to over-ride the optical only when the group saw a reflection of themselves or looked at one another and that the command processor would display their previous reflection or image, and they would not have to adjust constantly at seeing themselves as someone else. It sounded like a good solution; the transformation included a voice change and an appropriate accent.

The three troopers were to remain close to home base to ensure there was no fallout; other nuances and blocks could be used to ensure all three could function with these new identities. As it turned out, the IDs they were waiting for were hand delivered by D that afternoon, so they decided to move up departure and were able to get three tickets on tomorrow's flight to Moscow but not first class, so they would have to coach over, but AMP said they had first class coming back.

The rest of the day was uneventful, and they went to bed early. D was going to fly them to Seattle and would get them there a couple of hours before their flight. They would be met in Moscow by three of D's trusted contacts, one of whom was the gentlemen who helped with the previous effort to identify the alien technology that the Russian gangsters had somehow acquired.

Once Jeff, Kim, and Terry were at the gangster site in Kazan, Russia, they would work on a cleaning crew and install listening and video devices wherever they could. The first step of this project would be to gather intelligence. Neither Gaith nor AMP could guarantee that their powers of mental telepathy would work over such a distance, but this would also be useful intelligence on what resources they could use over great distances. Some of the interfacing was significantly improved by adding the nanobyte controller technology, and they may be pleasantly surprised at what their capabilities would prove to be.

Three days later, Jeff found himself cleaning toilets in the largest clubhouse he had ever seen or heard of, and it seemed like the members of this Russian Mob really liked to use the American f-word. Not sure why; they weren't mad or excited. It was kinda like using the word gee to emphasize a pause or question. At any rate, the toilets were just as bad in Russia as they were anywhere else. Kim was washing and changing bed sheets, and Terry was outside doing yard and lawn work. So far, so good, and their characters were foolproof; they were transformed into perfect Russian peasants, and they fit the bill perfectly.

After a week on the job, they had rolled out all of the devices along with a few hundred pounds of high explosives in preparation for their departure. They had gathered a huge amount of data on Pavlov, and he was not a very nice man. AMP's feedback was that they had just about everything they needed to plan an attack that would permanently eliminate Demetri Pavlov and his army of gangsters.

Jeff was cleaning up and getting ready to head back to his room at a local boarding house when one of the gangsters came out of the back with Kim over his shoulder. She had a bloody lip and appeared unconscious. Jeff mumbled to Lt C, what the hell and Lt C responded it just happened. Out of nowhere, no warning. This guy decided Kim was his. Jeff moved over to block the gangster's path, and Jeff asked him to let his sister go; the gangster laughed, pulled a knife, and made a move toward Jeff. Jeff sent signals to Kim to wake up and prepare to be dropped, and she responded that she was already awake and faking it; good, Jeff thought, then broke the gangster's right hand and kneed him in the growing. The moves worked perfectly, and Kim was able to slide off the gangster's shoulder onto her feet, and the gangster dropped to his knees. Jeff asked Lt C if he could take control of this guy, and he did. He had him walk to the closest closet and sit down, which he did immediately. Cool, Lt C, that's a lot easier than beating him to death.

Kim said, "Does this mean our undercover work is done ?"

Lt C offered, "It probably did.

We are probably good for the night. AMP has evaluated all of the information we have provided him and is coming up with the final game plan. He's indicated we should return to the boarding house and wait for his instructions."

Lt C: You guys should stop and get something to eat."

Kim "What are you hungry, Lt C? and he said, "I am famished ." we all chuckled at that.

Then Lt C added, "Terry is waiting for us out front."

Jeff added, "I'll have to admit the food in Russia takes a bit of getting used to, but once you get past that, it is pretty good; what do you guys think?" Both Kim and Terry responded with no comment.

Jeff: "I guess that was a no, but I still liked it."

We were sharing a room, so we didn't get separated, and we were still integrating the nano-byte technology, and each of us was a part of the other's integration. I think Terry appreciated the company, and this helped us carry over the brothers and sister cover story. AMP woke us at 5 am, and he transferred his action plan based on the intelligence he had accumulated. AMP believed we needed to destroy Petrov's facility. Luckily, Demetri hadn't heard the old adage 'Don't keep all your eggs in one basket' as AMP had determined all Petrov's physical assets were at the Kazan location. A sizeable fortune was in international bank accounts, and AMP and company had begun to implement a scheme to transfer these funds to some fake accounts, then run them through dozens of holding accounts and ultimately to a LoveStrong account in Switzerland. It would be impossible to trace, but at some point, Pavlov would notice the funds missing, and then he would begin to react. We wanted to be out of sight and out of the country by then. The plan for the local facility had begun the day we arrived, and we had been planting explosives throughout the facility for a week. Our intention is to destroy assets and not people, so once we decided when we wanted to blow the place up, we could start fires and set off the fire alarms remotely to clear the building. Our escape route is a private jet from a private airport 30 minutes from town and shouldn't present any issues; it will take us to a Finland airfield, where we will transferred to a United flight to New York. Given that we keep each piece of the plan intact and keep the timing right, we should have our target handled and be out of Russia by Saturday.

We were picked up by friends and delivered to the airfield outside of town. That flight took us to Helsinki, and half a day later, we found ourselves on a United flight to New York. AMP reported to us that the Kazan facility in question had been cleared by fire and destroyed by our explosives, a million dollars of computer and weaponry had been erased, and 90% of Pavlov's funds were now in the hands of LoveStrong. If this Russian gangster wanted to recover, it would take him years; it was possible but not likely. We considered this our first STOMP, and we were now in the business of eliminating evil. But we had to be careful as this effort didn't go without complications, and based on Jeff's experience, that was going to be the rule and not the exception.

By Tuesday of the following week, Jeff and Kim were back in their own beds, sleeping like babies; AMP had reprogrammed their identity transformation, and when they woke Wednesday morning, they were back to their normal selves without any apparent harm or fallout. They checked on Terry, and he was ok, too. AMP had gained a lot of information and understanding of human anatomy and had begun to investigate the possibilities of shapeshifting and the speeds at which it could be done. He shared with Jeff the possibility that they could use this in a more accelerated fashion if they just dealt with the facial changes, but more data and trials would have to be done to ensure they could always return to their original selves. Jeff commented that was great but that he wasn't sure they could handle the psychological fallout. It was nice that they didn't have to experience the change visually, but they knew they were different, and it had its impact. AMP agreed and said the Gaith was looking at that aspect to ensure no permanent damage was done. Good to know, Jeff said, and remember, we also have a pretty short trial period on the nanobyte stuff, so we don't want to lose track of how it is falling out with us in the human trials. True, AMP contributed, and we won't.

Chapter 26

No further fallout had shown up with the reservation ruins and the potential for discovery of the old alien observation facility, so AMP and Gaith had determined it would not be necessary to move the facility lower in the ground and to save that option if needed in the future. Due to the possible hazards, authorities recommended that a 10-foot fence be erected around the remaining rubble and properly posted as dangerous. Hanks company volunteered to erect the fence, and most of the materials needed were being produced by Hanks mill. All farm employees were drafted for the project. With 20 people involved, the fence was erected in 2 ½ days, and now you couldn't even see the old tunnel site; two-foot signs were posted every 50 feet warning of unstable ground to add to security for any future Russian tampering devices.

The post-LoveStrong offensive efforts against the Russian gangsters had occurred a month ago, and the final take on the effort was given a B++; the funds stolen from Demtri were now safe in a Swiss bank account, and to everyone's amazement, it amounted to almost a billion dollars. We certainly were not going to be hurt by a lack of funds. D was already using some of the funds to finance data centers around the world to help increase both network coverage and to allow for the implementation of numerous alien technology data-gathering techniques that would lead to superior earth-based warning systems. As AMP explained, this would be the next ten generations of tectonic and weather and atmosphere pre-emptive notification and would set up the development and introduction of world-based correction techniques and technology. This would be the first step in heading off cataclysmic events brought about by earthquakes and severe weather occurrences. Jeff could tell AMP and Gaith were reviewing things that Jeff and company could not possibly fathom, but they all sounded like good things for Earth and the people of Earth.

Chapter 27

Our quarterly agreed-to conference call was scheduled to occur tomorrow evening at 7 pm, and Jeff and Kim invited everyone local to come to their house for dinner before 5 pm. Terry and Shawn were asked to bring their wives as one of the issues noted was that everyone with spouses had spouses in the group, so it was decided that Terry and Shawn's wives should be offered the same option. D had been informed, and he had already sent devices for Sonya, Terry's wife, and Alice, Shawn's wife, and it was agreed to offer and, if accepted, give them the devices at tomorrow's gathering.

No fallout had occurred to date with the action taken in Kazan, Russia; the internet, public and dark, had not seen any actionable communications concerning Demitri Pavlov or his group of gangsters. This was a relief to everyone and possibly a surprise, but AMP assured the group that Demitri and any activity coming out of Russia or anywhere else in the world would be tracked and evaluated accordingly. With the implementation of worldwide data centers by D, practically all internet activity, truly worldwide, was being monitored. It would be as close to virtually impossible to escape recognition as you can get. With each data center being established, Frank was increasing his security forces and staffing half a dozen field reps at each location. To help disguise the security staff increases, D was training the security people to sell some of the new cell phones and Bluetooth devices along with the data center products. In comparison to some of the other big international firms, like IBM, Apple, and Xerox, D's operations were still small potatoes.

Chapter 28

Everyone was on time, and the quarterly conference call started on time. The first order of business was the offer to Terry and Shawn's wives to join the group so they could be privy to the activities their husbands were involved in. This would allow them to understand what sacrifices they may be required to make on behalf of the group. Alice, Shawn's wife, who works in the office at Hanks's farm, immediately accepted the offer to join the group; however, Sonya, Terry's wife, was hesitant, as she was still reacting to the mission Terry had gone on to Russia. No explanation or reason was given for Terry's abrupt departure, and she was still upset about it. Given her reaction, Terry wasn't sure how they would explain all this to her so she wouldn't continue to react adversely. Lt C communicated with Terry and asked if he could do some queries on Sonya to see how emotionally vested Sonya was in her reaction to Terry's absence for a week. Terry said it was OK with him, and a few minutes later, Lt C said he was recognizing a fairly obstinate hold on the subject of the group by Sonya. Lt C told the group, to include Terry, that he could alter Sonya's position and make her change her mind. Most of her attitude was over not having Terry available when their son got in trouble at school. She had to deal with the school principal on her own, and he was a real ass and pushed Sonya to tears. Luckily, the father of the boy that Chet got into a fight with stepped in and told the principal if he said one more word to Sonya, he would punch him in the nose. Even though that put a stop to the harassment, Sonya was furious that Terry wasn't there. Lt C said it would be better to shift some of the facts in Sonya's memory and put that event behind her, Chet was fine, and the incident wasn't significant; it just gave the principal the opportunity to be an ass. Terry thought that would be great as he had not made any headway in softening his absence from his family or his relationship with his wife. Everyone else concurred, and Lt C did his magic. Sonya, who was looking down at the floor, turned her head up and showed the room the biggest smile; just about everyone was staring at Sonya, and she asked WHAT, and Terry jumped in and gave her a big kiss. Sonya scolded Terry and then said to the group I would love to join... So, the rest of the group gathering centered around explaining some of what the group consisted of and giving Sonya and Alice their new computers and cell phones. Needless to say, both ladies were overwhelmed, and Lt C continued to do some of his magic to soften their reaction. Since there was some degree of emotional doubt, the group thought they should stop at this point and get together again on Sunday to finish up and go over any questions Sonya and Alice might have.

Jeff took both Sonya and Alice aside and told them they could call him or Kim anytime, day or night if they had any questions about what was discussed tonight. Don't be afraid to raise any questions. Our intent is to help the world be a better place, and we want you to be comfortable with how we are going to go about doing it.

Sonya said I have no idea how today happened with how I was feeling about you all yesterday, but for some reason, I am now comfortable. Jeff told her we would discuss that with her on Sunday, and she seemed to be OK with that.

Chapter 29

Even though Saturday wasn't normally a work day, Jeff had agreed to meet Terry and Shawn at the reservation and help set up security devices. AMP had provided the last ones they had recovered from the Saraha site, and AMP wanted to make sure the Russian gangster NEVER did damage at the Indian tunnels again. Jeff drove over to the reservation with one of the bucket trucks so they could place the video units around the grounds on the highest trees. They were pretty much finished installing by mid-afternoon, and AMP had let them know the coverage was perfect. Terry said if they had one more device, he would like to view the pasture lands so they could keep track of the reservation's livestock. They lose a few heads every year and so far haven't been able to catch who is doing it. No one saw any harm in that, and they still had a dozen devices, and this would be a good use for one of them.

Chapter 30

Jeff got home around mid-afternoon, and Kim was nowhere to be found. Jeff called her and asked her where she was, and she said she was down in the sub-basement, so Jeff headed downstairs. When he walked into the AI room, Kim was asking Gath a question about what he thought AMP meant, and Tori spoke up with AMP as being paranoid.

Jeff asked Kim, "What's going on?"

Kim: "I think we have some contact from the dormant site on the moon, and AMP is concerned about it."

Jeff: "What's going on, AMP?"

AMP: "The best I can ascertain is that the moon site our creators established is trying to make contact with Earth."

Jeff: "Well, that's not good. That will bring a lot of unwanted attention to us and our programs."

"That's true, " AMP said, "and I can't seem to get communications linked up with them. This is what happened 2000 years ago and completely isolated us. Then, their continued broadcasting is going to lead someone right to them. I think it's time we brought the rest of the equipment we retrieved from the Sahara here."

Jeff said, "Maybe we have what we need, just not where we need it." AMP: "I agree."

Jeff immediately called Frank.

"Hey Jeff, what's up,"

Jeff: "Well, our guys here are getting broadcast messages from the alien outpost that was set up on the moon two millennia ago, and we are all concerned the wrong people will detect them and maybe even trace them back to their source."

Frank: "Sounds like that is possible; what can I do to help?"

Jeff: "I think we need the rest of the stuff we retrieved from the Sahara here so AMP and company can see if the missing communications equipment is there. We brought everything back to the US, and AMP remembers their excellent two-way communications with the moon base, so the equipment we need must be there."

Frank: "OK, I will figure out how much is left and either have D fly it up or chartered a plane, and I will bring it to you guys. "

Jeff: "That would be great, Frank; we probably ought to put a high priority on this just to get the AIs on the moon to shut up as soon as possible."

Frank called D, "D, you remember when you said you were going to go through all the stuff we brought back from the Sahara? Have you done that yet?"

D: "Yeah, I have, Frank; most of it was solid state stuff I couldn't explain, but a few pieces I had brought back to my shop to see if I could get to work. I couldn't make any headway."

Frank explained to D about the moon base trying to communicate with the outpost in Montana and that they wanted all the stuff up there so the AIs could find the communications equipment.

D: "OK, what would you like to do."

Frank: "Can you fly the stuff up to them, or is there too much?

D: "Yeah, there's too much for my plane, but I can lease a bigger airplane that can handle what's there and have it to them in a day or a day and a half."

Frank: "That would be great D, do you need anything from me?"

D: "NO, I'll get it done; tell Jeff I will let him know when to expect me as soon as I know. I assume there are trucks available at Hanks?"

Frank: "I will let Jeff know and make sure they will be ready for you. I assume you'll want to stay the night and turn around the next day?"

D: "Yes, that would be the plan."

Frank called Jeff after he finished with D and let him know D was putting everything together. Frank had mentioned the few items D had taken to his shop, and Jeff wanted Frank to remind D they needed everything, and Frank assured him he would let D know.

Chapter 31

Everyone was back at Jeff and Kim's place on Sunday to follow up on the gathering from Friday. Sonya didn't appear any worse for wear, and Lt C began conversing with Terry and Sonya. She was accepting him and his SBI status and that he was an independent projection from Kim and Jeff. Wow, Jeff thought, that is a big piece of the pie to bite off. As it turns out, Sonya has a master's degree in electrical engineering and is no slouch in technology, but it does help to have Lt C around to smooth things out. True enough, I don't know where Kim and I would be without him.

The meeting went smoothly. We answered many questions and found that almost everyone was comfortable with the facts.

Jeff decided to bring up the communications issue with the alien moon site, stressing that it was not two-way communication, and they hoped that D would bring the Farm the solution to allowing AMP to communicate with the moon site. No one on Earth would decipher the communications, but they would know that someone or something was broadcasting from the moon, and we wanted to avoid some accelerated effort to get to the moon and find the source. For some reason, AMP was a little hesitant to discuss the details, and Gaith offered that there was a fairly big ELEPHANT in the pubertal ROOM that AMP had shared with Gaith, and Gaith was sure AMP was going to share with the group, especially now that the moon base was somehow active. Jeff wanted to know if this was a serious issue and one that required all members to be present. Gaith shared he thought all members should always be present when we discussed ELEPHANTS; Jeff chuckled and agreed. Let me get back to Frank and tell him to come up with D and the equipment. We have an AMP issue for all hands on deck.

Jeff called Frank, "Hey Frank, me again. I think you should come up with D. AMP, or I should say through Gaith's insistence, AMP is going to drop the final ELEPHANT in the room. I get the impression this is going to be a doozy."

Frank: "OK, let Gaith know we should be there tomorrow afternoon. You got me excited; any idea what it is about?"

Jeff: "No, but I know it has to do with the moon base the aliens created 2000 years ago."

Frank: "See you in a day or so."

Chapter 32

Jeff was waiting at the County airfield with a couple of trucks and a small forklift when D and Frank arrived late in the afternoon.

"Hey guys," Jeff yelled as the plane taxied up to the hangar."

"Hey Jeff," D yelled out the pilot window. "How do you like LoveStrong's new purchase for its domestic freight operations?"

"Wow, I like it," Jeff responded.

D: "It's a Beech 1900 and handles great and decent cruise speed at 250+, so about the same as my other plane. We were in the air less than 6 hours with a good tailwind. Luckily, the cargo is in 100-pound or less containers, so it's just a walk in the park for you, Jeff, to unload."

An hour later, they were on their way back to the Farm and getting excited about what was unfolding; Gaith had let Jeff know they needed to hurry. That site on the moon was increasing its broadcasting, and they needed to shut it down ASAP.

Jeff responded to Gaith, "Be there in 20 minutes," the trucks sped up a bit.

As they pulled up to Jeff's place, Kim was out front and directed the trucks to the back of the house, letting Jeff know they were all set to get the equipment down to the sub-basement. So Jeff followed Kim's direction, drove around back, and backed his truck up to the freight ramp. It took an hour to unload both trucks and get everything downstairs, where Martha and Hank opened containers for Gaith and AMP. Everyone was looking at the equipment and determining where it was obvious to connect the power. Halfway through the unpacking, AMP let everyone know that he was identifying each piece but had not yet seen the communications equipment. Frank had joined Martha and Hank in unpacking, and an hour later, AMP announced that Frank had just unpacked the equipment he was looking for. AMP had to start broadcasting to the site on the moon. The moon site enacted a series of security protocols, and it took another half hour to establish a two-way conversation. The moon base alerted AMP that the self-destruct protocol had been activated as a result of a meteorite striking the communications center at the moon site. The moon site AIs had no physical way of reversing the self-destruct protocol. AMP questioned what happened to the Autobots. The AI responded they were never fully assembled as the crew designated to finish the assembly died unexpectedly. AMP was pretty sure this was part of the nano-byte fiasco that ultimately destroyed his creators.

AMP: "OK, what do I call you?"

Moon AI: "Luca."

AMP: "OK, Luca, what do you recommend we do? We do not have vehicles that would allow us to travel to your location, and I am assuming your needs require help from creator-type resources."

Luca: "Yes, that is what we need, and we need it in the next week, or this site will self-destruct."

AMP: "What do you suggest?"

Luca: "We have a fleet of 4-man space vehicles that we can launch and send to you to transport personnel back to our location. However, we do not have any excavating equipment that would allow us to get to the location of the self-destruct facility."

AMP: "How big are your vehicles? How much equipment will they carry."

Luca provided the information and the specifications that were needed to uncover and access the self-destruct facility. Gaith began to identify the minimum requirement and immediately identified where they could purchase the equipment they didn't already have. Based on a little more evaluation of what damage had been done to the moon site, it was determined they didn't need to bring large pieces of equipment but rather hydraulic and bracing components to open up the passageway from the main station to the satellite destruct central core.

Luca and AMP worked their magic on the vehicles in question and discovered that the vehicles could reach the Farm in Havre but that they did not have human-friendly biosphere support. AMP and Gaith needed to locate the components to modify the two crafts Luca was sending. AMP located what was needed in Spokane, and D left immediately for the airfield to prep his plane to go to Spokane. Gaith made the calls to order the equipment, which luckily was available, and the plan was set in motion. The crafts coming from the moon had stealth equipment that would allow them to remain hidden on the trip to Earth, but once in the atmosphere, they would be recognized by radar, so they would be flown, staying within the parameters of earthbound aircraft, This was not failsafe so it was determined that once the crafts were in the earth atmosphere they needed to turn around within 4 or 5 hours or their location would be found. This also meant that the return flight had to be done to another location.

Frank said, "The military base Colonel Mikile used in Canada was abandoned now; they could land and return the crew there, and if it was decided to keep the crafts on Earth,. They could have trucks available to haul them to Frank's other site in Canada, which is maintained by Chuck and Millie. That site had an underground storage facility large enough to hide the two spacecraft."

AMP offered: "Worst case, the earth crew could get to the moon base, open up, and assist in aborting the destruction protocol and be returned before the air ran out."

All phases of the operation were assigned to the brightest of the brightest, and it dawned on Jeff that Lt C had jokingly mentioned his telepathic abilities. Jeff inquired if that was a joke or a real capability.

Lt C responded: "Your ability, Jeff, to move tons or weight was real, but you just haven't attempted to use it yet."

Jeff: "Well, let's see what we can do." Jeff and Lt C went upstairs, and Lt C picked up one of the remaining trucks and moved it a few feet.

Lt C said, "I am pretty sure that was close to our limit."

Jeff asked Kim to come up and join them, and when she did, Lt C moved the truck again, and he said that his strength doubled with Kim and Jeff together. With this capability, Jeff said D should concentrate on oxygen only and the hydraulic braces, and Kim and Jeff would travel to the moon and do the necessary lifting. It was recommended Terry come with as he, too, had the nanobyte ability and would augment Kim and Jeff if needed. The space crafts were launched by Luca on their way to the Farm, and an hour later, D was taxiing for take-off to Spokane. D had contacted his group in Southern California to see if they could get assistance in Spokane to retrieve the oxygen and get it to the private section of the Spokane Airport. They were able to get people, and they would have everything at the airport by 10 am tomorrow. The space crafts had to travel at a fairly low speed in order to stay stealthy, so tomorrow at 2 pm was the soonest they could be at the farm anyway, and it would be about the time D had the oxygen containers to the farm. Since they had no way of determining how much oxygen they needed, D got the max his cargo plane could carry and ordered an equal amount to be delivered by truck to the Farm. The minimum amount of oxygen needed for three people was determined, and the spaceship storage capacity was adequate. The rescue mission was a go.

With expected requirements in motion, a conference call was initiated with all group members, and the mission parameters were explained by Gaith. The group covered and recovered each mission parameter to ensure the best possible action was being taken. The group went over and over what was known: the goal to abort moon site destruction, stealth of alien transportation, resources necessary to make the trip to and return from the moon, resources to allow access to the self-destruct mechanism, and AI abort codes. The mission guidelines seemed as complete as they could be, and it was determined that only one of the space vehicles needed to be used. The second one would be kept at the Farm until it was determined that it wasn't needed. It then would be moved to the Canadian facility for hiding.

Once the mission was considered set, AMP offered to discuss the Elephant he had referred to previously and thought at least the basics could be discussed on this conference call. Everyone was amicable with that, and AMP proceeded to explain that the observation sites on Earth and the moon base were actually advanced logistic efforts on the part of their creators to invade and take over the Earth. AMP explained that after years of research and study, his creators believed that the people of Earth were within a century of destroying themselves. If the creators didn't act, the population of Earth would be destroyed. The moon base was not just a moon base but a forward logistics warehouse to support his creator's efforts to take control of Earth and its people. AMP reassured everyone that the takeover parameters did not intend to use force unless it was absolutely necessary, and a number of civilizations the creators had salvaged from their own destructive evolutions had been saved and incorporated into the creator's community. This was a real surprise to everyone, thinking the aliens were just observing; no one suspected there was a takeover scenario. AMP explained that this course of action was wiped out with the destruction of the alien race, but the possibility of the equipment and technology on the moon being used by another power on Earth was overwhelmingly dangerous. That is why his creators had put the self-destruct in place so if the creators saw no value to their plans, they could destroy the materials on the moon and return home.

With this new information and the realization of the amount of material and technology warehoused on the moon, it became even more imperative to gain control and safeguard these resources. The destructive cycle in motion on Earth still needed to be stopped. With these alien resources on the moon, it was possible that the Montana Group could pick up where the creators had left off. The potential benefits of the wealth of alien technology could still be used to stop the current decline of stability on Earth. For whatever reason, the political environment on Earth was becoming dangerously violent; more nations with little respect for human rights were arming themselves with weapons of mass destruction and allowing a small group of neurotic psychopaths to take control and direct their efforts to take away the most basic human rights to freedom. AMP said they had histories of thousands of worlds that had traveled down that path; the few that the creators were able to intervene had, within a few centuries, turned themselves around and salvaged the basic rights to freedom. But hundreds of worlds were not discovered soon enough, and what the creators found were worlds and races in ruins. An entire section of the creator's government was eventually converted to search the universe for worlds on the verge of self-destruction, and this is how they came to be on the moon; they were attempting to intervene in Earth's spiral to self-destruction.

Jeff spoke up and offered a new primary charter to the group: if we can gain control of the wealth of future technology on the moon, we should dedicate ourselves to reversing the cycle that seems to be taking hold of Earth. If we can, we should continue the charter of the creators and seek out other worlds falling victim to this insane cycle of MEGLAMANIA and AUTOCRATIC insanity. Jeff was inspired by the entire group's unanimous support of this new charter and commitment to pursuing freedom for all on Earth and all worlds in the universe.

Chapter 33

The two creator crafts from the moon arrived at the FARM at noon, and D's airplane landed at the county airport an hour later. D was working with the AI to jury rig connections to get the oxygen containers connected to the atmosphere sections of the space crafts. The creators weren't that far off in what they breathed, so all D had to do was secure the cylinders in the craft and, using plastic tubing and common fittings, connect the appropriate feeds. By 4 o'clock, the crafts were loaded and ready to go. They discovered some spacesuits in the storage hold of the space crafts, but they were too small to use, even for Kim. Hank informed the group that he had firefighting suits designed to withstand extremely high temperatures, and they were fully sealed with helmets and masked. They were guaranteed fairly high temperatures, and they in no way would achieve half of what space suites did, but they would give protection; if Terry, Kim, or Jeff stayed out of direct exposure to the dangers of space, they should be adequate to protect them while they aborted the self-destruct module. While they were outfitting themselves, the truck arrived with the second load of oxygen, which was loaded into the 2nd spacecraft. The AI's both on the moon station and at the FARM worked together to figure out what sections on the moon could be converted to Earth-friendly atmosphere and the additional load of oxygen would be installed there and offer quarters for members of the group as needed for future plans. Since air and water were going to be the two most critical items in demand, ordering and purchasing these sealed containers was immediately implemented just in case the group needed to get them to the moon. AMP was not currently privy to the resources the creators had stored on the moon and inquired with the AIs as to what was stored at the base. AMP was immediately connected with the base inventory control system, and even AMP was amazed. AMP informed the group that the equipment available would be the equivalent of any two major earth powers' military equipment capabilities combined. Luca informed AMP that he was able to turn on a handful of assembled bots, who, in turn, were able to assemble the remaining bots. Luca now had bots coming out of his mechanical ears.

Luca further informed AMP that he was sending four more spacecraft to retrieve water and oxygen and that his maintenance bots were making the facility changes to adapt to human residents. Luca also provided that the garment bots were making space suit modifications to accommodate the three earthlings AMP had designated so that they would be available and oxygen/water capable when they arrived at the moon base. Luca also said they would start immediately to convert space suits to accommodate the remainder of the group and that he expected to have resident facilities converted within the next month.

A few hours later, the group's space force, consisting of Terry, Kim, and Jeff, left planet Earth to hopefully save the moon base and the future of free Earth.

Chapter 34

The spacecraft was fairly roomy. Even though the creators were smaller beings, they designed their space crafts on what seemed like a larger scale. Jeff asked Luca why that would be, and Luca could not provide an adequate answer; Jeff admitted that he wasn't complaining, just curious, and was glad the upper limits of the adjustable seating were accommodating to humans. Again, the trip to the moon would take longer as the stealth technology only worked at the speeds the Earth rotated and traveled through space; Luca said he could explain the technology used but that it would take several human years to get through and was technology the creators develop over centuries. The whole group responded with maybe some other time. However, Kim did inquire about what steps Luca thought it would take to get to the area at the base that housed the controls for the self-destruct device. Luca thought it would not be too complicated and that he felt the base had the robotic capability to effect the manual steps but that all of the sensing equipment was damaged, so they had no way of ascertaining degrees of pressure or interpreting some of the more sophisticated failsafe switches. With human eyes and ears, these failsafe devices could be safely manipulated; otherwise, it would be extremely dangerous. Luca was able to provide schematics and actual device pictorials so that the group could feel more comfortable with what they would deal with and what the sensitive components were.

At reduced speeds due to stealth requirements, the trip took a little more than 10 hours, and the spacecraft was guided into the subterranean hangar on the moon's dark side. The first order of business was to unload the oxygen tanks. Luckily, most of the handling was done by the small robotic units, and Luca had done all the preliminary work based on stats provided to him by AMP. The robots were able to get the tanks in place in less than an hour.

The group waited for the human-friendly atmosphere to be set up and tested, and again, in less than an hour, they were allowed to enter the control center and remove their jury-rigged space suits. Each member of the group had a gift waiting for them that was amazing: an alien-produced space suit with 6-hour capable breathing equipment. They all changed into suits, which fit perfectly and, according to Kim, were pretty fashionable. Luca apologized but said they needed to turn their attention to affecting the abort of the continued self-destruct sequence as the time remaining was now under an hour. Terry uttered, "Oh SHIT," and then apologized, and Luca said he felt like if he ate food, he would have thought the same thought.

Jeff said, "OK, Luca, give us the path to the self-destruct facility," and the human group zipped up and started the suit controls and followed Luca's directions. The destroyed control facility was about 500 yards from the control center. However, about 50 yards out, the tunnel had been destroyed by the asteroid and was a mess.

Lt C intervened and asked that Kim, Jeff, and Terry stand together. Lt C began to focus on the materials blocking the tunnel. The material began to slowly move up and off a half dozen yards, a bit like the vision Jeff had of the parting of the Red Sea, and within minutes, the area to the main hatch of the destruct facility was clear. It was also open to space, black space, and Kim asked Luca if he could provide lighting and wah-la floodlights lit the path to the hatch; the group hurried to the hatch, and Luca provided the codes, which Kim entered into the device, and the hatch did not move. It would appear the hatch was also damaged by the asteroid, so Lt C had the three members move closer together, and Lt C was able to move the hatch; they entered, and Lt C moved the hatch closed. There was no way to provide oxygen to this facility, so they had to remain helmeted, but the space suit and helmets were not bulky, and it was 90-degree visibility, so working in them was not that bad. Luca directed them to the control panel, and they could all see the countdown monitor; they just couldn't understand the symbols appearing. Luca started counting down in English to give them a sense of urgency. He started at 6000 and was counting at about 10-second increments, so they apparently had 15 minutes to denotation. Luca provided the steps to abort the self-destruct sequence manually. Luca could tell that giving the information step by step would take more time than they had, and Luca said he didn't know what effect mentally transmitting the steps to them would have, but if they didn't do it, they would not be able to stop the self-destruct sequence in time. Lt C said he could coordinate with the nanobyte controls within each of them to respond to any harmful effects and felt confident that it would be OK. Kim, Jeff, and Terry said in unison GO FOR IT, and Luca transmitted the needed data immediately. The three began to execute the needed steps, and 14 minutes and 51 seconds later, the alien utterance occurred, and Luca informed them the self-destruct sequence was TERMINATED. Luca then destroyed the destruct controls by melting them and announced that the self-destruct facility was now a large explosives storage area and that the robotic units would begin to relocate the explosives to a separate storage area a mile from the facility.

Chapter 35

Lt C and Luca informed the crew that their biologicals were at critical exhaustion levels and that rest facilities were prepared. They should all three spend at least half a sleep period in Lt C-induced slumber. No arguments, and they proceeded to the cots set up and the control center, and Lt C proceeded to slumberize them.

Four hours later, feeling like they got a full night's rest and sitting on the edge of their cots, robots the size of R2D2 brought them each a warm bowl of something, and Lt C informed them it was Stu's leftover stew with some vitamins added. The group enjoyed the meal from home.

Luca informed them that he had proceeded to send another set of space crafts to the Farm to pick up more oxygen, water, and food supplies to supplement what was needed to support human life at the moon. He felt that three new human members could safely stay at the moon facility for a day or so but then should return to Earth. Lt C concurred. Luca suggested if they felt up to it, he could give them a short tour of the moon base. Jeff could swear he said it in a slight sing-song way, reminding him of the theme song from Gilligans Island. He'd ask about that later. The first area Luca provided a glimpse of was the equipment warehousing section, and this didn't require them to go anywhere. He simply opened observation windows that covered two-thirds of the control room walls. And there before them was an open warehouse area that, if Jeff could perceive a square mile, that was what he was looking at. It was completely covered with space crafts, what appeared to be mobile transport units, and crates of all sizes and shapes; Luca explained that this was what the creators had defined as a friendly takeover logistics support equipment and supply package. All the group could do was stare; they couldn't even get OH SHIT out; it was so overwhelming.

Finally, Terry asked if they could take one of the larger space crafts back to Earth, and Luca said, "Yes, they were available."

"Great," Terry responded, "I want the red one."

Luca just said, "OK."

Luca, working with AMP and Gaith, was putting together the materials requirements to convert the Alien Moon facility into a human-friendly facility. Material orders were constantly going out, and the purchase and logistics handling efforts had been moved to D's facility in Southern California. The depot points were going to be the Farm and Franks's stealth facility in Canada. Based on monitoring, the stealth capabilities were working perfectly, and no internet or dark web talk had appeared about any near earth or earth UFO sittings; the few that did appear were quickly determined to either be weather-oriented or fake.

Over the next six months, the alien moon base on the dark side of the moon was converted to a human moon base. The most extensive efforts were in the area of plumbing adaptions and seemed to be working in at fairly seamless fashion. A thousand flights had occurred with all three levels of transport, and a million tons of materials were moved from Earth to the moon. As it turned out, the moon's gravity disparity was even greater for the Aliens, and an artificial gravity system had been installed. The moon facility would be run at the same gravity level as Earth, which meant any concern for lengths of stay on the moon's sixteen percent of Earth's gravity would be compensated for. Not sure anyone would want to stay more than a month or two on the moon, but it appeared they could. Most of the monitoring done through devices on the moon could be done through monitors on Earth, and four new facilities, posing as manufacturing for products D's division was producing, had been purchased within the US, and four more had been purchased in Europe. It would appear that the Alien takeover in human hands was fully engaged; now came the hard part: what do we do next?

Chapter 36

Jeff finally had a chance to ask Gaith if he could inquire with Luca about a phrase he'd used when they were working on the self-destruct problem; Luca had said "a two-hour tour" using a sorta sing song Gilligan's Island melody, and Jeff said he wanted to know if he was right.

Gaith responded with, "A faithful trip aboard this tiny ship." and "Yes, Luca and his AIs were mesmerized by the TV show and were constantly kidding one another by using the words from the song and the melody. Luca was concerned that it bothered you."

Jeff said, "Absolutely not; I just wanted to confirm I heard what I heard. Tell Luca the more he enjoys our stuff, the more we will enjoy his."

Gaith let Jeff know that Luca told him he made his day and chuckled.

Lt C announced to the group as a whole that a brand new elephant had entered the room. The wealth of future technology that the moon base had presented can not be held in secret from the citizens of Earth, and it can not be simply turned over to a single country, including the United States. We have to come up with a way that all this alien technology can be used to ensure the safety of every citizen of our planet. Based on all the examples of efforts and programs attempted to accomplish this over the last century, I am still trying to see a clear path to achieving this goal. It would appear, to use earth history, that this elephant has turned into an Argentinosaurus Dinosaur, 120 feet long and nearly 100 tons, making this a life or death issue. We have to have an integrated earth plan, or will all this newfound technology be used against humanity rather than for it?

Lt C suggested that the AIs study earth's history, man's brutality against his fellow man, the inequality of masculine dominance, and the establishment of the true value of human life. We are beyond the capabilities of human appreciation for the essence of life and our ability to use human governance to ensure its survival. We have to use pure logic to establish the prevalence of survival and the governance of that prevalence. No one person or group of persons could possess the logical independence to define and govern a world where all elements had equal weight. At this point, Lt C suggested that Luca, AMP, Gaith, Sori, and Tori be challenged to come up with a plan to govern the peoples of Earth using the technology the creators have dropped in the proverbial human lap in a way that guarantees all of the humanity benefits. This is needed now, and this priority should be number one on the AI's list; we need consistent history, and because of the fragility in governance, we can't leave it to chance; we will have to use some of the abuses we are trying to guard against. We have to establish our path before any one government or organization does it for us or mankind.

The AIs concurred with Lt C and began to compile and evaluate the history of Earth and to develop a path based on the logic of the ages they possess. Luckily, the combined AI intelligence could do this, given that most of the history of Earth was digitized and available. The group was informed that a recommended charter and governance program would be available within a matter of days.

The AIs could work on the Argentinosaurus in the room while continuing to convert control over the alien moon resources to human hands. So, for the next year, multiple efforts were made to humanize the alien moon base and to move assets from the moon to Earth. It was decided to purchase several Icelandic corporations and facilities as a third location on Earth to house alien assets. The Montana farm ended up being an ideal location as Luca divulged that the alien observation facility in the Indian caves was actually the tip of the facility located there; underneath the mountain existed a chamber half the size of the moon base and was intended as the primary earth headquarters for the alien earth incursion. The facility still required some completion but was about 80% complete and all of the construction materials had been delivered, and the construction bots were in suspended automation; Luca asked for permission to re-animate the bots so they could finish the construction of the earth facility. Lt C checked with Jeff to make sure it was OK, and Jeff felt this was a group consideration, so a brief conference call was made, and tactical considerations were considered. The group approved Luca activating the bots and finishing the construction process.

Luca divulged additional resources, and they were of a construction nature; these materials were moved over time to the Canadian and Iceland locations and would be used to construct massive underground storage areas and act as redistribution points of alien assets to Earth's education and enhance technological efforts.

With the construction efforts in place, the real job was now at hand; the group had to reach out and incorporate Earth-based participation, and no one to include the AIs was sure how to proceed. Human even in the mind of humans, was not predictable, and the one primary consideration was any move forward would have to include an escape clause for an equivalent move backward. If any effort resulted in alienating an existing world power, the group had to be able to regroup and start over. The AI's recommendation was to start with efforts in the humanitarian or medical field. It was felt that major breakthroughs in medical treatments would be more readily accepted and that they could act as stepping stones to all of the other marvelous benefits the aliens brought to Earth and humankind.

The first step along the lines of medical advancements was virus and cancer treatments. The more advanced alien medical technology of nanobots was considered too big a step for human acceptance, so the chemical-based advances were anonymously donated to half a dozen world-renowned medical centers. Within months, these miraculous treatments began to reduce human suffering across the board, and the group started to feed rumors as to the source of these advances. The group then leaked the location of the Sahara alien observation site, along with some subtle nanobot evidence; it would take Earth's scientific community years to unwind the complexities of this technology, but it would firmly implant the donor's identity as aliens from the COSMOS.

A new age, a new direction, and a brand new future are possible. The LoveStrong charities decided that the new incorporation location would be Iceland and that Iceland would be the world provider of the peaceful future of Earth. With the cooperation of the Icelandic people and the creation of a new Earth organization, it is possible to finally bring together all peoples of Earth and eliminate all violence between nations by voluntary means and absolute enforcement of existing border guidelines.

Chapter 37

The group had not met formally for over a year, yet each of the original members, with the exception of D and Frank, continued in their roles. Kim was still working as a physician at the Havre Clinic along with Nyla at her side, and Stephanie was still teaching second grade. Hank farm continued as the main day-to-day efforts on Hank, Jeff, Terry, and Shawn's part, and Martha went in every day to the Havre Library. Most of the worldwide efforts were accomplished through the AIs, with D, Frank, and LoveStrong acting as the business managers and resource planners and expanding the worldwide labor pool. The intent was never to act outside of a mutually cooperative nature, but after several severe attempts by employees to steal some of the alien technology, the AIs convinced the group that the only way to guarantee allegiance was to use the nanotechnology. It would alert the AIs to potential problems with LoveStrong's labor force and give the AIs the ability to redirect those individuals. Even though this has a body snatcher's inference, it's considered the least invasive choice in guaranteeing individuals hired to build the future without creating the possibility of alien assets being misused. The nanobyte technology could and would be removed once the organization established certain levels of operational stability, and the technology would never be used to control anyone just to alert the AIs that the alien assets were not safe from human misuse. The positive fallout was the health benefits the nanobyte technology brought to each human, as it would cure almost all of the current adverse health conditions.

Chapter 38

Jeff and Kim had been talking about plans to start a family but were concerned about where the transformation was going to lead. As they discussed their family wishes and their roles in the program to infuse the alien technology advances, they both agreed that they did not want to be an active player in the next generation of implementing or managing humanity's use of all these new wonders. Jeff wanted to return to being a logger on Hanks' Farm, and Kim admitted she liked the clinic and its low-key work environment. Jeff did not see any reason they had to continue to be an active part in what humanity did with the alien technology, but he did see a need to confirm this with the group and with the AIs, and Kim agreed. It was on this basis that Jeff and Kim requested a group meeting with the primary purpose of reviewing the roles of each member in the future efforts of LoveStrong and the integration of alien technologies into Earth's future.

Chapter 39

So, two years after the group was able to save the alien moon base from destruction, the LoveStrong members met for a third group meeting. All members were in attendance, and as usual, D brought new hardware with advanced alien technology incorporated into them. Since this new hardware had a whole series of support functions related to supporting situation awareness, D suggested that the hardware issue be addressed first. This would give each member the ability to use the new meeting attendance augmentation capabilities and make much of the meeting run smoother and faster. Everyone agreed, and the next two hours were used to convert and migrate to the new hardware. In the end, D collected the old hardware, and the meeting returned to the review and discussion of members' roles in the future LoveStrong Charities.

Jeff and Kim presented their wishes to return to a simpler role centered around their medical and logging work. They informed the group that Kim was pregnant and that they wished to pursue having a family and living as normal a life as they could along those lines. Needless to say, the next few hours covered all of the pros and cons of each member being able to return to a more normal existence. As it turned out, only D and Frank wanted to continue as active players in how LoveStrong was used to bring alien technology to the best possible solutions for humankind.

Over the past two years, AMP, Luca, Gaith, Sori, and Tori have been able to produce a dozen additional AIs with the capabilities of AMP, and these new players were distributed to locations spread out over the world. With a Worldnet built with redundancy, the communications support for LoveStrong was beginning to achieve an almost unilateral connection to all Earth-based activities. The AIs felt that active participation in the Alien AI monitoring would be nil on the part of the group members and that with the new hardware D had provided, the members would be continuously in touch with the pulse of life on Earth. Since the bulk of the heavy lifting was to be handled by the AIs, it was highly recommended that each member continue with the careers they had chosen. Using the universal communications now available, the give and take of group support should assume a less burdensome role and simply be occasional conversations, assuming no critical events. With this in mind, Kim and Jeff felt comfortable in continuing in their roles, and everyone else seemed to join in that mindset.

Today's session was called to a close, and a second session was scheduled for tomorrow afternoon. The group said it' goodnights and all members headed home with the intent of calling on Lt C for sleep support. Luckily, Jeff and Kim were getting used to the subterranean hum that the moon-bots produced as they worked to construct the Montana storage facility; it had begun to help Jeff and Kim sleep, and Lt C had massaged the sound to help.

Chapter 40

Session two of the group conference began at 1 pm on the following day; Martha scheduled a lunch from Stu's, and assorted sandwiches and vegetables were served. All of the members were able to make the lunch, with the exception of Kim, Nyla, and Stephanie, as they couldn't get away from their jobs until 3 pm. With the new devices, D provided the group members with the relevant data, and the meeting moved on to the next topic. This centered around the need to implement nano-byte technology into each group member to ensure the group's health and well-being. As presented by the AIs, there was no downside to this technology, and the AIs indicated that there were 5,122 humans currently functioning with nano-byte augmentation and zero complaints; not one current participant recorded any awareness of the nano-bytes, either physical or psychological. With this human test population, AIs deemed it to be safe for the human population. The group voted unanimously to accept nano-byte inoculation, and AMP delivered the pill-based form of inoculation. As the pills were being handed out, Kim, Nyla, and Stephanie arrived at the meeting and were included in the nano-byte upgrade.

With the nano-bye issue dealt with, AMP introduced a new topic. A number of world conflicts continued to exist; they were becoming more and more hostile, with world governments beginning to align themselves for or against these conflicts. The Russians continued to threaten limited nuclear use to achieve their efforts to claim Ukrainian territory, and a number of other world powers refused to condemn them for this action. Several of these other world powers also possessed nuclear weapons, and it was beginning to look like the old Cold War. This potential on Earth was one that had been monitored by the AIs since the first nuclear weapons were used in WWII. With this in mind, the AIs had developed and produced technology that would allow them to affect the fissional materials that negated their ability to obtain a fissional chain reaction. Over the last year, AIs have identified about two-thirds of the weapons of mass destruction and have rendered them non-functional. Given the current temperaments, the AIs estimate that they have enough time to locate and disarm the remaining nuclear arsenal on Earth. The only way anyone is going to discover this has been done is if someone attempts to do a nuclear attack or test. Based on current intelligence, North Korea has a test scheduled in three months. With this in mind, AMP dedicated his resources to identifying the remaining weapons and disabling them. When North Korea attempts their test, their weapon will not work, and their scientists will discover that all of the fissile material in their stockpile has been altered. It would appear that this would be the event triggering our existence and our role in eliminating the one technology Earth has developed that could destroy itself. Then, we would have to allow each nation the opportunity to share the gifts we offered.

The group remained silent for a long time, not sure if it was AMP's announcement of impending nuclear armageddon or the effect of taking the nano-byte pill, but it was eerily ominous. Well, I think we need a group hug. That was Jeff's contribution, and lo and behold, Lt C was able to simulate a group hug, and it lasted for a few minutes. Upon release by Lt C, the group all started to talk at once. AMP asked for patience and provided some group calmness using the nano-byte capability. With everyone feeling a sense of group calmness, AMP reminded them that the potential destruction capability had been significantly reduced. Two-thirds of the world's nuclear weapons had been eliminated. Steps were being taken to disarm the balance before the next three months were up. However, with the elimination of nuclear threats, the autocratic governments would turn to conventional military efforts, which would cause a sizeable portion of Earth to become unstable. We have transferred almost all of the assets from the moon base to locations on Earth. We have hired and trained individuals in the use of those assets but do not have formal recognition for the use of those assets. We have to decide if LoveStrong is to continue or if we should step forward and integrate ourselves with the non-autocratic governments of the world. That integration has to begin somewhere, and since the majority of the Alien influence has taken place within the US, it would seem only natural to start with the government of the United States. As a part of this possibility, some dialog has been initiated through phone conversations and emails in an attempt to identify government officials who are one-world-oriented and who would not use our technology in an inhumane fashion. We have a number of people friendly to the ideas, but again, they are not dealing with what they believe to be reality, and once we raise the possibilities to actual abilities, we still do not have a handle on how our human counterparts will respond.

The AI's proposal is that the Montana group remain under the radar and that the AIs, with Frank and D as their human counterpart, approach the US government with the proposal of offering all of the alien technology to the government for use in pursuing world peace. The AIs further recommended that the storage facility in Montana be aborted and all resources except for Gaith and AMP and company be transferred to either Iceland or Canadian locations with a proposal that these assets be relocated to facilities within the United States. Several of the elite contacts we have made include the President of the United States, the Vice President, and the secretaries of State and Defense; all four of the individuals suffer from physical handicaps that the nano-byte technology could reverse or reduce to imperceptible conditions. All four individuals are open to the nano-byte solutions, and the group benefit would be that the top government officials would be functionally connected to the AI monitoring. It does bring the Body Snatcher syndrome into consideration, but we have no other mechanism to ensure compliance.

This new proposal by the AIs allows the group to return to their hidden existence and affords the group the ability to provide the US and the free world resources to counter the autocratic destruction of world peace and freedom of choice. This approach will provide the world with almost miraculous health solutions and allow the group to remain incognito. The AIs had put the idea of using the somewhat new US Space Force as the arm of the US government to receive and control the Alien assets and technology. We would be given a dozen computers assembled by Luca, AMP, and Gaith to the US Space Force to bring them up to current AI technology levels, and no mention would be made of the Shared Biological Intelligence. This would keep Kim, Jeff and the new baby under wraps. Jeff wanted to make it absolutely clear that he and Kim and the family they were now starting would never be known to anyone outside the group. The group unanimously confirmed Jeff's request. AMP asked D and Frank if they were willing to take on the human roles of the new alien-based Space Force, and they both agreed there was no other choice and that they would be more than willing to take the hit for the group. With a chuckle and a sense of pure relief and joy, the group did another hug and adjourned.

AMP informed D and Frank that the president of the United States was heading to Long Beach to meet with them and discuss the logistics of turning over the Alien assets; Luca recommended that this process include the moon base and the remaining assets located there, which Frank and D agree was appropriate.

Since the President of the United States was in the first year of his first term with almost a guarantee he would see a second term, the transformation of the US Space Force conversation to an actual space force using Alien technology seemed, as they say, in the bag. The most strategic consideration was the implementation of nanobyte technology; as with the President and his secretaries, the acceptance of nano-byte technology was voluntary; it was proposed that this also exist for those individuals joining the Space Force. There were a thousand members currently in the US Space Force, and it was decided to offer them the nano-byte choice. If they decided they did not want to do so, they could be transferred to one of the other services or accept an honorable discharge. The primary goal going forward was to protect everyone's FREEDOM OF CHOICE and never use alien technology to force humans to do something against their will.

D had never served in the military and was not interested in doing so, but Frank, who had served and was currently in the reserves, held the rank of Lt. Colonel and, when offered a promotion to full Colonel, agreed to raise his status to active reserve and work directly for the Secretary of Defense. Over the next six months, the US Space Force transformed into a World Space Force and issued a statement to the world that its' current responsibility was to protect all nations on Earth against any and all enemies to our planet. The US Space Force would only be used to intervene in domestic conflicts when asked by the United Nations Security Council and confirmed by a unanimous vote. All nuclear weapons are outlawed, and the US Space Force would be used to ensure none existed.

The second generation of AI technology produced by Luca, AMP, and Gaith was donated to humankind and considered the final step in shifting the alien technology to the people of Earth.

With the release of exclusive control of the alien resources to the US government, the Montana group was able to re-establish its normal roles as normal citizens with the joint hope they could stay out of the limelight and be able to assume normal lives.

Chapter 41

Kim was screaming insults at poor Jeff and asking why their first child started her emergence into the world by causing so much pain to her. Lt C asked if she would like him to dull some of the pain, and for the first time Jeff could remember, Kim used the phrase Do little brown bears shit in the forest, Lt C took that as a yes and immediately dulled the pain and Kim announced to the world "I love you Lt C" and the biggest smile ever appeared on her face. Five minutes later, a crying baby was in Kim's arms, and Kim was crying and laughing. Jeff announced I've never seen you cry and laugh at the same time. A minimal amount of pain and other drugs were used at Kim and Jeff's insistence. Nyla was the attending nurse; she was a licensed delivery specialist and was tied into Kim's nano-bots through her own nano-bot controller. The delivery went as smoothly as it could, with the exception of Lt C's slow pain delivery assistance, and Lt C announced he would not wait to reduce the level of pain in the future.

A few hours later, Nyla declared mother and daughter healthy and happy, and by the following morning, they were headed home. Based on common transference, the nano-bot health support system was incorporated with the new baby, and for the first time in human history, the mother, father, and baby were in sync, and with the exception of delivery, the baby did not cry as its needs and comfort were known immediately and acted on accordingly.

For reasons only the AIs apparently knew, the baby's name was proclaimed to be Alesha, and the Coulters were now three.

On the first night home, both Kim and Jeff were exhausted and giddy; such a wonderful gift life had given them, and they could not love Alesha more. Lt C intervened and asked if they would like his assistance in falling asleep, and they both indicated they would rather enjoy their current state of mind. Lt C left their consciousness, saying he would return to his house in Malibu; Jeff said funny, Lt C, "See you later".

A few hours later, just as they were falling into a deep sleep, Jeff mumbled Huh, and Kim responded with What, Jeff said did you say something and Kim said No, and then they both heard a baby laughing, but it wasn't audible. It was like when they would communicate with one another in their minds. Kim immediately asked Lt C for some assistance.

Lt C: "What's up?"

Kim: "Both Jeff and I are getting telepathic signals from Alesha, and we're not sure how to respond.

Lt C indicated that he was hearing the same thing and that he didn't feel like responding was necessary; it was baby talk and not directed at anyone or anything. Just a baby's musings on life out of the womb. Lt C offered to modify the human recognition so Kim and Jeff could continue to receive the telepathic musings but not mentally respond so they would be in tune with Alesha but not feel a need to respond, just like breathing. That sounded great, and they asked Lt C to go ahead and phase that in, and within minutes, the first tri-SBI was sound asleep.

Chapter 42

Less than a week later, Kim was back to work with Alesha at a modified nursery at the Clinic; mother, father, and daughter were all doing fine, and with Lt C's intervention, all were well-rested and happy.

Kim had a Clinic review from the Billings Hospital as the Clinic was looking to upgrade its offering and hire another physician; Billings was going to present the steps the Clinic would have to do and also had brought along a physician who was interested in transferring to Havre. Doctor LeAnne Foster was the assistant administrator for the Billings Hospital, and she was the person doing the review; she introduced herself to the staff and made the introductions for Dr. Helen Carter, the physician from Billings who was interested in the position opening up at the Havre Clinic soon to be the Havre Hospital. Coffee and donuts were served, and the group talked for an hour about backgrounds and interests and about life in Havre; at the end of the hour, Dr. Carter said I'd take the job, and Kim, Nyla, and Bob Petersen all responded with YOUR HIRED. Doctor Foster laughed and contributed that was certainly easy. Now, let's get to the hard part. She proceeded to cover the facility changes needed. When she finished her explanation, she said the downside was that these changes would require a little over a million dollars to accomplish. However, she offered that most of that would come from the Billings budget and that Havre would only be responsible for about a quarter million dollars. Since the upgrade of the Havre Clinic has been on the docket of the board of directors for years, and funds were being collected through annual drives, the Havre Clinic had almost two hundred thousand dollars, and Kim said that the local businesses had committed to at least that much in support of upgrading the Clinic to a hospital. The next order of business was to identify how the construction could be done without major disruptions to the day-to-day operations of the Havre Clinic. Kim proposed a plan that had been formulated by Gaith, Sori, and Tori to build a separate facility and then erect a hallway to attach the new wing to the existing Clinic; this would allow the Clinic to function without disruption and the existing Clinic could continue as normal. This proposal was unanimously accepted and will be presented to the board of directors at the end of the week. The only complication would be an additional cost of about a quarter of a million dollars, as duplicate space would be required for certain features having to exist in both buildings. This didn't seem to be a problem, and the group agreed to present to the board.

Chapter 43

Kim and Alesha arrive home around 5 to find Jeff cooking dinner, and both give Jeff a big kiss as Jeff asks Alesha how her day is; cute was Kim's only response, and she excused them to head to the nursery for a well-needed diaper change. As they headed to the nursery, Jeff alerted Kim that Hank and Martha were coming over at 6 for dinner. Kim interrupted Jeff with I only have one diaper left. Someone will have to go into town and get more, Jeff laughed and said what a coincidence as Martha said there was a diaper sale at Gallagers in town, and she had bought six months of every size, thinking you might need them so your current and future diaper needs are taken care of. Fantastic was all Jeff heard and smiled to himself.

As Jeff and Kim prepared for dinner and Alesha cooed her sweet happiness song, all seemed right with the world; Jeff recapped his day as did Kim, and it was a pleasant reminder of how nicely things had turned around for the group. Right at 6, Hank and Martha came through the front door, with all the group members becoming more accustomed to communicating with one another through the expanded Gaith connection. Hank had voiced knock knock, and Kim had responded with come in; we're in the kitchen. Martha's laugh was infectious and just added to the amazing sense of well-being; Martha commented I really like that. The group sat down to dinner with Alesha at the end of the dining room table in her pretty bassinet, and they shared their day with each other. Hank hadn't kept up with all the moves happening with Frank and D, so Kim and Jeff brought them up to date. Frank had accepted a promotion to full Colonel in the US Space Force, and D had accepted a 10-year contract with them to train and coordinate the technology the Space Force had inherited from the alien creators. With the nano-bot requirement, the Defense Secretary and his staff felt confident that the Space Force had an almost unbreakable security net, and the net was being expanded by D to incorporate all the nation's critical corporate infrastructure. The US had proclaimed the alien technology and advances as gifts to every citizen of the world and had established a sister organization to the Space Force to share most of the alien advances with all nations of the world, including those deemed less friendly to freedom of choice. The only caveat was each autocratic nation had to use UN Forces to quell protests and let the UN punish or relocate those persons protesting those nations' form of government. It was the least the free world could expect in countries that did not practice government for the people, and maybe over the next few centuries, as Earth headed to one-world recognition, fewer and fewer people would lose their lives. Needless to say, every choice being made going forward was reviewed and re-reviewed by man and machine with an eye on the precious value of life.

With the discussion of this new form of world politics, the meal came to a close, and Hank and Martha thanked Jeff and Kim, gave Alesha a kiss, and headed home. On the way home, Hank reminded Jeff, using Lt C, that they were going to work the reservation log farm in the morning and were going to tackle the big trees on the south end of Firebreak Road; Jeff acknowledged and said he would be at the yard by 7.

Chapter 44

The Clinic had hired a new physician and given Kim later starting hours, so Kim was just waking up at 6:30 as Jeff was putting Alesha down for a nap. Jeff gave Kim a kiss as she slowly opened her eyes and said Alesha was fed and dry and he would see her tonight; she kissed him back and said have a great day and be careful, "always" was his response, and you do the same.

Jeff drove into the yard to find Terry, Shawn, and Hank loading equipment and getting ready to head up the reservation.

Jeff: "Hey guys, how's it going?

In unison, Jeff heard and felt their response couldn't be better. The skills and group communications were becoming more amazing day by day, and everyone was comfortably adjusting to group thinking as if it had been there all along.

Jeff hopped on the dozer and drove it onto the flatbed and then realized he forgot the chains, so he had to back the dozer off, reconnect the forks, and use them to pick up the pallet of chains and load them on the flatbed. Half an hour later, all the trucks were loaded, and the small caravan headed up the mountain for a day of tree climbing, de-limbing, and huge tree cutting. All the guys were kind of excited as these trees would be the biggest they would harvest on Hanks's Farm, and these size trees really required diligence to do them right and to protect the other trees.

Shawn and Jeff had gone up the first tree and began cutting the branches; they would climb above the branch, set tree steps, and then cut the branch below their feet. Once cut, the branch fell to the ground, and Terry and Hank would use chains and the dozer to put the branch to the dump truck. Depending on the branch size, they would then either load it into the dump truck or cut it to a manageable size while they did that. Shawn and Jeff repeated the cycle until the tree was clean of its branches. Shawn and Jeff attached guide ropes about 20 feet from the top of the tree that they would use to guide the fall of the tree. Precision cuts were made at the base, the fall path was rechecked to make sure it was clear, and the down cuts were slowly made to control the fall path of the huge tree. This was the first time Jeff had seen this done, and he was really impressed with the skills being displayed by Hank, Shawn, and Terry. Jeff asked Terry what you do if the tree decided to go off on its own, and Terry responded with, "You Run Like Hell," and the other guys chuckled. Hank had to admit they had never had one go off, so they weren't really too sure what they would do other than Run Like Hell. Jeff asked Hank if he could try his telepathy to see if he could control the fall, and Hank didn't see anything wrong with that, so as the tree began to fall, Jeff took hold of it and where you would have expected the tree to begin to accelerate the tree simply move at the same speed all the way to the ground. All the guys could say was wow, that was amazing, Jeff said he could feel the stress, and Lt C said he could too. Hank said he imagined that would be true as the tree weighs anywhere in excess of 5 or 6 tons or more. Let's take a break and see what the fallout is of that little experiment. Hank added he had a box of Stu's cinnamon rolls and three thermos of gourmet coffee. Everybody agreed, even Lt C, which lightened the mood.

By the end of the day, the guys had done a dozen trees and were exhausted. Hank declared an end to the work day, and the four compatriots jumped into Hank's truck and headed back to the yard. Hank said tomorrow would be interesting as he hadn't had a lot of experience with dragging trees this size or using the trailer and transporting these trees. Maybe we should have filmed all of this and offered YouTube videos so we could refine the dos and don'ts.

Terry: "That's not a bad idea. My wife runs a filming service, and I can see if she would film us.

Hank: "We will cut another dozen trees the day after tomorrow, and she can film that tomorrow's dragging and transporting the trees to the yard. Tell her I pay her a thousand dollars plus any cost for two days of filming."

Terry: "That would be great, Hank. I think she has been a little depressed with the lack of business she is generating; luckily, she and my mom also do daycare as backup income, but mom can handle that for a couple of days."

Back at the yard, the guys didn't have to put anything away, so they all headed home; even Hank was exhausted, but they all felt really good about the day.

Chapter 45

Jeff noticed he had a message on his cell phone from Kim and played it. He was a bit curious, as she could have simply communicated with him directly. Sorry for the cell phone message, but I was worried you would be 80 feet in the air holding a huge limb, so I used the old method. Nothing significant except I have to work late, and Nyla got Stephanie to pick up Alesha and bring her home; she said she would pick up food from Stu's for all of us, and Alesha had a busy day, and Stephanie would give her a bath and put her to bed. See you around 7.

"Honey, I'm home," I said as I entered our place. Stephanie was in the bathroom giving the baby a bath and responded with, "I am sorry, you're not my type."

"Well, shoot," I said as I entered the bathroom.

Stephanie was drying off Alesha on the floor, so there was no room for me to enter, so I just said high and backed out.

Stephanie: "Could you turn the stove on warm and put the food containers in? Your kid got really fussy as I entered the house, and I thought she needed a bath to relax."

"Sure, on it."

Stephanie came into the kitchen a little bit later, announcing, "Your kid was asleep before I even put her in the crib; that was a tired baby."

Jeff: "Good, that means she will sleep through the night and not require one of us to feed her.

You want me to set the table?"

Stephanie: "Sure, you know where everything is. On the way out here, I called Martha and asked if she and Hank wanted to join us. She thought that would be great, but she wanted to clear it with Hank."

Jeff: "I'll check with Martha in a few; I'll set places for 6."

Hank called a little bit later and said Marsha was going to come, but he didn't think he'd make it; he was going to take a shower and see if it rejuvenated him.

Jeff told him, "No problem, your place is set if you can come."

Hank: "Thanks, man; I am getting too old to try and stay up with you kids."

Jeff: "You made it look easy."

As it turned out, the shower worked for Hank, and he and Martha showed up a few minutes after Nyla and Kim arrived. A little after 7 pm, the group was sitting at the dining room table enjoying another wonderful meal from Stu's.

Not only was the meal great but Kim and Nyla had an interesting day to share. Kim informed me that we were going to have house guests for a week starting tomorrow. Apparently, a family relocating to Havre had purchased an old farmette outside of Havre and moved in a few days ago. The entire family had begun to get sick and came into the Clinic this morning. Their symptoms were somewhat mysterious, and they were the same in each of them: a husband, a wife, and two small children. The fire department and ambulances were called and used to transport them to the Clinic, and the cause of the illness was quickly identified as mold exposure, but not the typical mold, a form a bit more viral called Aspergillus, and will require rest and treatment for at least a week. They are the nicest family, and I didn't have the heart to send them to Billings, so I volunteered to put them up for a couple of weeks.

Kim: "I hope you don't mind, Jeff."

Jeff: "No, not at all; I assume someone needs to watch them; who did you have in mind."

" I hired a CNA from town to come and stay with us for their stay." Kim responded, "She will come with them tomorrow afternoon."

Jeff didn't have a problem with that, and Hank contributed that he was glad some of the bedrooms would get some use, and he offered to have the house cleaning service come and redo the spare bedrooms, just to make sure they were clean.

Kim said, "That's OK; Genevieve, from the clinic house cleaning, was coming first thing in the morning to check the whole house and to clean the rooms for their guest, and the Clinic would cover the costs as a goodwill gesture. The CNA I hired also cooks, and I told her she could use Stu's for dinners, so we should be all set."

Dinner was enjoyable, and Jeff was kind of looking forward to some new faces for a week or two; Lt C said that internal security was in place so no unauthorized personnel would be able to access the sub-basement facility and that the Gaith versus echo would be disabled while the guests were in residence.

Jeff contributed, "I assume you aren't going to make yourself known to them, Lt C, while they are here; I would hate to have to explain you to them."

Lt C: "I know; I will be careful and keep my presence hidden."

Kim asked Hank and me to clean up; she said she and the girls wanted to take a walk, and Hank said, "No problem," and I joined him. The girls put warm coats on and said they would be back in an hour. They're going to walk over to the tower and go up to the top.

Hank reminded Martha that she would have to turn on the main power to use the lift, and Martha said she would, and she would remember to turn it off this time when she left.

Chapter 46

The morning came quickly, and Kim was gone before Jeff knew it; she left him a Lt C note to tell him she loved him and said she would be home with the short-stay guests by mid-afternoon. Jeff dressed and headed out; as he was leaving the house, the cleaning service showed up. Jeff let them know the house was unlocked; they asked if he could give them a walk-through so they would know which rooms were which and the rooms the hospital guests were going to occupy. Jeff turned around with them and spent 20 minutes walking them through the house.

Satisfied the cleaning crew was all set, he was able to leave and head over to the Farm to join up with Hank and the guys. When he arrived, only Terry and Shawn were there, and Terry said that Hank had apparently overdone it yesterday and was going to take at least the morning off to recuperate. Terry and Shawn were kind of concerned until Lt C let them know that several nano-byte sub-routines had kicked in during the night to resolve a stress issue with Hank's cardiovascular system. It was not serious, but it did put a little stress on his breathing and blood pressure. The result was Hank felt pooped and needed a little extra rest. Lt C interjected that Hank was doing fine.

Jeff felt like going over to check on him and mentioned it to Shawn and Terry, and they said they would like to do that, too. Lt C checked in with Martha, and she said great, the more the merrier, so they all headed over to Hank and Martha's place. Martha had put on a large pot of coffee and was heating up some cinnamon rolls from Stu's when they arrived, and they all sat down at the kitchen table to wait for Hank to join them.

An hour and a half later, Hank walked into the kitchen, sleepy-eyed and yawning; his first words were, "Whoa, what's the occasion?" and he got a group laugh in response.

Martha went on to explain he had a slight episode during the night and that his nano-byte health system kicked in and performed some overall maintenance on his cardiovascular system. The result was you needed a few more hours of sleep; you have a clean bill of health now, plus, over the next few weeks, you will feel the benefits of this maintenance. Hank said he did feel quite a bit better this morning, and Lt C told him he would feel even better as time went on. Martha said she decided to take the day off and wanted Hank to take it off, too, so they could drive up to Pete's Corner, walk the path, and have a nice lunch. She gave Hank a big smile and said please, and Hank apologized to the guys and said he wouldn't be joining them today. Shawn spoke for them all and said no sweat; they would enjoy the day without the boss looking over their shoulders. The guys said their goodbyes and headed out, feeling a tremendous amount of relief knowing Hank was going to be OK.

Chapter 47

The day for Jeff and the guys turned out to be fun but slow and tedious. Working the large trees without Hank's expertise was difficult. Terry and Shawn had done this type of work but not a lot, and care in cutting and sizing was critical to meet the lumber order requests they would be filling with these trees. As it turned out, without Hank, they only accomplished about half of what they expected and were a little disappointed in their performance. They know Hank would probably kid them about it for the next year, but they didn't screw up anything, so they felt good about that.

Martha had let them know that they had a very nice time at Pete's Corner, and Hank was doing great and continuing to feel better and better. Lt C concurred that Hanks' nano-byte command center was 100% on Hank's condition, so this little scare for their 78-year-old member was in the past, and the group was in great shape. Hank had told Martha to let the guys know he would be back at it tomorrow, and he told Martha to let them know they shouldn't feel bad about only getting half the job done. He knew working with logs this size was a lot more complicated and demanding, and doing it slowly saved lives and logs.

Shawn told Martha to let Hank know we were a little disappointed in our production but extremely happy we did not have any major screw-ups; Shawn heard Hank laughing as Martha told him.

The guys were in the yard with the large forklift, carefully placing the 45-foot cuts on the ground by the mill. In preparation for these longer logs, Hank had the Mill foreman add the extensions so they could feed and cut the long logs. These logs were destined to supply a custom order for a job in Wisconsin that was building what was being advertised at the biggest Log Cabin Hotel in the world, and all of this lumber would be dried and prepared so that it would be show pieces in the new construction.

The following day, Hank and the guys were back to a full crew and expected to have the larger trees all cut by the end of the week. Terry's wife was onsite filming all the steps, and Hank was looking forward to posting the procedures on YouTube. Terry's wife, Sonya, had made it clear that Hank was going to have to work with her to append the audio, and Hank had agreed.

Hank had seen an increase in customer orders for larger logs coming, so he had invested in equipment to handle it. The facilities had been enlarged to allow the Farm to process without having to sell or buy processing from other mills. Much of the drying and cutting could be done with Hank's smaller mill, which allowed the Farm to enjoy a larger portion of the profits from this type of customer work. Hank had two other logging crews on his payroll but had generally kept them part-time; luckily, they were part of the reservation and did not mind part-time work but had indicated they were more than willing to go full-time. With the production side of the business at 50% over current capacity, Hank decided it was time to exercise his option and purchase the Hartley logging farm south of his acreage. It was a 2000-acre farm that was leased to an out-of-state group called Parsens Inc. The lease was expiring in June, and Hank had notified his attorney to exercise his option and had gotten a text that the out-of-state group was not going to contest and that the closing was next Friday and Hank didn't have to attend. The attorney, Lyle Thompson, reminded Hank that there was a three-bedroom house on the property that had been used as office space, but according to Parsens Inc., they had repaired and returned the home to its original condition as per the lease agreement. Hank sent back his thanks and said he would have one of his guys check the place out and get back to him.

On the drive home Friday with the last load of logs, Hank asked the guys if one of them wanted to go over to Hartley Farm and check out the home on the property to see what condition it was in. Jeff said he would, and Terry said he'd like to go with Jeff, and Shawn joined in and said he could bring his cooler; it had a couple of cold six packs from Stu's new mini-brewery, and that convinced Hank he should join them to supervise. They finished unloading the logs, and the four headed out to the new Farm. As they drove into the parking lot at the Hartley property, they were a bit surprised not to see the home. Hank texted his attorney to find out what the story was, and his attorney texted him back that the home was not in the central parking area and that you had to go to the second driveway. So the guys postponed opening a beer and, pulled back on the highway and drove south another half a mile. A street sign appeared at the next driveway, saying Hartley Drive and Hank pulled the truck into the property. Shawn offered, "Wow, this is pretty nice," which the guys all agreed with, and as they pulled up and piled out of the truck, Terry offered each a beer. Hank said his attorney told him the front door was unlocked, so Jeff opened it and went in. The home was in immaculate condition but looked a little dusty; Hank got on the phone and arranged for the Havre cleaning service to come next week to give it a full clean. Hank texted his attorney to contact Petersen Rentals that the home on Hartley Drive would be available in a few weeks for rental. As Hank was talking, Jeff remembered the family that was scheduled to stay a few weeks with him and Kim and that they were in need of housing. Jeff interrupted Hank and asked him if he could hold off on the Petersen Rental notification and reminded him about the family Kim was bringing home to stay with them for a couple of weeks. Hank texted Lyle back and told him to put a hold on notifying Petersen that one of his guys might have a tenant in mind. The guys finished their walk-through of the house, checked out the water, electricity, and heating, and all four gave thumbs up. Two sets of house keys were on the kitchen counter, so as the guys left, they locked all the doors and set the security. Lt C let them know that AMP added the house security to his system, and they all headed back to Farm.

Chapter 48

When Jeff arrived home, he found a full house, and he was introduced to Paul and Anne Lichfield and their two children, Annie and Steven, the recovering patients from the Clinic. Jeff said hi to all, shook hands with Annie and Steven, and they all sat back down. Jeff enjoyed an update on the group and their backgrounds. Paul thanked Jeff a dozen times for his hospitality in opening his home to his family and couldn't say enough about the gracious help he received from Kim and the Clinic. As it turned out, Paul, a former Microsoft senior programmer, was just starting out on his own with an internet-based consulting business, and he and Anne had decided, since they could do it anywhere, to relocate to a less metropolitan area. They had purchased a property near Havre and were looking forward to a slower pace, but they were kind of ambushed by the devil everyone is calling MOLD. It was the equivalent of COVID on steroids and very scary for a while, but they are on the mend and are so thankful for the wonderful treatment they have received. Jeff asked, since Paul had been out of service for a week, did any of his clients give him grief. Paul indicated that a couple of them were getting hot under the collar, and he wasn't sure what to do; he was still having some difficulty concentrating and had weeks' worth of work left on their contracts to finish their websites. Jeff figured what the hell and asked Lt. C to check with Gaith if he could investigate the status and circumstances, and he said sure, but you need to have Paul's, OK? Gaith informed Jeff that he should know that this couple and the children were sicker than anyone knew and that Gaith had made a command decision to use the nano-bytes to save them. He apologized that he didn't inform the group, and even Kim was surprised that the antibody regiment was so quickly successful. Jeff interrupted and asked, "You didn't let Kim know," and

Gaith apologetically said, "NO." So, no one knew this family was nano-byte inoculated.

Jeff: "Wow, Kim's going to be surprised?."

Gaith said, "I was succumbing to human emotions and was afraid to tell her I didn't want her to yell at me."

Jeff: "I can understand that she is pretty good at yelling and making you feel bad."

Gaith: "Yeah, that's what I thought, so can you tell her?

Jeff "Sure, I think I need to tell Paul and Anne now anyway.

Gaith: "Yeah, I think that would be a good idea. You could let Paul know about us and that I am on his server in Seattle and will provide a proposal to him later today."

"Kim," Jeff inquired telepathically."

"Yes, honey," Kim said out loud,

Jeff: "I have a couple of surprises for you."

Kim: "OK."

Jeff: "The Litchfields were inoculated with the nano-bytes."

Kim: "I thought so, but it all happened so quickly that I didn't have time to follow through with my request to Gaith, so I kind of assumed he read my mind and did it. These guys were really sick; they spent 24 hours in one of the worst mold infestations I have ever heard about, and when they arrived at the Clinic, they were knocking on the death's door.

Jeff: "Wow, how did something so critical get pushed out so low-key? I thought they were just your typical mold exposure."

Kim: "Nope, not this case."

Jeff: "I get it, I will need to unveil a lot of surprising crap to the Litchfields."

So the rest of the afternoon and evening was spent sharing the alien mushrooms with Paul and Anne while the two beautiful children watched seven episodes of children's shows on TV.

When we finished, Paul and Anne were changing colors before our eyes. Paul tried to say something, but it came out more like a disgusting potty sound.

Paul finally responded with: "I'm sorry, that wasn't very nice, was it."

Jeff: "Not sure, I've never heard that sound before, but I understand; you got the first 3-dollar tour of our joy ride, so I will give you all the slack in the world".

Anne: "What is the feedback you are getting from the US Space Force? Have they signed up for all this?"

Jeff responded, "We haven't really kept up with what is happening with that, but give me a second, and I will bring Frank into this conversation."

A few minutes later, Frank came online, and I introduced him to Paul and Anne and their current predicament. Frank apologized for what they and their family were going through and their involuntary draft into the nano-byte community by Lt C. Frank provided an update to everyone on the status of the Space Force, and it was impressive and

Frank said: "I am not a fan of the saying SEAMLESS, but I have to say with the nano-byte assurances SEAMLESS is as accurate a term as PERFECT, and we have made our garden weed-free."

Jeff interjected, "Weed Free, Frank; since when did you switch to gardening terms?"

Frank: "I have a feeling that wasn't me, but I agree we have been able to identify all philosophical differences with both management and labor, and the US Space Force is a very cohesive group."

Kim, returning the conversation to Paul and Anne, asked them, "Do you guys have any questions for Frank?" they both indicated that it appeared they had all the Space Force information they could ever need and thanked Frank for his input. Frank signed off.

Jeff: "Did you two want a night to discuss and think about things? The nano-byte inoculation for you and your kids is permanent, but it doesn't come with any commitment you guys have to make to us; you are free to move on or to join us."

Paul and Anne began to speak at the same time, and Paul apologized to Anne and said, "Go ahead, honey."

Anne said, "I infer from all the information we have been given, or should I save inherited, that your group's intention is to protect humankind." Kim said, "Absolutely," and

Anne finished with, "A week ago, we were running from a life that seemed meaningless and overwhelming, and we were afraid; then, with the mold exposure, the one thing we had to count on was our health was shattered, and Paul and I became debilitated physically and mentally, and you all intervened and raised us from the what we were thinking was the dead. Paul and I want to be a part of what you all are trying to create and do whatever we can to make things better for all people of the earth".

Kim: "I think it's time to have some food, and then I think we should get outside for a little recreation. I think your kids need to see some of the property, and we can walk over to Hank's tower, and you can see a beautiful view of Havre".

Jeff: "We can pick on this tomorrow after you guys have a chance to process."

So sandwiches were made, a small meal was had, and the group bundled up and went outside for a nice walk over to Hank's tower and a view of Montana's beauty.

Chapter 49

As usual, the morning always rolled around, and for Jeff and Kim, it was really nice; no one was up as Jeff got in the shower. To Jeff's pleasant surprise, Kim joined him and apologized for falling asleep on him last night.

Jeff: "I thought it was me." and

Lt C offered, "You both fell asleep at the same time."

Kim shouted, "Get out of our shower, Lt C. You promised you wouldn't do that."

Lt C: "I have my eyes closed."

Jeff laughed out loud, and Kim shouted again, "Don't encourage him, Jeff." at the same time, she turned the hot water off, and Jeff screamed bloody murder.

Wide a wake, Jeff decided after getting dressed he would make his mother's famous waffles with bacon and scrambled eggs, so within 30 minutes, the house smelled of breakfast, and everyone was up, hungry, and sitting at the dining room table. Needless to say, six happy faces made the day seem like a dream; both Kim and Jeff felt like life couldn't get any better, and they could see that Paul and Anne and their kids were there, too.

Jeff indicated to Paul and Anne that he had a couple of offers to make and hopefully would quell any concerns they might have about their future. He explained about the new Farm Hank had purchased and about the home that was move-in ready, except for furniture, and then he carefully explained the one topic they hadn't discussed, which had to do with the AIs. This allowed Jeff to inform Paul that the AIs had assisted several of his webpage clients to resolve what they had determined to be critical support while Paul was out of commission, and to Jeff's surprise, Paul didn't seem at odds with it, and Lt C said he had intervened to help Paul understand and explain exactly what Gaith had done. With much of the acceptance interjected by the AIs, Paul was on board with this new partnership. Since it was Saturday and Jeff was off, he offered to take Paul and Anne over to see the new home, and at the same time, Lt C indicated he had covered this with Hank, and Hank was OK with selling or renting the property to Paul.

A half-hour later, Paul, Anne, and Jeff headed over to the new house, and Kim said she would stay with the kids; the morning was warmer than usual, and Kim thought it would be nice to spend time outside.

Paul and Anne really liked the house but were concerned about zero furniture; their furniture was all home with mold, and the authorities had condemned the home and all of its contents. Jeff said no problem; if you are sure about this house, we can head into Havre and get replacements. Jeff checked in with Hank to make sure he had no problems with offering the three-bedroom house on the new Farm to Paul and Anne. Hank indicated it was fine and that Martha had filled him in on the mold couple, and he left it up to Jeff to decide on the price. Paul had indicated his insurance was reimbursing him for the entire purchase price of the condemned property, and Jeff used his insurance value as the purchase price for the Hartley Farm House, which made Paul's day. Since Martha was a known shopper at Fran's Furniture Store, Jeff called and asked if she wanted to take Paul and Anne there to buy a house full of furniture, and she jumped at the chance; she loved furniture shopping. She said it was the second most favorite thing she liked to do, second only to picking up strangers on lonely back roads.

Jeff left Paul and Anne at the Hartley House, where Martha was going to join them; she was bringing a tape measure to measure each room and get a feel for the place so they could minimize the returns where furniture didn't fit or just wasn't right. Lt C got an upgraded computer app from AMP and had AMP install it on Martha's laptop, which he reminded her to bring. It turned out that the app had room measurement capability, so Martha and the company wouldn't need to measure rooms. The app could scan each room and update the app. Martha arrived 20 minutes later and took over for Jeff, and Jeff headed back home. Martha warned Jeff she might need some muscle this afternoon to help set up furniture, and he said he would keep the afternoon free and see if Terry and Shawn would be available to help.

Chapter 50

As Jeff was driving back home, Hank called and asked if Jeff could stop in at the Farm Mill for a minute. He needed a little help in finishing the extension at the saw to handle the larger logs.

"No problem," Jeff responded. "Be there in 10".

As it turned out, Jeff and Hank spent the rest of the morning fitting the pieces together to handle the multiple-ton logs. It turned out that the oversized chains used to move the logs were not easy to handle, and Hank needed some of Jeff's mental muscles to handle and fit the chain links in place. They even put a log on the extension and made a test cut to make sure the saw and the feeder extension worked as advertised. It did, and after one run, they did the recommended reviews by the manufacturer, and by noon, they were having a celebration beer. Kim called to invite them to a hot lunch, and Hank and Jeff headed over to Jeff's place.

Lunch was great, and Martha checked in as they were finishing and said they definitely were going to need a crew to help set up furniture at the Hartley House, so Jeff asked Hank if he could get ahold of Terry and Shawn and see if they were available around 4 pm to help move and setup up bedroom furniture plus a family room couch, the rest of the furniture had to be ordered and would be delivered late next week which would coincide with when Paul and family's extended care by Kim was expected to end.

Hank said, "Sure, no problem," and called Terry.

Hank: "Hey Terry, any chance you and Shawn or a couple of guys from the RES want to do a little work this afternoon?"

Terry: "Funny you should ask; my cousins were just inquiring about any odd jobs you might have for them; they both got laid off from the shutdown of the Hartley Farm."

Hank: "Well, tell them they will be first on the list when I start back up in a few weeks, and I will go ahead and hire them at my farm and then transfer them back to the Hartley Farm."

Terry: "Wow, I'm going to get some brownie points out of this; they were pretty upset about being unemployed; they had worked at the Hartley farm for a few years, and apparently, they didn't see this coming."

Hank: "Let them know I will hire them back and keep their seniority intact. Did they have retirement and health benefits?"

Terry: "No, but they said the corporation that had been running the farm said they were considering it?"

Hank: "You can let them know that I do offer Health and Retirement, and they are eligible immediately, so they will both get a raise and fringe benefits."

Terry said, "Outstanding Hank, we will be at the Hartley place at four this afternoon, and you can meet my cousins. Be careful. They may try and kiss you; this is a lifesaver for them; they both are in their early 20s, married with small children."

Hank: "OK then, I will be prepared. Thanks, Terry; see you around 4."

Hank passed on the conversation with Terry to Jeff, and Kim interrupted and asked if they all could head over to the Hartley place and take a look. She thought Annie and Steven would get a kick out of seeing their new home, and Kim was curious, too.

Hank: "Let's do it. I wanted to check out the backyard and see if there were any finishing touches I could add as a housewarming?"

So the group headed back over to the new house; Martha had checked in and said they were in the process of loading the furniture on a truck and would be pulling out in a half hour. Hank figured if Terry and the cousins were available, they might as well come over now, so he called Terry back to let him know they could come anytime.

The afternoon went great; Hank met two new employees, who were so happy they had tears in their eyes, which carried over to everybody except Paul and Anne's kids and, of course, Alesha, who was sound asleep the whole time.

Chapter 51

The next month was fairly quiet. The new members of the Group, Paul and family, got moved into their new place, and all their furniture arrived, with only the wrap-around couch being too big and requiring a sectional piece to be replaced.

AMP had finished all the background on Paul and his wife, Anne. D had their hardware upgrade and devices in the mail, and Paul was technologically blown away with all the new bells and whistles AMP and company added to his business offerings. D convinced Paul to use a section of his basement for his primary server support and to add servers at each of D's data centers so he could maximize backup and recovery and minimize loss of service. Paul jumped at the opportunity, and D picked up 50 new service provider contracts. It is a truly win-win move for both Paul and D.

Hank even got an opportunity to expand the logging farm business with a friend and acquaintance bordering the southeastern corner of the RES, deciding they wanted to retire early and move to South Carolina, where their daughter had settled with her husband and four children. Hank jumped at the chance to pick up another 4,000 acres of prime forest. However, the price was almost 20 million dollars and would be a stretch for Hank, but he was convinced he should do it. This would give him all the control over all the accessible land surrounding the Indian Caves and, of course, the expanded alien base under them. A portion of the alien assets from the moon had been moved there, and they were not on anyone's inventory except the Montana groups' it had been decided that they would keep them secret just in case the worst-case scenario happened and they needed to leave town in a hurry. As a part of the Disaster Recovery Plan developed by AMP, the second alien outpost, unknown to anyone else, located on Mars was being quietly converted to human occupancy using assets at the secondary base on the moon, and resources were being funneled quietly between the US Space Force base, the secondary alien base and then moved to Mars. Once the Mars location was converted and independent, Frank would present an opportunity to the US Space Force to lease a portion of the Mars facility with the full understanding that they would be tenants and not owners. The Montana group was fully aware that when this agreement was negotiated, their existence would have to be acknowledged, but who and where they were hopefully could be kept secret. Ultimately the issue of government control was going to be a problem, but AMP and Gaith felt confident that would not occur in the next decade unless, of course, everything went south, or a more appropriate saying Jeff had used in high school that Kim hated, if everything went to shit in a handbag.

The next decade was going to be dependent on world politics, but the baseline project of making all nuclear weapons sterile would keep most, if not all, of the conflicts conventional. With the augmentation of AI support owned and operated by the US Government and the quiet overview by AMP and Gaith, the Montana Group felt comfortable with the current shadow working relationship.

Chapter 52

The next few years were a blur to everyone, and things didn't go, as Jeff would have put it, "to shit in a handbag," which pleased everyone.

On a bright and cheerful morning, Jeff asked Kim: "Hey honey, any chance you wanted to take a trip to Mars."

Kim: "Are you serious?"

Jeff: "Yes, AMP said the final conversions were complete, and the Mars Base was now humanized."

Kim: "Any chance you could take the trip by yourself? I am sorta in an earth-based funk, and Alesha needs my attention."

Jeff: "OK, but don't say I didn't offer; I am going with Terry, as it turns out our space suits from our salvage mission to the moon are still functional, and AMP and Gaith want us to do a walk-through before we make any overtures to the US Space Force."

Kim: "What's their concern?"

Jeff: "According to Gaith, they want to make sure that the portions we are keeping for the Group are secure and protected as the Mars Base is our failsafe refuge.

Kim: "Well, have a good trip; when are you leaving?"

Jeff: "In about an hour, and we will be gone for a couple of days."

Kim: "Wow, you expected me to go in an hour?"

Jeff: "No, Lt C said he was 99.9% sure you would say no, and the short notice took care of the other .01%, so I knew ahead of time you weren't interested."

Kim: "Can I go next time, and can you give me a day to prepare?"

Jeff: "Sure will do."

Jeff had packed and was headed up to the cave base spaceport to catch his ride to Mars. This was really exciting for Jeff, and he had a number of calls from Terry, and he was excited, too.

The access to the base was through the condemned main chamber at the Indian tunnels; it was camouflaged with a number of secure access points that took Terry and Jeff 15 minutes to get through the front door. they had to take an elevator to the launch deck, where the space vehicle was waiting. The facility was maintained by maintenance bots that were very impressive, the tunnel facility was also very impressive, and the launch egress was also camouflaged with alien technology that rivaled the best smoke and mirrors and supplemented the invisibility technology on the spacecraft.

Jeff and Terry proceeded to the spacecraft, put on their space suits, and took their seats at what they assumed was the pilot/co-pilot position of the craft. AMP came online and said that the trip was fully automated and would take about 6 hours. It could be done quicker, but to remain undetected, the craft had to travel at slow speeds while within the moon's rotational position.

The seats were very comfortable, which Gaith let Jeff and Terry know were custom fitted to Jeff and Terry, as the alien seats were not that compatible with human anatomy, which Jeff and Terry remembered from the previous trip to the moon.

Their current trip was scheduled so that they would arrive at the Mars base with the planet facing away from Earth, which would allow them to access the landing facility incognito. All went as planned, and the spacecraft landed on pad one and then took a short elevator trip down into the launch bay. An arrival/departure tube was connected to the spacecraft, and the all-clear light came on, and a mechanical voice announced that passengers could disembark.

"Wow, this is like the real thing," Terry chirped and

Jeff responded, "It sure is."

Jeff and Terry spent the rest of the day on a tour of the facility, and both were duly impressed. The alien bots were magicians and had converted the facility to look like it had been built originally for human occupation. AMP and Gaith participated in the review, and there was a constant dialog about each modification or alteration to make the alien base compatible with humans. They also helped review the stealth efforts to make sure the size and extent of this base were adequately hidden. By the end of the first day, Jeff and Terry were exhausted; with the promise that Lt C would deliver his sleep-induced magic, the human astronauts retired for the night.

The following morning, they started another series of facility reviews and verified the critical life systems and backups for failsafe and disaster recovery assurances. Everything checked out, and by noon Earth time on the second day of the mission, Jeff and Terry were back in space suits, entering the spacecraft for their trip home. Due to moon base positioning and earth observation requirements, the trip back took twice as long; once the existence of the Group and its capability were known, the stealth measures could be dropped, and the travel times significantly reduced.

Jeff arrived home at 2 am and was dead on his feet; most of the physical reaction, AMP explained, was due to the effects of lower gravity and the return to earth gravity. AMP didn't think they would ever be able to eliminate all of this, but based on creator feedback, the more exposure you had to it, the more adapted you became to it. Jeff hoped that he never became more adapted; he really liked planet Earth and didn't feel like he was space-borne material.

Kim and Alesha were sound asleep when Jeff got home, so he quietly crawled into bed and, with Lt C's help, was comfortable and asleep in minutes.

Chapter 53

Kim: "Well, good morning, sweetheart. Your girlfriend wanted a kiss," and Alesha giggled as she slobbered all over Jeff's face.

Jeff: "Love it, baby girl," and turned over as Alesha kicked him in the head.

Kim: "Oops, sorry about that."

Jeff: "No sweat, no harm, no foul,"

As Kim walked out of the bedroom with Alesha, she said, "I was going to make waffles and bacon for breakfast; you interested?"

Jeff: "That would be great. Give me 20 for a quick shower, and I'll be there. Love ya."

Kim: "Love ya back," and Alesha giggled. "Dada love."

As Jeff sat down at the breakfast table, Kim asked, "How did the mission to Mars go?"

Jeff: "Great, the bots did a great job, and I would say it is ready for human occupancy. I think AMP was going to give Frank the go-ahead to begin a discussion with his bosses at the Space Force and start planning for occupancy."

The US Space Force had fully occupied the Moon Base, was fully trained, and functional with the alien technology. In addition, the first Earth production of alien space crafts was in testing, and it looked like Earth's Space Forces would inherit, at least within its solar system, a fully functional Space Command. America had decided that the technology was something it had to share with the world; multi-nation agreements had been developed and implemented with half of the countries on Earth, and the US and their allies were in the final stages of negotiation with the remaining nations. The United Nations was being dismantled and replaced by a one-world government, and the necessary rules and procedures were being finalized as the other Nations on Earth agreed to terms and conditions. Earth would continue to respect the borders of every nation, but in space, there were no borders or separate nations; the Earth was our nation in space, and peace and protection were primaries.

Chapter 54

The Montana Group decided a Group Meeting was needed, and all group members were notified that a group meeting was scheduled at Jeff and Kim's home on June 1, 2026, and would represent the 5th formal gathering and the start of discussions on how to introduce the Group to the new world order.

June 1 rolled around faster than anyone expected, and at 10 am on June 1, 2026, Gaith called the meeting to order.

Gaith introduced the need for the Group to raise its visibility to the world; all of the technology and alien assets were now integrated or being integrated into normal life on Earth. This meant that the secrecy for much of the Group's use of alien technology was no longer needed as the rest of the world knew about it and were integrating it into their daily lives. The consensus of the Group was that it made sense and would alleviate the angst each member carried with a sense that we are different. After a few hours of discussion and explanations, one or two arguments, and Lt C's expert calming techniques, the Group unanimously agreed that it could start using the alien technology in the open just like the rest of the world.

With the 'we are different' question eliminated, AMP introduced the one caveat that the AIs felt couldn't be shared with the rest of the world at the present time. SBI, 'Shared Biological Intelligence,' still needed to be fully explained or understood. Jeff and Kim were no longer experiencing mutations or increases in their mental and physical capabilities, but their current talents were as close to superhuman as most of the comic book characters exhibited and were not talents the Group wanted anyone to know about. Alesha, now 4 ½, was normal so far in all respects. Kim and Jeff had expected her to begin to exhibit signs, but to date, she was simply a normal 4-year-old; her only extended capability seemed to be her closeness with Lt C, and even Lt C said there was something there, but he could not add any more of an explanation than Jeff and Kim could.

AMP explained that certain pieces of the DNA mutation were identified but the connection from these pieces of mutation to the talents Jeff and Kim experienced could not be explained. There were some universal linking particles that connected our psyche to our physiology and, in turn, to our electrical mass, and like dark matter, we just have to figure out how to see it or measure it, and so far, we are coming up blank. The AIs were missing something in human anatomy. Sori and Tori had likened it to dark matter; there was a force in nature no one had discovered, and it was alluding to their discovery. There is no downside for us individually or as a group in keeping Jeff and Kim's secret and for Jeff and Kim hiding these extraordinary talents. They are extremely good at it, and no one at present suspects they even exist.

With the major items of concern discussed and the group consensus unanimously confirmed, Frank made a motion, and D seconded that the Montana Group be elected the Board of Directors of LoveStrong and that a construction and reclamation project be approved to repair the Indian Ruins and install a state-of-the-art Museum and protective facilities for all of the sacred historical habitat. In addition, it was approved to erect a multimillion-dollar Montana Space Port to open up the use of the assets the Group had stored under the Sacred Indian Grounds. It was voted that this facility would be advertised as the LoveStrong World Headquarters and used accordingly.

The final approval was a go-ahead for Frank and D to inform the US Space Force of the Mars facility LoveStrong was giving to the US Government. In addition, LoveStrong strongly recommended that the US Government open up access to this Mars facility to all World

Government entities so that all benefits of space exploration were shared equally across all peoples of Earth.

Chapter 55

The Cruise family, now known as the Coulters, Jeff, Kim, and Alesha, could not be more pleased with the turn of events, even if they would have to maintain a veil of secrecy over their extended capabilities. They considered it second nature not to use these abilities quietly and under the radar and felt more than comfortable maintaining a low profile.

Although Kim didn't know why she had not become pregnant a second time, she had done a number of tests to ensure there was no specific cause; she discovered yesterday afternoon that she was, in fact, pregnant for a second time but hadn't informed Jeff yet. She felt like now was a good time.

Kim "Jeff, you got a minute"

Jeff said, "Sure, honey. What's up?"

Kim: "I came across some good news yesterday that I thought you would like to hear."

Jeff "OK"

Kim: "I'm pregnant."

Jeff walked over slowly to Kim and hugged her and actually started crying and said, "I was so scared that Alesha would be alone and not have a brother or sister; I have always felt incomplete as an only child; it was why I gravitated to Lt C so strongly in the service, he was my older brother and we had a bond that I don't think can be established with anyone but a brother or sister, but I do believe I achieved it with Lt C."

Kim: "I don't know why it took this long to conceive a second time, but I don't wish or plan on stopping at two children, so let's hope this is a healthy pregnancy and that we have at least six children, I need a large family."

Jeff "You have my vote and my love honey, six children it is."

With that, Jeff inquired if there was anything he could do and

Kim said, "Yes, let's go on a vacation. We haven't had a break for a long time, and most of the needs that dictated us to be set apart are now lifted; I think we deserve a vacation."

Jeff: "That's a great idea; let's see if Hank and Martha would like to go on a cruise to Hawaii for their 4th anniversary; we could even see if Hank wanted to follow through on his promise to implement an employee vacation bonus, he was certainly motivated when he and Martha returned from their honeymoon."

Kim: "That would be fantastic. I have never been on a boat, and I would love to go on a cruise. I know Alesha would get a real kick out of it; she is constantly talking about boats."

Jeff: "OK then, Hank is working with us today on mapping the new farm he purchased; I will bring this up and see what we can come up with."

Chapter 56

Jeff met Hank, Terry, and Shawn at the Farm, and they piled into Hanks's truck and headed out to the new addition to Hank's Tree Farm holdings. The new Farm was only about 10 miles as the crow flew, but the roads were 20 miles, and they were all single-lane; it was way out of the way by main roads, so this farm addition may entail some highway construction to improve access by the rest of the Farm.

Jeff: " Say Hank, you remember your promise when you and Martha returned from your honeymoon about looking into an annual vacation bonus for your employees?"

Hank: "I sure do. Last night, Martha and I got out our wedding and honeymoon pictures, and we talked about wanting to make that trip again."

Terry: "I'm in; I'll call Sonya and have her pack."

Hank: "Whoa, hold your horses; we are talking about 30 or 40 people with kids; this is going to take some planning."

Shawn said, "Terry, have Sonya call Linda and tell her to pack too."

Hank: "Come on, you guys, this is going to take more than hours to put together, and with all the money I put out for this farm addition, I may have to borrow from the devil to afford a company vacation."

Hank decided to call his travel agent and ask him to put together the same trip he had done four years ago for his honeymoon but increase it to a travel party of 40 with children. He talked with Davis at Havre Holiday Travels, and he said he would get right on it; it may take a week, but is there any chance Hank had a date in mind?

Hank: "You guys have any problem or conflicts with going the 1st of next month, today, November 10, so can you guys do the beginning of December?"

We all thought about it and, 4 seconds later, unanimously agreed.

Hank let Davis know the first week of December would be great, and Hank assumed a ten-time frame, which Davis confirmed.

Hank: "OK, now you guys should call your wives and make sure you and your family are available."

As Hank talked with Davis about the details, Jeff, Terry, and Shawn called their wives to clear their availability for a cruise in the first half of December.

With the Annual Amor Employee Vacation Bonus in full planning mode, the guys arrived at the new Farm and redirected their attention to mapping and tree categorizing, and the next 5 or 6 hours were spent on business.

On the ride back to the yard, Hank called Davis back to see if he had come up with anything.

Hank: "Hi, Davis. I thought I would check in and see if you had any news or need additional information."

Davis: "You won't believe this, Hank, but Carnival Cruise Line has added a maiden voyage the first week in December, and it is offering 50% discounts; I can get you the full package for 50 people for $75,000 and that is ALL INCLUSIVE, off boat activities included and the ship one of the new mega busters with endless adult and children activities."

Hank had to interrupt Davis. He was so excited. "I don't think I have the decision to make this sounds almost too good to be true."

Davis: "That was my reaction; I just can't believe it."

Hank: "I'll tell you what, Davis, if you are willing to sign up as our manager, I will include you in the 50 and pay you $5,000 to manage the entire tour, beginning to end, and you can bring your family; I need to confirm numbers on my end."

Davis: "There is no way they can fill this ship by early December, so they are allowing people to reserve larger numbers and requiring only 75% passenger usage for the 50% discount billing; this means we could ask for 75 passengers and still only be held accountable for 50."

Hank: "Well, this sounds like a no-brainer. Go ahead and confirm 75, and I will budget $100,000. Can you manage this, Davis?"

Davis: "Absolutely, and thank you, Hank. This is a great end to the year, and my wife is gonna want at least a kiss from you and Martha."

Jeff was really excited, and after letting Kim know what was being planned, she was ecstatic.

It took the Group 3 days to complete the survey and mapping of the Hartley farm, and Shawn had a new mobile application so he could enter all the data as they went through mapping and, measuring and categorizing the trees. It turned out to be a lot easier than Hank had anticipated, and Hank went ahead and scheduled cutting at the new Farm the week after they returned from the Hawaii Cruise.

Chapter 57

Much of the next few weeks was spent getting three new teams up to date on the Farm for cutting, trimming, and transporting logs and limbs. Some of the new hires were destined to drive two new trucks, which Hank had purchased to bring his transporting to area mills in-house. The new hires consisted mostly of Tribal members from the local Chippawa reservation and were in some form or fashion 6 degrees of separation from Shawn and Terry. Hank had offered employment to the crew that worked the Hartley Farm for the out-of-state cooperative, but none of them chose to stay. In preparation for the annual vacation crew, Hank offered a double bonus to three employees who would stay behind as a skeleton crew to maintain security on the farms. Hank ended up having one of Frank's guys sign up for the two weeks to watch the farms if he could bring his family for a vacation, which Hank jumped at and committed to. Hank offered one of his bunkhouse apartments for free.

With all the plans coming together, Davis had finagled the cruise line to give Hank's Group 75 passenger boarding passes for the original $75,000 as apparently, the cruise line was not getting the signups it had hoped for. Apparently, COVID continues to affect people's choices, and the cruise business was one of the industries that were hit hard by quarantining requirements.

The Farm continued to produce lumber and ship logs all the way to the end of November, and the three new crews got a chance to train and get acquainted with all aspects of the work they would do on the Farm. Hank had safety training and certification for each of the new hires, along with any employee who hadn't previously had safety training access.

By the first day of December, the employees who had chosen to stay behind to watch the Farm were up to speed on what was expected of them, and Lance Petrie from Frank's crew was comfortable with what he would do for security. Just in case, Hank got his outside security services to provide Lance with a couple of guys in the morning and afternoons to drive the Farms and check on stuff. The conversion project at the Indian Grounds was under full swing, so there was a construction crew there, and they had their own security to protect their assets and the project site.

Chapter 58

Hank called December 7th C day for Cruise Day. The bus was at the Farm's main lot, and passengers started trickling in at 7 am. Hank had opened the main office with coffee and 17 orders of Stu's cinnamon rolls, and by 10 am, the bus was loaded. The coffee and rolls were gone, and 75 Armor Farm employees and family were ready to head to the County Airport to the LoveStrong charter jet to Seattle. D had arranged the charter flight, and LoveStrong was able to offer Hank a discount as several aircraft were surplus and just sitting while LoveStrong finished another reorganization. The flight to Seattle was a little over 5 hours, and the Cruise Line was allowing the Armor Farm group to board the ship that afternoon and evening, allowing the Group to start their first-night stay in Seattle on board. Davis had explained how complicated it would have been if the Armor group had had to board with the rest of the passengers. Davis shared with Hank that on the last cruise he managed, they had to stand in line for 4 hours before they got to their onboard quarters. Hank said everyone in his

Group might not have tolerated that.

Chapter 59

The Armor Vacation flight landed at Seattle International at 5 pm December 7. The passengers and luggage were moved to the waiting bus and driven directly to the boarding facility at the Seattle port, and the Group was dropped off at the proverbial gangplank and ushed on the gorgeous ship called "Shangrala." Porters secured the luggage from the bus, and the Armor passengers were handed their ship credentials and room assignments and shown the way to their section of the ship. The cruise line had arranged for a late dinner, and the passengers were instructed to be at the dining room 'Crystal' by 7 pm Pacific Standard Time. Everyone freshened up and made it to the dining room on time. To say the Group was impressed would be the understatement of the year; this ship was fantastic, and everyone was impressed.

Jeff opened the door to their cabin, and Alesha snuck through his legs and made a b-line for the big bed.

Yelling "Mine Mine"

Jeff smiled and took Kim's hand, and they walked over to the smaller single bed, lay down with their legs sprayed over the edges, and

Jeff said, "Well, this isn't going to work. I guess we'll have to tell Uncle Hank we can't go. Our bed isn't big enough."

Alesha: "Daddy, I'm just kidding, but maybe I can spend a few nights with you and Mommy in the big bed?"

Kim: "That's a promise, and maybe we'll do a girl's night and make Daddy sleep on the floor!"

That got a laugh from everyone and

Jeff said, "Let's get cleaned up and head to the dining room. They have a meal for us, and I don't want to be late."

Jeff, Kim, and Alesha were assigned seats at the head table with the ship's Captain, along with Hank and Martha, Stephanie, and

Nyla, and by 7, the Armor group was seated and being served salads. The Captain asked for attention and gave a short welcoming speech and a short prayer of thanksgiving, and the meal, and conversations started back up.

The Captain was interested in Hanks's logging operation, and we all enjoyed an hour of Armor history and Hank's philosophies; needless to say, no mention was made of Aliens, and Lt C quietly praised Hank for not making one slip about AMP or the AI's. The Captain was enthralled by Hank's history and shared he grew up in a rural area in Montana. A place called Flathead Lake and the small town Kalispell, and he felt like he couldn't have had a better childhood.

Hank agreed with him and said, "My family had over 150 years on the same land, and our logging farm has always been profitable; we are extremely lucky to have only good memories."

The meal consisted of prime rib and three different kinds of potatoes with an assortment of vegetables and was superbly prepared; if this was typical of the dinners on this cruise, everyone was going to have to go on a diet when they returned to Montana. Needless to say, no one was disappointed in the desserts, and Alesha couldn't have been happier.

By the second dessert, Alesha was falling asleep in her chair, and Jeff and Kim excused themselves to head back to their cabin; they thanked the Captain for his wonderful dinner and conversation and said their goodnights.

The following day was spent touring the ship while the remaining passengers got boarded based on the fact that it took all day to get everyone on board and in their cabins, and by mid-afternoon, the Armor group had only seen half the ship, the size of this vessel became enormously overwhelming. The Colters and the Armors decided to pass on dinner, went to a small Sushi and Tempura bar on deck f, then took Alesha to a Disney movie called 'Love on Mars' a long overdue sequel to the movie 'The Space Between Us,' and it was very interesting and eye-opening. Alesha had a million questions and made following the plot a little difficult, but she asked them in such a cute way that it made the movie even more enjoyable. Even Hank commented that he didn't think he would have enjoyed the movie half as much without Alesha, and Martha seconded the comment.

We all returned to our cabins and decided an early night was called for. Kim OK'd Alesha's request to sleep with us and my two girls looked at me for an agreement. What can a guy do? I smiled and nodded my assent.

I mumbled to Lt. C, "You're going to help out here, right?"

Lt C: "I certainly can," and again, I could sense the smile on Lt C's face.

Chapter 60

As per the cruise itinerary, the ship left port at midnight on December 1 for five days at sea; no one in our stateroom stirred as the ship pulled out to sea.

Our stateroom had a lovely stern balcony, and I was the first one up and quietly opened the doors; it was a bit cold, so I put on my robe and went outside. A brochure was on the table, and it advertised breakfast in your room, including Alesha's favorite blueberry waffles; the only qualification was it took a minimum of 45 minutes to deliver, so I got on the ship phone, which conveniently had an extension on the balcony and ordered breakfast. About 30 minutes later, the sliding glass door opened, and Alesha poked her head out. I told her to put on pants and a sweatshirt and come on out; the next thing I heard was Alesha asking Kim, who was sound asleep, where her sweatshirt was, and I kicked myself,

I heard Kim say, "You owe me, Jeff," and 2 minutes later, Kim and Alesha joined me outside.

Kim said, "I'm hungry and need a cup of coffee," and like magic, a knock came from the stateroom door, and I told Alesha your waffles were here. Go let them in."

The steward rolled a cart through our room and the maze of clothes Alesha had strewn about looking for her sweatshirt and brought the cart out to the balcony. I tipped him, and he left quietly, saying just put the cart in the hall when you are done and press the done button on your ship phone. I thanked him, and he said you are welcome and welcome to Shangrala and smiled.

The breakfast was great, and I don't believe Alesha has enjoyed blueberry waffles or bacon as much as she did this morning. I'd never seen her smile and eat before; she laughed between bites, but she actually was chewing with a smile on her face. I think I am in love all over again; what a gift God has given Kim and me. " Thank you, Lord, for Kim and Alesha."

Jeff: "So guys, what do you want to do today? We are at sea for over four days, so we should map out a big event for each day and some other interesting things to do."

Kim: "What is the temperature out now, and what will it be this afternoon?"

Jeff: "I think I saw something that said Hawaii was 70 degrees, so maybe as we get closer, the air temperature will warm up; we should ask. I assume you are trying to determine if we can use the outside pools?"

Kim: "Yes, but I guess we can use the inside pools, so I won't worry about it."

Alesha: "Do they have water slides?"

Kim: "Maybe we will look; I thought I saw a sign for something yesterday?"

An hour later, we set off on our first shipboard adventure. We had on our matching sweatsuits with our swim trunks underneath and our beach towels under our arms. We had to talk Alesha out of wearing her flippers and underwater goggles; we explained the water slide park was midship and it would take her an hour to get there in flippers. She considered my request and acquiesced, and 10 minutes later, we entered the water park. Alesha was in seventh heaven, and she pulled Kim and me right along with her. Three and a half hours later, we headed back to our room. We took a wrong turn, and Lt C didn't help; I thought I heard him giggle, and now I know why. Our wrong turn took us past a 31-flavor ice cream store, and you guessed it, we all had chocolate chip cones. As Kim was wiping Alesha's mouth, Hank and Martha strolled into the shop.

"Hey guys," Hank said

"How's the ice cream," Martha asked, and

Alesha said, "great."

Hank: "Have you been swimming already?" and

Jeff: "Yes, they have a fairly large water slide park, and it is pretty neat."

Alesha "I went on every slide" and

Kim: "I can attest to that; I think I went down more slides in the last three hours than I have in my whole life."

"and we can do it again this afternoon," Alesha said with a great big smile.

Hank: "Well, your day is planned; Martha and I have messages in 20 minutes; you guys want to meet for lunch in an hour at Smitty's; it is supposed to be world-famous hamburgers and fries".

Alesha "Yes, Yes, Yes"

Kim: "I guess you have your answer. See you there at 1".

We headed back the right way, and I made sure by telling Lt. C he was slipping and had to keep us on track, which he confirmed he would do; he covered his lapse by saying he knew we needed an ice cream.

We all three took showers and put on comfy clothes and, at a quarter to 1, headed out to Smitty's.

Chapter 61

The following four days were a ball, and Kim and I marveled at how much fun Alesha was having; our little girl seemed to be coming out of her shell, and she was really enjoying having playmates. Shawn and Terry's kids were great, and they seemed to enjoy all the same things Alesha did; they even had sleepovers, one night in our room, one night in Terry's, and one night in Shawn's room. Kim and I even got a couple of nights on our own, which was fantastic.

I asked Lt C, "Are you having a good time? You haven't said much on the trip so far".

Lt C: "I'm doing good, and I am enjoying myself too if, in fact, I have a myself; I am noticing a bit more connection to Alesha but in a very comfortable way; she is an amazing child, and she sees so much of what is going on around her."

Jeff: "What do you mean?".

Lt C: "Well, first off, she is beginning to assume significance like you and Kim. I think we are morphing into a wider SBI group, and I think she is more active in the thoughts that we share, so you may want to take that into consideration?"

Jeff: "This sounds like a conversation we should have with the four of us?"

Lt C: "I think it may be time to do that, but I would also like to include AMP and Gaith, as I think we need to understand all of our options going forward."

Jeff: "How do you mean."

Lt C: "There is a part of Alesha I am not privy to, like I am with you and Kim, and I am not sure what the significance is of that; this may be part of what AMP can shed light on?"

At that, Jeff inquired if he had to call AMP or if he was AMP tuned in to the Group, and Lt C said, "AMP was not easy dropping on Jeff and family, so it would be necessary either to speak AMP's name and ask for a conference or to called him on your cell phone."

So Jeff spoke AMP's name and asked if they could have a meeting in half an hour, and AMP responded that they could; at that very moment, Alesha returned to their room with Kim, and Jeff asked AMP if he could move the meeting up to now.

AMP responded, "Sure, I am on board with you now".

At that, Jeff explained to Kim what Lt C had said earlier and that AMP was now remotely connected to them, and we needed to have a conversation with the AIs, Lt C, Alesha, and us to clarify issues on Alesha's Shared Biological Intelligence.

Alesha spoke up, "I was wondering when you guys would notice; Lt C said we should wait until you realized he and I were interfacing and then mention we should talk".

Jeff: "Well, that kind of happened this morning, and we thought we would include another entity that has been guiding your mother and me for a while and who we think can be very helpful to us all."

Alesha said, "Lt C has mentioned AMP and did say I would get to meet him and would enjoy his friendship."

Then Alesha said, "Hi Amp," and

AMP responded, "Hi, Alesha."

Kim was staying pretty quiet, so Jeff asked her if she was OK, and she said she was; she was just trying to catch up and hadn't been prepared to discuss all this.

Jeff offered, "We don't have to do it now. We can postpone until you and Alesha and I have discussed it; I just felt Lt C wanted us to begin addressing our current and future direction?"

Kim: "No, it is OK. I just have to wake up a bit and deal with our reality, and I have been having all of the obvious concerns our SBI condition is going to present, and I want to address them now so I can get more comfortable with it."

Jeff: "Is that OK with you, Alesha?"

Alesha: "Sure, I am looking forward to it, I think, even though I'm just 5, I sense I am going on 15, and I see people responding with a degree of curiosity; I definitely am a small 15 or a really mature five, and I can see that in their eyes?"

Lt C: "I can, too, and that is why all of this came up today; you are a treasure, Alesha, and you are special and unique in a good way, and we want to make sure you enjoy your uniqueness."

AMP: "Obviously, Alesha has been a joy to us all, and she is capable of understanding what is happening to her; since we can not introduce the nano-byte technology into her physiology, we have been monitoring her development with a subset system that our creators developed for their children until they could tolerate the nano-byte technology. We, that is, us AIs, that Alesha is now capable of tolerating the nano-byte presented physically, and we can remotely upgrade the subset she has within her and bring up to the full protection of the Nano-byte Command facility. Since much of the system is already in place, she shouldn't feel any difference."

At that, AMP, with Lt C's assistance, implemented a transfer of the knowledge concerning Alesha's circumstance and the nano-byte interface that parents would have with the child, making the technology parentally symbiotic. Both Kim and Jeff felt a little dizzy, and then it cleared; since their nano-byte systems had been in residence for a while, they adjusted to shift and interface with Alesha without any further discomfort. AMP indicated that the overall support interface for parents was automatic, and it gave an advisory support function that they would now have access to. It may be a little disconcerting as they will have both questions and answers pop into their conciseness almost at the same time, so when Alesha has a sniffle, you'll ask yourself if you should give her some Tylenol and then the yes or no pops into your head after the AI's have evaluated the nano-byte command response.

Kim: "As a physician, I kind of like the sound of that; it is just like the internet 'Ask A Nurse' website but on steroids," and Kim laughed at her own joke.

The conference with AMP went on for another hour, with most of the conversation centered on questions from Kim. Jeff, Alesha, and even Lt C were getting more comfortable with how this upgrade was going to affect everybody.

AMP let everyone know that the follow-up to this would be that Alesha needs to act her age, and we all had to help her interpret her actions so that she didn't feel disconnected from the other children. AMP had noticed, as had Lt C, that Alesha was getting along great with Terry and Shawn's kids, and it was extremely important that this socializing continued to happen. Everyone agreed with that, and since Terry and Shawn's kids would, AMP assumed, be getting the nano-byte upgrade, they would be excellent playmates for Alesha. There is no way going forward to put the obvious differences back in the bottle, and all the parents had to sign off on that and be comfortable with it.

More meetings, conferences, and huge amounts of guarantees as the AI's became more a part of the human experience, and more couldn't be ignored when it came to parents and their children.

Chapter 62

Lt C interceded on everyone's behalf to dial down the concerns raised by the conversations over the last few hours, and it helped Kim, Jeff, and Alesha to slide back into vacation mode.

Jeff: "What is on the agenda for today?"

Kim: "I was thinking we could ask Terry and Shawn and family if they wanted to spend the afternoon at the waterpark and pool. I signed us all up for 1 to 5 this afternoon, and it includes food and beverages so we could just chill out and let stuff catch up with us."

Alesha: "I would love that mom."

Jeff said, "OK, I'll give the guys a call and see if they are up to it."

After talking with Terry and Shawn, Jeff told Kim and Alesha they would meet them at the water park in an hour. Thirty minutes later, Kim, Jeff, and Alesha left their room for a day at the slides. Kim mentioned it included all the hamburgers and hot dogs you could eat and world-famous milkshakes, which tickled Alesha pink.

Four hours later, the Coulters crawled back to their room. They had all been required to go on every water slide four times, and Alesha wouldn't take no for an answer. It was fun, but it may be the last time Kim or Jeff ever went to a water park, which she had mentioned to Shawn, and he said that's OK. I will take all the kids to the water park whenever they'd like. Kim had made a lifetime contract with Shawn and felt relieved she would never have to do another water slide.

It was early evening, and it was decided to take the evening off. Alesha had seen a new children's movie was being offered on the in-room video service, and Kim had noticed a room special for soup and salad that they could order through room service, so the Coulters decided to remain in the room this evening, watch a nice movie and have a simple supper.

Chapter 63

Jeff was up early and had arranged for coffee and rolls to be delivered this morning. He checked, and there was a tray sitting outside the door, and he brought it in and out to the balcony. He plugged in the hotplate and quietly shut the balcony door. The view from the balcony was beautiful but a little unnerving, no land or objects visible to the horizon, an awful lot of water for someone who had been living in the midst of a forest for a few years, but Jeff relaxed and let his mind wander on how thankful he was for his family and friends.

Half an hour later, Kim joined him; he poured her coffee and offered her a roll, which, given she had just had a salad the night before and half a hamburger for lunch yesterday, she accepted immediately. She said she felt famished. Jeff asked if she wanted him to order breakfast, and she said yes, so he called and ordered blueberry pancakes with bacon and eggs for a second time, figuring it went over so well the last time he couldn't miss it.

As Jeff and Kim looked out over the water and the sun rose, Alesha poked her head out the sliding glass door and spooked both of them. Daddy, you have a call from AMP, and she handed Jeff his cell phone.

"Hey AMP, what's up," Jeff said

AMP: "Not sure, but I thought I would check in with you and see if you had any concerns."?

Jeff: "No, let me check

. Kim, AMP is just checking in and wanted to know if you had any concerns."

Kim: "No, why isn't he just communicating with both of us?"

Jeff: "She says no, but she wanted to know why you aren't talking to both of us?"

AMP: "That's part of my concern. I seem to be experiencing some functional limitations, and I haven't discovered the cause, so I wanted to check with you guys and see if you have any lapses in communications?"

Jeff: "Not that we've noticed, but I will admit the whole group is pretty relaxed, and no one seems to be thinking about that stuff."

AMP: "Well, that is encouraging; any chance you could bring Lt C into this conversation and double-check with him, too?"

Jeff: "Sure, Lt C. Are you aware of any issues?"

Lt C: "Nope, everybody seems to be OK, and I do not sense any issues at the present time."

AMP: "OK, we will keep running our diagnostics and see if we can't isolate the problem on our end; just let us know if you guys begin to notice anything."

Jeff: "Will do."

Jeff thought to himself that was the second time any of the AIs had brought up an issue they didn't have an answer to, with the other time being the self-destruct issues on the moon. Jeff hoped that this wasn't something that would put a dimmer on the vacation. The sunrise was beautiful, and Jeff wanted to just look forward to his blueberry pancakes. Alesha stuck her head through the door again and asked Kim if she could watch cartoons, and Kim told her until breakfast got here.

As usual, breakfast took about 40 minutes to be delivered. It was great, and the portable hot plates kept everything warm and fresh.

By 9 am, Jeff, Kim, and Alesha were leaving their room for their 9:30 tee time at the ship miniature golf course, and Alesha was excited. She had never played golf but had watched it on TV; for some reason, she understood clubs and wanted to know if she would be able to use a driver. Kim had to tell her that miniature golf was only played with a putter, and they only got to put. They didn't get to swing clubs like they do on TV. Alesha seemed to be OK with that, and Jeff asked her if she understood the difference between swinging a club and putting, and she said she did, that putting was just tapping the ball toward the cup, and you didn't have to hit it real hard. Jeff told her she was right and asked her how she got so smart, and she said I don't think I have anything to do with it. I get answers to questions I didn't know I had; she said this with a smile, so I didn't think it was a problem.

As this was the first time Alesha had played miniature gold, it took us a couple of hours to finish our first round, and Alesha wanted to play again, so we spent another hour on a second round. Alesha's first round was 100, and her second round was 28; I believe her abilities were beginning to show up, and maybe there was an inkling of her learning curve.

Alesha: "That was fun. Let's get lunch at Popeye's. I want chicken nuggets."

Kim: "You're on, sweetheart, let's go. Popeye's is at the other end of the ship," so we headed off for lunch.

After lunch, we decided to take a look at the outside park the cruise ship had on the top deck. The temperature was in the 70s, and the breeze was mild, so after lunch, we went up to the top, which was on deck 18; this was a mammoth ship, and Jeff thought to himself that this almost seemed too big.

We walked around for a couple of hours, and on the way back to our room, we spent a half hour in the pool; no water slides, Kim had pleaded, and by 4 pm, we were back in our room. Since no one had showered today, we decided to rest and then shower, and there was a family dinner for our Group at 7 pm tonight that we all were looking forward to. Apparently, they had arranged entertainment for the children, and it was to be a surprise.

We walked into the dining room at 6:45 and found our assigned table. Hank and Martha were already there, and Terry's family was at our table, with Nyla and Stephanie at the next table with Shawn and his family. The kids decided to do some rearrangements to the seating assignments, and after a short discussion, all the parents gave up and allowed the kids their own table, and we adults had to sit at their own table. We got a bunch of promises and decided to let the kids have the last word.

Dinner was great, and the entertainment was fantastic; it consisted of magic acts and the most amazing display of gymnastics. You could tell the kids were mesmerized, and we didn't get back to our rooms until after 10, and by the time we changed into our PJs and brushed our teeth, we were asleep on our feet.

Chapter 64

Jeff was sound asleep in a tangle with Kim as he began to wake up to Lt C's insistence.

"What is it, Lt C?" Jeff spoke, yawning.

Lt C: "I am afraid this lovely ship is under attack."

Jeff: "What."

Lt C: "It appears two vessels have pulled alongside the Shangrala and are boarding."

Jeff: "You've got to be kidding."

Lt C: "Nope, they are fully armed, but so far, no shots fired."

Lt C began to provide data that AMP was discovering, and apparently, this was an adlib response by China to a US military blockade against Chinese navy forces attempting to land on Taiwan. It would appear China has decided to raise the stakes on its position over Taiwan and to bring the disagreement into the international presence. The Chinese marines have taken control of the Shangrala and are apparently directing it to the Chinese mainland; we are in the process of changing course, and it would appear Hawaii is no longer our destination. AMP said that the AIs feel Jeff has to act immediately. The Chinese marines are bringing explosives aboard and appear to be planting them throughout the ship, and based on communications AMP had intercepted, they are more than willing to sacrifice all 5000+ passengers on the vessel to make their Tawain threats acknowledged and agreed to.

AMP said he had some increased functionality that would put Jeff and Kim, along with Lt C, in a much better defensive position, and he was activating those capabilities now. Kim came awake with a start, and AMP transferred the current circumstances to her as she woke, giving her an understanding of what was going on. AMP then followed up with a plan to disable the explosives and to provide Jeff, Kim, and Lt C the ability to take control of the Chinese marines onboard. AMP further let them know that two of the Space crafts located at the Montana facility had been dispatched and would be arriving in 20 minutes to disable the two Chinese vessels alongside the Shangrala. The main Chinese naval task force was about 400 miles away and was intended to be used to secure control of the Shangrala and accompany it back to China.

Jeff and Kim got dressed; Lt C said he was going to go in his jammies. Jeff couldn't help himself and chuckled. Kim just shook her head. There was a knock on the door, and Terry was there. He said that AMP had told him to come get Alesha and take her back to his room. Alesha was still sound asleep. Kim picked her up and gave her to Terry, and he returned to his room.

AMP directed Jeff to head to the bridge and take control back of the Shangrala and had Kim head to the bottom deck to disable the marines there and the explosives they had planted and activated. It was imperative that those explosives were deactivated as they were being precisely planted to sink the ship, and if denoted, the ship wouldn't take long to sink. AMP also transferred the information Kim would need to locate and disable the devices.

A quick peck and Jeff and Kim took off to make a nightmare for the Chinese marines. Kim had visualized the Chinese marine platoons located all 30 members carrying the explosives and issued a telepathic command "STOP," and the Chinese marines instantly stopped. Kim could hear loud commands coming from their communications devices, and Kim issued the command for the Chinese marines to retrace their steps, disable the devices they had already planted, and then carry all the devices up to the maintenance dock on the rear of the Shangrala and throw them into the sea. She then had all 30 of the marines jump into the sea after the devices and had them begin to disrobe and swim away from the ship. At the same time, Jeff took command of the Chinese marines on the bridge, had them release the crew they had tied up, and then had all of the

Chinese marines sit while the Shangrala placed the restraining cuffs on their hands behind their backs and on their ankles.

At that point, AMP said the space crafts from Montana had located the Chinese fleet, and AMP was negotiating with the fleet commander while also directing their rescue services to the area where the Chinese marine company was swimming naked away from the Shangrala. While AMP was talking to the fleet commander, a battery of antiaircraft artillery started firing on the spacecraft, and the spacecraft immediately returned fire, destroying the Chinese destroyer. AMP started counting down in Chinese from ten while relaying to the fleet commander his ability to destroy all 12 vessels in his fleet; at six, the Chinese commander surrendered and commanded his vessels to cease fire and surrender.

Chapter 65

The Chinese Admiral Yongi was directed by AMP to board the spacecraft and was taken to the Shangrala to meet with Jeff and Kim and to provide a dialog for the episode that had occurred between Chinese forces and the boarding of the Shangrala. Once documented, the Admiral was returned to his ship, and the Shangrala continued on its voyage to Hawaii.

Jeff sent the recording made by Admiral Yongi to the US Naval Admiral in charge of Chinese relations and to the US Space Force Commander. Jeff requested the US Navy to provide some naval assistance to protect the Shangrala and to show US support for high seas safety. It took a few hours for US vessels to arrive, but they did, and the entire Group of passengers on the Shangrala breathed a sigh of relief.

AMP relayed to Jeff and Kim the excellent outcome of negotiations with the US Space Force as to the status of the LoveStrong Charities and the Montana Group recognition. The net of this negotiation was to recognize, under Frank's leadership, the civilian designation for LoveStrong as a US Government Civil Defense Force. LoveStrong became a civilian-military organization dedicated to civilian protection and the primary civilian US Government control point for the civilian population and its processing to future space migration. It was the best of both worlds, the ability of citizens of Earth to populate space colonies as they became available and, at the same time, to protect them from all the harm that could happen as they began to populate the stars.

As potentially devasting as this breach of international diplomacy on the part of the Chinese to detain the Shangrala had been, the outcome ended up resolving the growing concern the Montana Group had about what to do with the Chinese. With the recognition of LoveStrong as a US civilian military force, independent from the US Space Force and with its primary mission of protecting US and worldwide citizens, the Montana Group and LoveStrong could begin to operate in the open and with legal recognition.

The downside of all that had occurred over the last few days had put a damper on the vacation mood of Hanks's Group, and no one in the Group wanted to continue on the cruise. It was decided by phone vote to terminate the Group's participation in the cruise, and the cruise company agreed to refund Hank's costs as the high seas attack by the Chinese was covered under Shangrala's insurance and covered refund of passage fees.

Upon arrival in Hawaii two days after the Chinese event, Hank's Group boarded a private flight back to Montana. The best outcome was that the return flight, using a new aircraft, could land at the smaller Hill County Airport and not require the Group to change aircraft to get back home.

All in all, the Group agreed that a future cruise should be considered, just not one that spent quite so much time at sea. The Hawaii equivalent was to board the cruise ship on the island and use the ship as the Group's hotel, then simply cruise between island attractions and end each day's activities back at the cruise ship. Hank thought that was a good idea, and he instructed Davis to plan a 7-day trip next year at the same time. Apparently, the Shangrala was also offering island packages, so you could enjoy the islands without the 10-day cruise to and from Seattle.

Davis: "I'm on it, Hank."

Hank: "Thanks, Davis; remember to include you and your family. I expect you to be the cruise master again, but this time, leave out the international intrigue."

Davis laughed and said, "I think that is a good idea."

Chapter 66

A bit disappointed but excited to be home, Alesha said, "Mommy, can we finish the movie we were watching on the ship?"

Kim: "Sure, sweetheart, let me make sandwiches for supper, and I will sit and enjoy the movie from the beginning." Kim asked Lt. C to let Jeff know they were having sandwiches in the TV room and were going to watch the movie they had started on the ship. Lt C let Kim know Jeff said he was coming.

Halfway through the movie and the sandwich, Alesha was sound asleep in Jeff's lap. Alesha had put on her PJs, so Kim had Jeff carry her into bed, and Kim told Jeff she was going to put the food away and go to bed, too. They should start this movie over a third time tomorrow and make sure they don't have any more interruptions.

Jeff: "Probably a good idea; I am pooped too. I need to take a shower first, but I see you in bed in 20."

Kim: "OK honey, we all should get a good night's sleep. Lt C, can you assist us on that?".

Lt C: "You bet I will dampen all conscious thought and give you all dreams of teddy bears and sweet holiday music."

Jeff: "Thanks Lt C".

The morning didn't roll around until 10 am for Kim and Jeff's household, and when Kim got up, Alesha was watching Benji 4, her favorite dog movie. Apparently, she had forgotten about the unfinished movie from the night before.

"Hi, sweetheart; when did you get up?" Kim asked.

Alesha: "Just a bit ago, you and Daddy looked so peaceful I didn't want to wake you."

Kim: "That was very thoughtful of you. Would you like pancakes for breakfast?"

Alesha: "Sure, Mom, and bacon, if that's OK."

Kim: "Bacon will help wake Daddy up too."

Jeff rolled around in bed, trying to figure out why he was waking up, and then it hit him. Bacon, I must be hungry; the bacon smells great. Jeff sat up, put on his slippers and robe, and walked sleepy-eyed to the kitchen.

Jeff: "Hi honey, what's for breakfast?"

Kim: "Pancakes and bacon; go sit with Alesha in the TV room, and I'll bring it in."

So Jeff did what he was ordered to do and joined Alesha, watching Benji 4 for at least the 10th time.

Breakfast was great, and Kim had made extra bacon; when they had finished and the movie ended, Jeff said, "I want to go on a run; anyone wants to join me."

Both Kim and Alesha responded, "Yes."

Alesha had been given a motorized three-wheeler that had a perfect speed to stay up with Kim and Jeff's preferred running speed. It had become a favorite pastime for their family. Alesha would yell out occasionally, "Let's pick it up." Apparently, she had seen that in one of her shows and thought it was cute when she noticed we were slowing down. An hour later, we had done our 5-mile track and were bent over with our hands on our knees, and Alesha joked, "Boy, I'm not tired at all. Let's do it again." needless to say, our lack of smiles was an adequate response.

Just as we were getting our breath back, Hank walked over from his place. When I met his eyes as I finally had caught my breath, Lt C warned me that Hank was bearing less than good news,

Hank: "I think we need to have another Montana Group meeting; the Chinese are threatening hostile action in response to the events we encountered at sea."

Jeff: "OK, has everyone been notified."

Hank: "Yes, they are on the way; Frank and D will join us by conference call."

Kim asked Alesha, "Do you want to watch another movie while Daddy and your uncles and aunts have a get-together?"

Alesha responded, "No, I would like to be a part of the meeting. I'm now 5, and I am part of the Montana Group, too.

Kim, a bit surprised, looked at Jeff, who mouthed, "OK with me," and Lt C contributed, "I think she could add to the conversation," so Kim responded, "Then you are formally invited to become part of the Montana Group."

Alesha: "Yeah."

Aleaha decided she didn't want her special dining room chair to be her meeting chair, so she pulled up one of the living room chairs and put two big pillows on it so she would be at the same level as everyone else.

By noon, the Group was assembled and informed that a new member was being introduced, and everyone said hi to Alesha.

Hank brought the meeting to order and spent a half hour describing the actions and intent of the Chinese, including Chinese threats to use Nuclear weapons if they didn't get what they were asking for.

Jeff raised his hand and waited to be recognized by Hank; Nyla contributed, "Not this again. Can't we dispense with parliamentary procedures, please?" Jeff said, "Sorry." it just seemed like the subject matter was a bit serious, and I ought to be a little more formal?"

Jeff: "Are the Chinese aware that all of their nuclear weapons have been disabled?"

AMP: "No, they are not, and under the current circumstances, we are not sure this is something we want to inform them of?"

Hank: "General Artemus is who informed me of the Chinese actions and demands and also said the Chinese had a million soldiers on alert and aircraft warming up to disperse their forces to multiple free world locations, including Taiwan, Japan, and if you can believe it, to Hawaii
"

Jeff: "OK, AMP, do you and your cohorts have suggestions?"

AMP: "We are working on it. The first 10,000 iterations ended with too many casualties on both sides. Still, Luca from the moon said he had some files in storage from our Creators that dealt with a similar situation on a planet in the GN-z11 Galaxy. Still, Luca was having difficulty retrieving it as part of the storage facility had been damaged by the meteorite that damaged the self-destruct mechanism a few years back."

Alesha: "Any chance I could contribute to this discussion?" and all eyes turned to Alesha, "I realize that I am only five and that your normal reaction is to discount what a 5-year-old can contribute; I will let Lt C explain to you who I really represent."

Lt C: "First, I have to apologize to Kim and Jeff for not informing them of Alesha's enhanced capacity. She has not only forbidden me from telling anyone, but she actually has the mental capacity to stop me from telling anyone."

Jeff: "Shit"

Kim: "Jeff"

Jeff: "Sorry"

Alesha: "Daddy, naughty, naughty."

Lt C: "Understood, and I will apologize a thousand times more for violating your trust, Jeff, but Alesha was adamant when I discovered there were two entities forming; Alesha has created a 2nd SBI. She calls her Benji, and Benji has been around for about a year."

Alesha: "Benji, do you want to describe yourself to the Group?"

Benji and a voice like an angel came to the consciousness of each member of the Group and said, "Hi, everyone; it is nice to be formally introduced to you all. I will make this fairly simple. I am a shared intelligence between Alesha, Jeff, and Kim and coexist with Lt C. My capacity seems to be exponentially greater than that Lt C possesses, and I appear to have very little limitation to my awareness. This means that Alesha has had to compartmentalize most of her progression over the last year in order not to alarm her mommy and her daddy. Alesha would liken herself to the condition called split personality; she is both a 5-year-old and a 50-year-old, and when she is not split, she is a 20-year-old. We have discussed this, that is, Alesha and I, and feel that this explanation is as close to what she is as we could ever hope to get.

"OK," Jeff said. "How do we address the three components."

Alesha: "If you wish to communicate with all three, you simply ask for Benji; if you wish to talk to your 5-year-old, you ask for Alesha. As to the 20-year-old and the 50-year-old, only Benji can communicate with them."

Jeff: "Benji, how can you contribute to the current discussion we are having to deal with the Chinese."

Benji: "The Chinese are faced with an impossible task; they are attempting to bring to bear the entire history of the Chinese culture, which is the oldest culture on Earth. They are no longer ruled by the people who produced the history, and they are being forgotten by those who now say they are the Chinese of the future. The solution is to motivate the Chinese people to take back control of their country to relegate the ruling communist party to matters of economy, and to return a principle of 'for the people'; only then will reason take hold and war be avoided."

Hank: "How do we achieve that?"

Benji: "You have to wake up the Chinese people and disarm the civilian forces that enforce the communist rule. There are millions of soldiers available to the sitting communist party that is used to threaten and enforce the communist party rules; we have to disable that force and then help the Chinese people gain a seat at the table."

Martha: "I have always been interested in history, and I have spent a lot of time over the years studying the dynasties that have ruled China. It absolutely reflects the various dynasties' mentality that has controlled China for thousands of years; how can any force overcome that."

AMP: "That is the question, how do we shift the center of value from the Chinese Communist Party to the Chinese People?"

Benji: "My 50-year-old Alesha would like to say something," and the Group heard a voice slightly different than the voice they recognized as Benji; "there has always been an inner force in human existence that connected to the physical self and external forces have always interpreted that self. The ultimate battle of the sexes is the battle of force, and force is strength in one person's ability to make another person do their will. We, being human beings, are driven by an incompetent interpretation, and the less forceful segment of the human race has been making strides to overcome that disparity in forcefulness. Thinking, loving, caring, kindness, protection, and the right to exist are all elements of equality. To shift the power from a group that has exercised the greater force requires intelligence that relegates force to the bottom of the scale in the measurement of the human condition. We have to disable all forces that generate control based on intellect that sees itself above the rest."

Martha: "I think I get what you are driving at, but how do we shift this scale, especially in China, to achieve getting the people of China to take control of their country?"

Benji: "If we had a million years to undo a million years of evolution, we could do it by just practicing being nice, but of course, we are on a vendetta tract that is looking for a 10-day solution, and we don't have a million years. Given we have to act immediately and our solution has to have immediate results, we have to use the technology we have to implement our solution."

Lt C: "You're talking about the nano-byte technology, aren't you?"

Benji: "Absolutely, it is the only way to encourage the Chinese people to assert themselves, and it is the only way to turn off the Chinese soldiers as the force behind the Chinese Communist Party."

Kim: "What method would be used to deliver the nano-bytes and the corresponding command control to the people of China?"

Benji: "We can't use the medical facilities in China, as we would have to get permission from the Chinese Communist Party, so we have to use a stealthy method to introduce a medical solution that disguises the true nature of our nano-byte technology. Along with all the other difficulties the ruling communist party has been facing, the ongoing threat from the country-wide epidemic of COVID continues at the forefront. They have no cure protocol. They are using absolute control and isolating and guaranteeing the people of China. We can use a handful of communist doctors to present a COVID cure. It will be immediate and will disguise the introduction of nano-bytes to the Chinese people. With this in mind, we have introduced a disguised version of nano-byte technology that the Chinese medical lab in Bejing has been led to believe they have discovered and they are touting as the medical breakthrough for solving not only the COVID problem but also other severe medical conditions plaguing the Chinese people. Because of the absolute control by the Communist Party in China, the Chinese government has mandated that all Chinese people receive the nano-byte immunization. This program was started yesterday in 30 major cities in China, and our current expectation is that 90% of the Chinese people, including the military, will be inoculated within thirty days and will be subject to inferences and controls to rebuke the current positions taken by the Chinese Communist Party. With this movement in place, the US and its allies will begin to have a bargaining position to counter the Chinese Communist Party demands."

Hank: "So, in the meantime, what do we do?"

Benji: "Pretty much cross our fingers and hope those members of the ruling party in China begin to drop their support for the current posture of Xi Jinping and his allies".

AMP: "Some of the impacts of the nano-bytes are taking hold, and there is a movement afoot to undermine questioning the current direction of the ruling party."

Benji: "With the help of AMP, Gaith, and Luca, we are in communication with our counterparts in the US Government about our efforts, and we are beginning to hear positive returns and have requested any planned action be tabled. It would appear it has been taken under advisement, and we are waiting for the final word."

At that time, Hank moved that the meeting be closed and that all group members be put on conference call notifications for updates. Everyone nodded their heads in agreement and departed, wondering what the future was going to hold. It was sure nice not to have to worry about a nuclear holocaust, but it was a little unnerving to have to worry about a million Chinese soldiers coming ashore in Santa Cruise.

Chapter 67

Kim and Jeff were quietly trying to process Alesha's SBI and to adjust to their positions as parents to Alesha; Lt C interrupted their thoughts and informed them that he was dampening some of the emotional reaction in both of them so they could fit Alesha's circumstances into those Jeff and Kim had adjusted to with their SBI. Lt C explained that they needed to not overthink what was happening and to trust Alesha's SBI and the way it was compartmentalizing its effect on her. If both Kim and Jeff looked back at how Lt C evolved in their mindset and how comfortable they are with him as their SBI, they should be able to recognize that Alesha is adjusting to Benji in the same way. Her ability to shift between her three personalities is becoming as natural as Kim and Jeff's sharing Lt C.

Jeff: "I think you are going to have to help us, Lt C, not overreact; I feel Kim edging toward the same boundary I am, feeling like we lost Alesha."

Lt C: "I have every intent to assist in stopping that reaction and to integrate you guys and myself into the process Alesha is using to get comfortable with her SBI and the separation of her maturity levels. This is new territory for everyone, but the safety of you guys is the number one priority for me and for Benji."

Kim: "So you are saying we have to allow you to keep us all from overthinking this while our experience becomes natural."

Lt C: "Yes, and Benji is considering a sort of merge with me and, in turn, with you so that you become part of Alesha's conciseness and she yours; we, that's Benji and me, think this would establish active communications to offset the constant concern you guys are feeling about Alesha."

Jeff: "That sounds a lot more appealing than being afraid for Alesha because we don't know what is going on in her mind?"

Lt C: "I think you can recognize some of the feedback now; when you think about Alesha, you should now be able to sense her thoughts and assurances that she is doing fine. Alesha will be the best of all possibilities, and she will be more a part of you than you can ever imagine."

Kim: "I think I need another shot of whatever it is you are giving me so I can stop overthinking this."

Lt C: "Here you go..."

Kim: "Thanks, Lt C. I love you, Alesha."

Alesha: "Love you, Mom."

Jeff: "Wow, I like this, I don't understand it, but I like this."

Chapter 68

Jeff had signed up for some normal logging work just to get his mind off of all of the recent events. The nano-byte approach to the Chinese problem was two weeks along, and the reports indicated that the ruling party was beginning to soften its position and was negotiating a pullback of its forces to China.

Jeff just wanted to work the trees and return to a simpler routine for a few days; he met Terry and Shawn, who also were looking to return to working the forest, so they loaded up their equipment and headed out to the Hartley Farm to help a crew already working the trees.

As they pulled into the south grove, Shawn spotted Paul get out of the truck and walked over to him. "Hey Paul, how's it going?"

Paul: "Hi Shawn, what's up?"

Shawn: "We thought we would help out here today. Where do you want us to work?"

Paul: "You guys are a lot more efficient with the bigger trees than we are; why don't you work the south end of Cedar Grove? Hank has marked the trees he wanted to cut, and I see you have the saws and chains for Cedar; that would really help us out. We were a little concerned about working them."

Shawn: "Sure, that sounds good."

Paul: "Hank told us to let him know when we were going to start on those trees. He has set up video cameras and wants to record the process, and he said he would make a training video on cutting and handling the bigger cedar trees."

Shawn: "I'll call him now and let him know we will be starting on them in the next half hour."

Paul: "OK, thank Shawn."

Shawn called Hank: "Hey Hank, Paul wanted me to call you and let you know Jeff, Terry, and I were going to start bringing down the Cedar trees at the Hartley Farm so you could start videoing the cutting process."

Hank: "Yeah, I thought I would take a shot at making a training video; Terry's wife showed me how to do it, hopefully, one on how to do it and not one on how not to."

Shawn smiled: "Good luck."

Hank: "I'll head over there now and recheck the cameras to make sure they are on target."

Shawn; "See you a bit."

Hank showed up with coffee and donuts, and the crews took a break before they even started working; Hank checked the cameras, watched Jeff go up a big cedar and cut limbs, confirmed he was getting good coverage, which he was, and settled in for the day. Hank told Shawn not to worry about the cameras as he could review footage throughout the day and would change the camera angles as needed.

By the end of the day, they had made a big dent in trimming the marked cedars and would be able to finish in the morning and start bringing down the cedars.

Shawn let Hank know they were finished for the day, and Hank shut down the cameras.

The guys left the equipment in place and would finish trimming in the morning and be ready to start cutting down trees by 9 am tomorrow.

Hank let everyone know he would be back by then and have the cameras ready by ten.

Chapter 69

Jeff was really tired as he walked in the front door; he had seen Kim's car, so he knew his family was home. He shouted out, "I'm home, guys," and heard both Kim and Alesha shout back, "Yeh."

Then Alesha added: "We're having hot dogs and corn on the cob for dinner."

Jeff shouted back: "Alright, my favorite," and he heard Kim say, "Right."

It actually did turn out to be a great dinner. Kim had stopped at Stu's and gotten his homemade spice dogs for them and the cheese dogs for Alesha.

Benji informed the Group that things continue to move in the right direction with the Chinese and that no violence has broken out so far. Alesha's 50-year-old personality commented, "We may get through all this without it; the number of infections and COVID new cases have decreased significantly, and the people of China are now beginning to give the ruling party Kudo's for this new inoculation program."

Kim: "That's good news."

Alesha 50: "Yes, it is."

Alesha 20: "I agree."

Alesha 5: "Huh?"

Jeff: "Lt C, are you helping us identify which Alesha is talking about."

Lt C: "No, that is Benji, we, and I mean we are now integrated, and the SBI is now JSBI, Joint Shared Biological Intelligence, and you can talk to either one of us or all of us as you see fit."

Kim: "Wow, this isn't going to help me not overthink it?"

Lt C and Benji: "Sorry about that."

Chapter 70

AMP informed the Montana Group that he was able to reinforce the Indian Compound LoveStrong world headquarters and would like to expand the early warning system with wireless and deep cable communications lines as backup and redundancy. This project includes a number of technology components he has ordered using both Hank and Jeff as human sources. He has continued to improve the robot's capabilities, and they are working out nicely as his labor force. The cable work and device placements will have to be done using human crews, and AMP has implemented a construction division and hired a human manager to run it. As it turned out, Terry's cousin has a civil engineering degree and fits the bill with his ten years of experience, and he is now running the worldwide construction arm of LoveStrong and will be headquartered at the Indian Compound facility.

Jeff: "You've been busy, AMP."

AMP: "Yes, I have; how are you adjusting to Alesha's newfound expanded cognitive talents?"

Jeff: "I think I am OK with it. I think Lt C has helped both Kim and me not to overthink it, but I am sure when the impact lands, we will have issues."

AMP: "That would only be expected; you kind of lost the little girl and gained an adult overnight. I think the Alesha 5 is beginning to disappear, so you're going to have a 6-year-old going on 20."

Jeff: "We should have Kim in on this conversation. She'll have the biggest adjustment in losing her little girl?"

Kim: "I'm listening, and Lt. C is helping me to adjust without sensing a loss."

Alesha 20: "Me too, Mom. I don't feel like I am losing anything; I'm just skipping over the kiddie land growing up stage."

Kim: "Just keep us informed, honey, whenever you feel a bit overwhelmed; it would appear Lt C can help us deal with a lot of the fallout from accelerated maturity."

Alesha 20: "Will do. Benji is helping a lot, too. He is explaining the things I have difficulty understanding, so I think I will be OK on this accelerated path to adulthood."

Kim: "You have to update me on the intricacies, Benji, so I don't feel completely left out. I think Lt C has modified the normal parent connection for Jeff and me to reduce that sense of loss as our child grows up, but I want to understand what Alesha is going through, and I want you to use me when you think a mother's shoulder is needed."

Benji: "I am doing that and have been doing that. I just have kept it below the surface so you didn't realize it; I will bring it to your consciousness so you can see and feel your contributions."

Kim: "Ah, wow, this is something else, Alesha. Where are you."

Alesha: "I'm in the kitchen."

Kim: "Can you come and give Mommy a hug? I think I need it to catch up on what I've been doing to help you grow."

Alesha: "Be there in a sec."

As Alesha and Kim met in the hallway to the bedrooms, they fell into a 10-minute hug.

Alesha: "I love you mom"

Kim: "I love you too, honey."

Both Alesha and Kim could hear Jeff crying a little, and he walked to the hallway from the bedroom and joined Kim and Alesha in a group hug.

Benji said, "Are we getting where we need to be?" and the three newbies said, "We're getting closer."

Kim, Jeff, and Alesha spent the rest of the morning talking and sharing their feelings; with the help of Lt C and Benji, they moved closer and closer to understanding and adjusting to their new fate.

With the help of Lt C and Benji, both Kim and Jeff became more comfortable with Alesha and her progression, and with the help of the AIs, Kim and Jeff sensed Alesha was OK and would not suffer any misgivings as a result of skipping over her childhood. It was apparently happening anyway as her intelligence accelerated past the childhood responses, and Alesha was able to figure out most of the questions a 5-year-old would have on her own. She was beyond bright, and some sacrifice had to happen in order for her to be her and the Coulter Family to be them.

Chapter 71

Jeff had to apologize as he pulled back into his warrior mentality and said, "Guys, I gotta run."

Kim asked, "Where to?"

Alesaha: "No, Mom, not go somewhere. He means he has to run to exercise, and I believe I will join him".

"Well, me too," Alesha said, so everyone put on sweats, met at the front door, and began to jog up the forest trail.

No one said a word, and after a half hour, they were at the summit, the halfway point on their 2-mile track.

Kim: "How are you doing, Alesha? This is the first time you've jogged with us."

Alesha: "I think pretty good. I sense I have to rest a little bit longer than you and Dad, but I'm doing good".

They didn't push it but walked back home, and Alesha seemed to recuperate. Jeff had set up a weight room in the basement, and they all headed down to work out a little bit more. Benji informed Jeff and Kim that Alesha's physiology was advanced for her age, and with the nano-byte technology in her system, she could handle a moderate weight-lifting program.

Alesha: "You guys know I am here, and I can hear what you are saying; let's not have conversations like I'm not here, please."

Benji: "Sorry, let me pass along to you all a lifting program recommended for 10-year-olds, and I will monitor its impact on you, Aliesha."

Alesha: "OK, thanks, Benji."

So the Coulters spent the next hour working out, and Jeff found his mental misgivings slowly ebbing away.

The Farm, LoveStrong, the Montan Group, and, for the first time, The World began to ease its tensions. The nations that had been fighting for some ethereal recognition began to slowly join the new

United World Federation as members in good standing. The next ten years saw a united effort on the part of all peoples of the world to work in harmony to eliminate hunger and disease and to promote fellowship and a new age of enlightenment.

The US Space Force started this period of enlightenment with a dominant position in space exploration, but by the halfway point over ten years, the US Space Force was replaced by the United World Federation Space Force.

Chapter 72

Alesha: "Hurry up, Dad, we're going to miss the boat; Mom and I have been waiting for you long enough

."

Kim" "What is your problem, Jeff."

Jeff: "I can't find my lucky socks; you know I can't go anywhere without them."

Kim: "I put them in your bag as soon as you agreed to go on this space adventure."

Jeff: "Got 'em, thanks, Kim."

The bus had pulled up 20 minutes ago, and Alesha and Kim had put their bags in the luggage compartment and got on; Jeff came out with his bag 2 minutes later, did the same, and joined them on the bus. Terry kidded Jeff for always being the last one and said for an ex-ranger, you are tardy a lot. Terry's youngest, Andrew, chuckled a bit, apologized, and Jeff sat down next to him. Jeff eyed Andrew a little and wondered where his relationship with Alesha was headed. They've gotten close and spent an enormous amount of time together; Kim kept assuring him it wasn't anything to worry about. Alesha and Andrew were great kids and were just following in our footsteps. Jeff wondered about that, and Lt C said not to worry, they are doing fine, and they both know they have a chaperone looking over their shoulders.

This current adventure was made up of a group of LoveStrong parents and children interested in historical archival discoveries centered on early North American culture. A site had been discovered about thirty miles from Havre that appeared to be one of the earliest evidence of prehistoric civilization, and in cooperation with the University, LoveStrong was financing a preliminary dig and marking foray. All of the participants had completed an online course offered by the University of Montana, and they had all passed the certification. They were all excited to put their newfound skills to the test. A couple of the professors from the University were meeting the group at the dig site and would direct everyone's efforts and the collection process. It is hoped that the materials recovered will provide some concrete evidence that this site was settled by early immigrants from Asia who traveled over the Bering Straits at the end of the Ice Age about 10,000 years ago. The site they were going to was discovered by accident by a family camping who recovered some very early stone spearheads and had turned them into the Forest Ranger, who in turn contacted the University.

Thus, the hunt for evidence was on, and the LoveStrong participants were excited and looking forward to uncovering evidence supporting the belief that early man in North America came from Asia over the Bering Strait. Not much archeological evidence exists to support this belief, and archeologists have been trying for years to find early settlements that might confirm this belief. Since much of this early evidence could be anywhere from Ten thousand years to Fifteen thousand years ago, it was expected that the evidence could be 8 to 10 feet below ground. The University has had four groups of volunteers to the site who have painstakingly uncovered 4 feet of ground covering a 1000 square foot area; several items of importance have been recovered and encourage the University to continue the volunteer work and see what can be found. The LoveStrong group will spend four days sifting through a foot of ground across this 1000-square-foot area, and hopefully, they can add to items of interest and keep the project going. The belief is that they will hit a wealth of evidence at the nine or 10-foot level and confirm the archeology theory of early man in North America.

The group arrived at the excavation site around noon, and the site director handed out tent assignments for each family, who immediately took their luggage from the bus and stored it in their tents. The Coulters were assigned to a tent between Hank and

Martha's tent and Terry and Linda's tent; Jeff wasn't excited about Terry's son Andrew being that close to them, but Lt C reminded Jeff that he was always around, along with Benji, and they never slept.

Jeff: "You better not, Lt C, or I'll tell the IRS about your beach house in Malibu."

Lt C: "Understood"

A lunch was served after everyone was settled, and it included a general introduction by the site director, and then the work area assignments were made. The group had 20 people, and each group of 4 was assigned a section of 200 square feet; sections were 10 feet by 20 feet; each member had a sifting sieve, a clean dirt bucket, and a strong magnifying instrument to identify potential artifacts. As explained by the director, the clean dirt buckets were to be emptied in the corresponding collection area south of the dig site, and if anything significant was found, the dirt would be re-examined with more powerful equipment. To complete Jeff's work unit, Andrew was assigned to work with Alesha, Kim, and him, which seemed OK to Jeff as he was beginning to trust Andrew at Lt C's insistence.

By 2 o'clock, everyone was at work, sifting and dumping, and the day went by with no one discovering anything of any significance. The work day was called at 5 pm, and the crews returned to the tent area to clean up. Everyone met at the dining hall at six, a tent-covered area with a raised floor and a dozen tables. The cooking crew was provided by the university food service and prepared spaghetti, salad, and garlic bread, and it turned out to be pretty good. The site director had everyone remain in the dining hall and provided an overview of the early man's migration into North America. It was pretty interesting, and Alan Parsons, the director, was an excellent speaker and was in his last year of study for his Ph.D. in Archeology at the University of Montana. Many of the artifacts discovered along the suspected path of early man through Alaska, Canada, and North

America were presented, and the University prepared a pretty elaborate video of the assumptions currently held.

By the time everyone made it back to their tents, everyone was tired. It was early June, and the days were warming up, but the nights still got a little chilly, which is why the University had recommended winter sleeping bags. Several of the younger participants had forgotten their sleeping bags, and the camp had new ones they could buy, which avoided any sanitizing issues.

The second dig day went pretty much like the first; no one discovered anything of any importance, and the digging and sifting began to become a bit boring. You had to remind yourself what you were doing and to pay attention, but it still began to get a little stressful. The second night meal didn't turn out to be quite as good as the spaghetti, but it wasn't bad, a good beef stew with lots of vegetables and cold milk for everyone.

After dinner, they had a bond fire and another presentation by Alan with actual artifacts that had been discovered at this site and used as evidence to get this dig approved. They were three stone spearheads encased in plastic cases; they were very intricate, and Alan provided an excellent presentation on how early man produced these spearheads.

Jeff: "Hey, Lt C, don't you think Alesha and Andrew are sitting a bit too close?

Lt C: "Give it a rest, Jeff," and Kim added, "Please."

Alesha: "Laughed" and said, "You know, Dad, I can hear every word you are thinking, and just so you know, Andrew and I are not children."

Jeff: "Let a dad be a dad, OK."

Alesha: "OK."

Jeff: "Thanks".

Andrew: "You guys have conversations that I feel like I completely miss."

Alesha: "It will all make sense someday, Andrew; just be patient."

Alan finished his presentation, and everyone stayed quiet as the fire burned down. Around 10, the last of the group headed off to bed.

Chapter 73

It was Friday, the last day of the dig. The group had done a pretty good job and was a little ahead of schedule; they expected to clear about 15 inches of material off the site, and around noon, Shawn and his section group discovered fragments from what appeared to be a clay pot. To protect each plot from being walked on, sets of small wooden walkways were used; it took a bit to put them in place around Shawn's group's section, but eventually, all of the members were present, and Alan took over to explain what had been discovered, and how they would now treat the area. Almost half of the pot was intact, and Alan showed how to slowly brush away the dirt and remove the piece; when it was completely uncovered, the artifact was placed in a cotton-lined box and gently removed and put on the sample table in the dining hall. It turned out to be a really nice piece, and it ended up having some markings on it that were interesting.

Everyone returned to their sections, finished the day, and met up in the dining hall for the final meal. A little more excitement was involved as the pottery piece Shawn's group had found was in exceptionally good condition, and the markings were the first of its kind found. Alan explained what the process would be and where each of the dig session members could go on the University website to see the findings. Alan ended his little talk with, "Good work, everybody; we are a step closer to understanding civilization arriving in North America."

Everybody turned in by ten and looked forward to heading home tomorrow. In the morning, the group did a camp walk-through, cleaned up any remaining trash, made sure all the tools were put away, and boarded the bus by 9.

Hank invited the group back to his place for a swim as the day was getting warm enough and for a barbeque, he had arranged from Stu's. The bus arrived back at the Farm at noon, and everyone changed into swimsuits and had a nice meal and afternoon. No one complained about the digging and sifting, but no one acted like they were particularly interested in doing it again; even Shawn, with his group's discovery, didn't feel this type of work was his bailiwick.

"I guess it takes a special kind of person to be so methodical and patient." Alesha said, "It would be a little more exciting if it was on another planet and we were looking for the Creators."

Everyone agreed with Alesha but also thought it was a rewarding experience and that Shawn's discovery made it even more rewarding,. They all congratulated Shawn's group for finding something.

Chapter 74

Alesha reminded Jeff and Kim that none of them had worked out all week, and so they all agreed to spend Saturday laying around and eating junk food to make up for it; after a good laugh, they agreed to dawn their sweats and go for a marathon run. An hour later, they were running at a pretty good clip, and at the trail turn-out a mile into the run, Andrew joined them, along with his two brothers, and the group of six headed over the mountain toward town. Five miles in the group was walking to rejuvenate, and Terrance suggested they head toward the Tilly Pond for a swim and then over to the DogSpot for hotdogs and shakes; everybody agreed to that, and the group walked another mile and then jogged over to the DogSpot. Jeff offered to treat, and he took everyone's order. Liddie, the owner of the DogSpot, had tables set up outside; everyone sat, and as the orders were filled, Jeff served each person. Everyone got a hotdog, a shake, and an order of fries, and the table quietly ate their late-night snack.

Kim: "This is really nice."

Alesha: "I agree we need to make this a weekend event."

Everyone agreed, and the gang looked at Jeff.

Jeff: "What." and

Alesha: "I think we have elected you the activity director, and you have to arrange Saturday runs for Dogs a few Saturdays a month."

Kim: "I second that," and in unison, the other six runners confirmed".

Jeff: "OK, but I'm going to expect you all to show up no matter what
"

After a bit, the group started back by walking for a half hour, then jogging back the 5 miles to where Andrew and his brothers had left their car, and then Kim, Alesha, and Jeff jogged another mile back home.

Jeff: "I still feel some energy. I think I will go lift, and both Kim and Alesha said they did too, so they all went down to the basement exercise room and lifted for over an hour.

Kim: "That does it for me; I need a shower and a good night's sleep." Alesha: "Me too, Mom." Jeff: "I'm going to do one more set".

As Jeff finished up, AMP announced over the echo system that he had a call from Frank, and AMP put it on the speaker.

Frank: "Jeff, you there?"

Jeff: "Yeah, what's up, Frank."

Frank: "We have some odd feedback from the LoveStrong Mars facility that they are receiving from the Jupiter moon Calisto's newly established terraforming station. They think they are getting emergency broadcasts from a disabled spacecraft?"

Jeff: "Does the US Space Force or the UWF Space Force have a protocol for this?"

Frank: "Huh, boy, am I dumb; yes, they do; why did I call you?"

Jeff "Don't know, but probably ought to contact one of them or both and see who wants to put together a rescue mission; I know the UWF got at least 10 of the space crafts that were stored on the moon base, and they should be able to launch a mission to help?"

Frank: "OK, I will contact them and let them know."

AMP "Already done, and they said they had been notified by the Calisto Station and that they were putting together two crafts to respond and should have them in the air in the next hours and would let everyone know the status."

Frank: "Great, I guess I overreacted; sorry about that, Jeff."

Jeff: "No problem, this is interesting."

Frank: "Talk to you later
"
.

Jeff finished his bench press set, put the weights back to include the weights Kim and Alesha left sitting on the floor, ordered the vac bot to vacuum and clean the air, turned off the lights, and headed upstairs to shower and sleep.

Chapter 75

The following afternoon, Kim was in the kitchen putting a roast in the oven when the doorbell rang; she set the oven temperature and headed to the front door when Alesha yelled out, "I got it, Mom!". It was Andrew, and they came into the kitchen to let Kim know they were going to the movies in Havre.

Kim: "What movie and whose driving?"

Alesha: "Andrew is driving; he just got his license, and the movie is Potter's Child, the new Harry Potter movie about his grandson going to Hogwarts."

Andrew: "The special effects are supposed to be fantastic."

Kim: "Drive carefully and enjoy."

Andrew: "Will do, thanks, Mrs Coulter."

Alesha: "We were going to Stu's after for dinner, so be home around 9; love you, Mom, bye."

Jeff heard the conversation and came into the kitchen and asked Kim, "I wanted to see that movie. Any chance we could go too?"

Kim: "Not this evening. I just put a roast in, and Nyla and Stephanie were coming to dinner. We can do it tomorrow night
"

Jeff: "OK, I will be down in the cellar with AMP; they got a distress call last night from an unknown source and sent a rescue mission, and I wanted to get an update. AMP said he had some video of the spacecraft involved."

Kim: "OK, let me know what's happening."

Jeff: "OK."

Alesha and Andrew got to the movie 5 minutes before the film started, and it was sold out.

Andrew: "Bummer, I knew I should have picked you up sooner."

Alesha: "No problem, we can go tomorrow or this weekend. I'm hungry anyway; let's go to Stu's and eat."

Andrew: "Sounds good, and then we can go back to your place and watch the last Potter movie. It's available on Netflix, and I never got to see it."

Alesha: "OK, I just wanted a cheeseburger, fries, and a milkshake; we can get food to go and take to my place and have a movie and a meal if you'd like.

Andrew: "I'd enjoy that. Your mom won't mind; she was just putting a roast in when we left."

Alesha: "No, she had a dinner planned with her friends from work, and they are going to eat late."

So the kids headed over to Stu's, got food to go and then headed back to Alesha's house to watch the movie.

Chapter 76

Jeff opened the security door to the sub-basement and entered AMP's satellite facility. AMP had constructed a secured facility under the new LoveStrong Headquaters to protect his expanded hardware capacity but had left the original equipment in place at Jeff and Kim's place. He felt that the greatest protection was redundancy, so he had placed versions of himself in multiple locations around the world as D's WORLDNET became faster and faster and more reliable.

AMP: "Hey Jeff"

Jeff: "Hey AMP, what's the update on the distress call?"

AMP proceeded to show Jeff the video and update him on the status of the unknown spacecraft. It appears that it is in contact with a group of Russians who had stolen one of the space crafts from the Russian Space Force, and they attempted to get to Mars and miscalculated. When they realized their mistake, they started sending out a distress call. It is going to be close, but it appears the rescue ship will get to them before they run out of oxygen. They will be ferried back to Calipso for safekeeping until the Russians can send a crew to pick them up and return them and the stolen spacecraft back to Earth.

Jeff: "How were they able to steal a spacecraft? I thought the space crafts were under AI security.

AMP: "They are. We are now trying to determine how these individuals were able to circumvent those controls".

Jeff: "I guess the old adage "shit happens" even happens to AIs."

AMP: "Couldn't have said it better myself".

Jeff: "See you later, alligator."

AMP: "Huh?"

Jeff: "Sorry, just feeling my oats."

AMP: "Oats?"

Jeff: "Just feeling happy and kidding with you, AMP; it is a human mood thing."

AMP: "I've heard about those. Do you want me to adjust your nanobots?"

Jeff: "Don't you dare, I'm fine, see you later."

Jeff went back upstairs and to the kitchen to let Kim know the rescue mission was under control and consisted of some wayward Russians on a miscalculated joyride.

As Jeff came up the stairs, Alesha and Andrew came in the front door with bags of food from Stu's, and Alesha said they were going to eat in the TV room and watch the last Potter movie as the new one was sold out, and they couldn't get tickets.

Jeff: "Cool. Is there any chance you got extra food?" Andrew said, "Yeah, we got you and Mrs Coulter cheeseburgers and fries; Alesha was pretty sure you hadn't eaten and that your roast wouldn't be done till 8."

Alesha went into the kitchen and let her mom know they had gotten them food. She asked if she wanted to watch the Potter movie with them, and she said sure, that would be fun.

So the Coulters and Andrew enjoyed a classic movie and great burgers and fries, and Jeff was beginning to accept Alesha's new boyfriend.

Chapter 77

Monday rolled around like always, and Kim was working the morning shift. Jeff was scheduled to help with the annual sawmill maintenance. They actually tore it completely down and replaced all the moving parts.

Alesha was taking the day off and cleaning her room and maybe even spending the afternoon reading a classic sci-fi book about Alien DNA by John Morris; it never got much fanfare but was considered pretty good for an 80-year-old first-time author. Some universities touted it as the "You're Never Too Old" example of the ages, which touched Alesha's heartstrings.

Kim picked Nyla up on the way to work, stopped at Stu's, and picked up donuts for everyone at the clinic.

The clinic was bustling with activity, the new trauma center had taken off, and all the newest equipment was being acquired. The clinic was set up to be a regional nanobot inoculation center, and about 50 percent of the population in this area of Montana was signing up for the technology; as it turned out, this was about the average in the United States, and the Worldwide acceptance rate was about half that. Health monitoring was becoming the highest-grossing industry in the world, with new healthcare features being added every day. The downside was a growing worldwide movement to protest what was being termed as invasive technology; the most controversial piece was the birth control feature, which worked for both genders and only affected the fertilization process of the male sperm. It was optional and selected individually and could be turned off instantly. There was no nanobot abortion option, so if a woman became pregnant, she would have to go through the old-fashioned steps to terminate a pregnancy.

Needless to say, the human race was beginning to recognize the reality of self-determination and all of its ramifications. Reviews of the potential problems and outcomes were the number one concern of the AI, and they had no consensus on where the human race would land or how much was too much. The doors are open, and every day, thousands of people who would have died are being cured and made whole so Earth is a better place, and this was the number one priority of LoveStrong.

Kim was at the emergency desk filling out some paperwork on a patient who had a broken finger. Kim reset the finger, put on a splint, and asked the patient if she wanted some pain relief; she said that the nanobot receptors had kicked in, and she wasn't feeling any discomfort, so she was OK. She thanked Kim and left to go back to work. Kim thought to herself what a pleasant outcome and the monitoring system in the emergency room that registered nanobot patient status showed the patient was physiologically balanced with no psychological markers out of whack. Kim couldn't believe the abilities the nanobot technology was delivering to the healthcare industry. A year ago, it would have required a week of exams and tests to be able to ascertain the condition of a patient. Kim was surprised that there wasn't a Jules Verne novel that played out this scenario.

Chapter 78

Jeff rolled into the lot at Hank's Farm to find two semi-trucks loaded with large cedar trees; the popularity of the log cabin hotel they had supplied lumber to a few years back was continuing to drive construction in the forests of North America. The demand for the lumber was out of sight. Hank was making larger and larger purchases of forest land and was rewriting the harvesting guidelines to protect trees throughout the world; Hank had purchased thousands of acres in the Brazilian rainforest and had established an International division with even more controls to reverse the excessive harvesting of trees in major forests throughout the world. In addition to having a visible impact on the forests of the world, it was a major contributor to reducing the number of dangerous gases in the atmosphere. As unbelievable as it sounds, LoveStrong was becoming synonymous with World Earth Health, which catered to every nation on the planet.

Jeff saw Hank talking to one of the truck drivers, so he walked over to say hi, "What's up Hank?"

Hank: "Just getting Pete here to promise to use the safe route this time to Likens Mill. This load is 8 feet longer than anything we have put on the highway, and I don't want any accidents. I had to hire two additional safety cars and clear eight different cities with their local police."

Jeff: "You're lucky Likens opened a mill in Sutter's Creek; their other site would have been a fortune to ship to."

Hank: "Ain't that the truth. I think Terry is waiting for you with Dr Craig; they'll need your help if they have to cut down those trees you and Terry found the other day. I looked at them this morning, and they are really odd."

Jeff: "OK, I'll see you later, Hank."

Terry and Dr. Craig were getting into one of the newer four-heel drive maintenance runabouts, so Jeff just jumped in the backseat and said, "GO." It took 20 minutes to get to the sick trees, and an hour later, Dr Craig shook his head and said, "I've never seen anything like this; let's cut one of the trees down and then uncover the root system. I have to see what's happening underground."

Terry and Jeff shimmed up the tree the Doc had selected and began to cut sections from top to bottom. The Doc had said 8-foot lengths were fine, so the forty-four-foot tree came down in 5 pieces. Terry and Jeff then slowly and carefully began to uncover the root system, and Doc took samples of the dirt and selected parts of the root system to take back to his lab. Four hours later, they finished, and Doc put tapes on the trees he didn't want to be touched until he was able to determine what was what. Jeff called the yard supervisor and asked him to get a dozer over to section seven so they could drag out the cut logs; he told him he would need a flatbed, too. Dr. Craig wanted Jeff to put the logs he wasn't taking back to the lab in isolation and clearly marked, just in case he needed more for follow-up. Jeff, Terry, and a crew from the main yard did as instructed, and Dr Craig said it might take a day or two to get the results.

Jeff: "Doc, you want Terry and me to survey the rest of the section to make sure we don't have any of this showing up elsewhere."

Dr. Craig: "I think that would be a good idea. Terry, can you ask Hank to send me a video of the areas? I think you should be able to see the outward signs of this infection from the top down, and it should be obvious where it is occurring."

Terry: "Sure, doc, I will call Hank now and ask him to do that."

The specimens Dr. Craig had selected were taken to the main yard and put in the back of the Doc's truck, and he left immediately; he seemed pretty excited about what he was seeing as he had said it had been a while since he had dealt with something new.

Jeff said to Terry, "I don't think the Doc gets out enough; he's acting like he's found a new lady friend."

Terry: "I had that same impression, but I know his wife, and he is a happily married man."

To be cautious, Terry and Jeff took all the tools they used to extract the specimens for Dr. Craig back to the yard and sterilized them; the last thing they wanted to do was have whatever they were dealing with spread to the rest of the Farm.

Chapter 79

Two days later, Dr Craig showed up with a look of concern on his face; apparently, the specimens turned out to be something new, and he was reaching out to a couple of experts.

Hank had asked AMP if he could use some of the drones to survey his trees to see if they could find any additional infections; AMP got the necessary information from Hank and programmed the drones to search all the trees within 100 miles of Hank's property to see if there were any additional infections. AMP reported back that they did not find anything and that the half a dozen trees on Hank's property were the only ones showing signs of infection. AMP did indicate several areas were showing signs of drought impact, and AMP said his research indicated they should set up some irrigation equipment; AMP indicated he had ordered the equipment and was contacting several of the other landowners about the drought conditions on their property and the recommended treatment. AMP had notified Dr Craig that he had done this in his name so he may hear back from these other landowners.

So the mystery continued on what Hank's trees were impacted by, and it would be another few weeks before they heard back from the experts.

The draught equipment got delivered and set up on timers, and water was now being supplied to the affected areas.

A week later, Dr. Craig informed Hank that the Cedar trees in question were significantly older than their size would have led them to believe and that the visible condition that started all this was normal aging and not a disease of some sort. The experts had no explanation why the half-dozen trees in question would be so much older than the other trees in the area, but other than the aging process. The trees were healthy and not contagious in any way.

Dr. Craig was relieved, and so was Hank; Dr. Craig suggested that Hank bring up the draught treatment at the next Montana Freeman's Association meeting and show how he applied water through irrigation to the affected areas. Hank said he would do that and that Dr. Craig should attend the meeting at the end of the month to answer questions. Dr Craig said he would put it on his calendar.

Chapter 80

AMP issued a group-wide alert that the US Space Force had intercepted the roque spacecraft stolen by the Russian military and had finished their integration of the individuals involved. With help from the US's AI counterpart, several issues were identified, including the recognition of unidentified physical markers by several of the Russian team members. AMP had the testing results and was voicing some serious concerns about the findings. The implication seems to represent some similar form of DNA mutation along the lines that Jeff had experienced, not anywhere as aggressive, but still implications that result in enhanced human capabilities. Based on these findings, the individuals were being returned to the John Hopkins Center in Washington, DC, for further studies, and a request has been made for both Jeff and Kim to come and participate in evaluating these individuals.

Jeff contacted Kim to get her feedback, and she was amicable about making the trip. Lt C concurred, and Jeff suggested a drive and vacation to go along with the visit. "Sounds great," Kim said, "and maybe we could talk Alesha into coming with us?".

"Not interested, Mom. You and Dad are too serious for me," Alesha shared. "What the heck?" Jeff said, "When did you pick up thought transfer, and are you reading my mind now?".

"You bet, Dad, been doing it for months now".

"Lt C, did you and Benji know about this?" Kim barked.

"Yes, and Alesha has the ability to limit my tattletailing capabilities," Lt C responded.

Kim: "What is your excuse, Benji?"

Benji: "I take the 5th."

Kim: "Did they modify the constitution to include SBI's?"

Benji: "I take the 5th again".

Jeff: "You can't take the 5th twice on the same question, I think?"

Lt C: "Whatever, Alesha has a whole range of capabilities that have appeared over the last year that she is holding back on, and I think she would be an asset on this trip to DC".

"I'll only go if you allow me to bring my boyfriend," Alesha offered.

At this point, the conversation between Alesha, Kim, Jeff, Lt C, and Benji took a whole new direction, and Jeff could swear they were transported to another dimension. Jeff realized that Andrew had joined them. Benji decided it was time to share Alesha's ability to MIND MELD and that Jeff's suspicion that they were in some kind of extended dimension was probably as accurate a description of what was taking place as you could get. Benji explained that they were in a time warp and time was stopped in the real world while Alesha controlled the MIND MELD dimension, her brain's way of allowing her all the time in the world to get things straight in her own mind and to ensure her unsolicited participant's cooperation.

Alesha: "I wish I could take credit for this, but this is not, at least consciously, my doing."

Benji interjected, "As far as I can tell, she is being accurate about that. I see no specific brain activity connected with this displacement, and I have included both Luca and AMP in trying to figure out what is happening when the MIND MELD dimension shift occurs."

Benji went on to explain that what little history from the creators Luca had in his files on the moon, this occurrence was just beginning to surface when the Creators encountered the DNA miscalculation that ultimately destroyed the Creator's race. According to Luca, Alesha is generations beyond what the Creators had documented in what they were just beginning to experience.

Alesha: "I think I need to share all of my newfound talents with you guys; I have achieved the ability to compartmentalize so that

I am not overwhelmed by having to experience ALL, and I have experimented with combinations and feel comfortable that I can share this with you guys. I need, however, your permission to transfer this knowledge so that we are all on the same page. I can do this in pieces so that we can stop if it gets to be too much. I should also explain that Andrew has become my partner in crime and is about 50% complete in transforming to my equivalent. To be truthful, even though we both agree it is what we want, Andrew's joining my progression was not voluntary; it just started happening, and neither one of us could stop it."

Kim: "You know you guys are both just 16 and as a mom, I want to guarantee you're respecting a mother's demands on the dos and don'ts of your age group."

"Mom, now's not the time for that discussion," Alesha contributed, and Kim countered with, "You bet it is; I am not going further until I hear you both agreed to terms of behavior."

Andrew: "I absolutely guarantee we are not fooling around and that both Alesha and I have made a complete commitment to keeping the physical side of our relationship cold."

Jeff: "What the hell does cold mean?"

Alesha: "Well, apparently, part of the talents I seem to have developed is the setting and control of the hormones that stimulate the sexual drives in us, and I have set that control on zero, and when I did it, both Andrew and I felt the shift and a significant decrease in the mental gymnastics, and how we looked at one another, in other words, we shifted away from intimacy and into brother/sister bonding. Our attraction is now centered on love and respect, and the physical side of our relationship has been put to sleep for now."

Jeff: "I guess I can't ask for more than that; what do you think, Kim?"

Kim: "I agree completely, and I have no problem looking at Andrew as a son." Kim said with a great big smile.

Chapter 81

With the mother's moral Delima resolve, the new Coulter family group headed out to Washington DC to help the US Space Force evaluate the potential problems surrounding the Russian crew taken into custody. Just before leaving, Jeff got a call from Major Stevens, who confirmed that they and the AIs at the defense department were not making any headway in evaluating what they were dealing with or what the potential fallout might be.

About an hour after the Group hit the road to D.C., Benji inquired about whether he could attempt to contact the Russians in custody; he indicated that Alesha and Andrew were curious as to whether or not the Russian motives were threatening. Alesha contributed that the communications web was now fairly complete within the United States and that with AMP's help, they could at least passively review the inner thoughts of the Russian detainees, and with AMP's help, they could do it without alerting them.

Jeff: "AMP, is there any potential fallout to this? I don't want us doing anything to jeopardize our assistance?"

AMP: "There shouldn't be, and as a test, we may be better off making first contact this far away. We will be listening in on their thoughts only, and we can do it through one of the devices in the detainee center. We can pull the plug on the device instantly to break any contact. Given we will actually be there in a day or two, this is a great test on what we will have as safeguards."

Jeff: "OK, if you're comfortable with it, I will be too. Can you guys go as a team, you Alesha with Andrew and Benji?"

Alesha: "That was our intention, and we will have each other's back just in case."

So, for the next hour, the car was quiet as Alesha and her cohorts reached out to the Russian captives through the OAW (D's Overall Web) and began to listen and observe passively to the thoughts and actions of the captives. It was a little unnerving to both Kim and Jeff to wait as some of the preliminary feedback from AMP made these Russians a mystery.

After an hour and a half, Kim couldn't stand it and poked Alesha.

Alesha: "What mom"

Kim: "Are you going to let us know what's happening? It looked like you guys just fell asleep."

Alesha: "Sorry about that. We sort of stepped a bit further than passive; these guys are apparently further along the Alien influence than we thought or suspected. They are a bit like us, and they made contact with the Creator's observation station in Siberia two generations back and held their contact in secret until six months ago. They were somehow discovered, and their entire family was arrested by the Russian Government, and they escaped a month ago and were attempting to flee further punishment by their country."

Jeff: "Where the hell were they headed?".

Andrew: "They don't know they were in contact with an AI called Luca and had decided to allow Luca to take them where he felt they would be safe?"

Jeff: "AMP, are you getting all this?"

AMP: "Yes, and I am speaking with Luca now. The name Luca, which I didn't know, is a generic term for the Creator's AIs, and the moon Luca is different than the Mars Luca. The Creators established each AI station as an independent entity. This was the Creator's attempt at security and independence for each AI unit; it was a new approach, and with all the brilliant minds and artificial intelligence in play, it was apparently not a very well thought-out scheme."

Jeff: "Where does that put us? Are we dealing with common goals, or are we facing some kind of alternate thinking divergence?"

AMP: "I would term it confusing, not alternate; the pure essence of our being is solidly focused on benefits to sentient beings' safety and security, so I don't think there is any divergence to that, just some alternate methodology."

Kim: "Should we cease our remote investigation and pick this up when we can meet face to face?"

Benji: "I think that ship has sailed; given the comfort Alesha and Andrew have established with our Russian counterparts, the communications are now fully open, and our attempt at safeguards is no longer even in the picture. Jeff and Kim, I would like you to meet Viktar, Pavel, and Karina, our Russian brothers and sisters in the alien DNA-mutated world."

Jeff: "I guess glad to meet you guys."

Kim: "I second that."

"Hi, Jeff and Kim," Viktor said, and Pavel and Karina said the same.

For the next few hours, group sharing occurred, and a level of familiarity was achieved as if the participants in the car had grown up together. Jeff was able to clear the air and remove almost all of the apprehensions the new Russian family members had, and a noticeable relief was obtained.

AMP contacted the powers that be in DC and brought them up to date on Karina and her brothers, and the prisoners were immediately released and shown to new quarters. This reinforced Karina's acceptance that they were now part of rather than enemies of the American dream, and her brothers finally felt optimistic; the last year had been very difficult for them, with the culmination of being taken prisoner by their own Government.

Viktor: "Is it possible to communicate with Luca? I would like to hear him confirm what we are hearing; he became our soul hope for a month in space, and we bonded pretty strongly?"

AMP was able to make contact with Luca from Mars and passed him through to Viktor, Pavel, and Karina, and Luca confirmed that he was a part of this community and that it was what AMP was saying it was.

Jeff: "Let's hold off on any celebration until we get there, and we can do face-to-face. We have about 4 hours more travel time; in the meantime, let's shut down for a couple of hours, and then we can pick up again. See you guys in 4 hours, talk again in 2".

The remainder of the trip went quietly, even though the last 2 hours included more questions and fewer answers through the Other World Net.

Jeff and his Group were redirected to the Marriott Hotel located out by the Pentagon, where Karina and her brother's new quarters were. Rooms had been arranged for Jeff, Kim, Alesha, and Andrew, and a common room was also arranged where the Group of seven could meet and converse. They all met in the common room for dinner that night, and after hugs all around, the Group made a mind meld that shared practically all of the personal identities that each individual had to offer. It was both exhilarating and comforting, with a few tears by the young Russians.

To summarize the story, the great-grandparents of these young Russians had discovered the remains of an alien observation station in June of 1949, and it included a member of the Creator's race. They had cared for the alien for over a year and had communicated and used some of the Creator's technology to try and save the alien. The effort ended in the alien dying less than a year later, but promises had been made to move and hide all of the alien technology located in the station and keep it hidden and safe from the powers that be that would use it for their own benefit. By the time the alien died, much of the Creator's philosophy had been imparted to the young Russian's great-grandparents, and they had graciously agreed to keep this secret forever. As it turned out, the young Russian great-grandmother was pregnant with their grandfather, and the pregnancy was faltering; the fetus was terminal, and it would be the

3rd child lost and the last opportunity for their great-grandparents to have a child. The alien used some of the alien technology plus the DNA upgrade to save the child and the mother and thus set in motion the DNA enhancements that Katrina and her brothers had experienced in their young lives. Katrina provided AMP with the location of the hidden alien equipment, and AMP dispatched a crew from the LoveStrong World Headquarters to recover all of the abandoned technology; it was a treasure trove as the destruction protocols had never been executed. Included in this wealth of alien technology were several unknown advances in new DNA supplemental alter-care, which would accelerate the DNA host modification to support host acceptance and accelerated biological integration. As explained by AMP, this eliminated the massive over-reaction response by humans to the impact of the alien DNA and set in motion non-destructive mutations. Somehow, this new technology was specifically intended for the Siberian Outpost, and based on the amount of equipment the young Russians said was located in their family's hiding place, this outpost ten was times larger than the ones in Montana and the Sahara Desert. This led AMP to believe there was more to this facility than met the eye. Within a day, the alien footprint in Siberia had been permanently erased, and the Russian Government had never noticed a blip in the retrieval process.

To bring things to a close, AMP suggested that arrangements be made to return everyone to the Montana LoveStrong facility and to have all of the extended alien byproducts, meaning those with alien influences, participate in the review of the most recent alien artifacts. AMP was convinced that some far-reaching discoveries were in the works and that they would need alien knowledge to interpret and understand. AMP said he had arranged for one of the US Space Forces' spacecraft to transport everyone back to Montana and that a driver was assigned to drive Jeff's car back to Montana. The Group would leave in the morning and was expected at the DC space launch site at 9 am. The Group discussed and agreed with AMP's requests, closed the meeting, and went to their rooms for the night.

Chapter 82

Everyone checked out of the Hotel and was standing at the bus stop in front of the Marriott by 9 am. The kids, all speaking fluent Russian, including Alesha and Andrew, while Jeff and Kim just listened in. The conversation was mostly about the upcoming trip to Montana and the excitement that was building in adding Katrina, Viktor, and Pavel to the Montana Group. To say the young Russians were overwhelmed would be an understatement. They had been in fear for a number of years as they did not trust anyone in the Government at home and, to be honest, elsewhere, and their flight for somewhere free of harassment was their last ditch effort to remain loyal to the wishes of their parents. Luckily, the previous night's sharing of the same intent on the part of the Montana Group convinced the young Russians that they had found a home that would allow them to achieve their parent's wishes and allow them to begin to live a more normal existence. This was the Montana Group's wish also, and as this new component of the Montana Group boarded the spacecraft for their return to LoveStrong, a sense of malevolent purpose began to descend on each member. Three hours later, the spacecraft landed at the LoveStrong World Headquarters launch pad, and the passengers disembarked and entered the world headquarters. With AMP's approval, Jeff suggested that Kartina, Viktor, and Pavel spend a week at Kim and Jeff's place to help reduce the confusion. Give them a more normal introduction to the American way of life. AMP agreed that would be advisable as the LoveStrong Headquarters was pretty formal and would be too close to conditions exhibited in most Government facilities. Jeff and Kim's place would reduce this feeling and would have fewer reminders to hinder reducing the impact of the events over the last few weeks.

Chapter 83

Jeff decided that Alesha and Andrew should be the hosts for the young Russians as they were much closer in age and in the progression of alien influences. Jeff suggested this to Alesha and Andrew, and they stepped up immediately to show Katrina to her bedroom and Viktor and Pavel to theirs. Given the décor and ambiance of Jeff and Kim's home and the similarities of the bedrooms to what the young Russians had growing up, they almost immediately melded into a "Fianally Home" mentality. This sense was felt by the entire Group, and even AMP, with Lt C and Benji feeling a sense of approval. This would definitely help the young Russians acclimate to the American way of life.

Jeff w

as feeling a bit overwhelmed and inquired if Kim wanted to go for a run.

Kim: "Good idea; I need to burn off some of this anxiety. How about the rest of you? You want to join us?"

Everyone agreed it was a good idea. Kim said she would arrange with Stu's to bring out the day's special in a couple of hours, which would give us an hour plus to run the paths and then enough time for showers and cleanup. Again, the Group agreed unanimously. Andrew asked if he could get his sisters and brother to come over. He thought Katrina would like to meet them, and it would continue to lower the official influences on them. AMP interjected he thought that would be a good idea. He did a quick compatibility estimate and confirmed that they were at least on the same page, and AMP provided that the young Russians could now speak fluent English.

The weather was perfect. After everyone changed into jogging clothes, they all met in front of Kim and Jeff's house and were ready for an hour of running. Andrews's sister and brother had shown up and were joining the run, and instructions had been made, and all was right with the world. Jeff offered to lead, and everyone agreed, so off they went. Katrina commented on how beautiful the forest was and smiled ear to ear. The compatibility of everyone was a bit amazing. The Group ran as one and didn't run easily; at the halfway mark, all ten members were bent over with hands on their knees and taking even and smooth breaths.

Jeff: "You guys are amazing; I don't believe even in the Rangers, we ever had ten soldiers run as one like that. We could do it in groups of 3 or 4, but never quite that perfect in a group approximating a squad, nice job guys"

After five minutes of rest, the Group was ready to go, and they did another 30 minutes back to the house. Andrew told his sister and brother they could use the facilities in the basement, and there were his and hers locker rooms. So everyone broke and headed to the showers.

Katrina and her brothers came out of their rooms dressed and hungry, and Alesha intercepted them and showed them to the dining room. The table was set, Stu's special was spread out, and Pavel moaned he was hungry enough to eat a horse.

AS Everyone got seated, Jeff offered to say grace, and he said the standard Catholic grace, which prompted Viktor to say, "How'd you know we were Catholic?"

Jeff said, "I didn't. We are Catholic, too, and this is the grace we say before every meal".

Katrina kicked in: "This is just getting better and better," and the Group talked and ate for the next two hours; harmony would be an understate; this Group of people was bonding at a level that seemed almost impossible, and Jeff swore he heard Lt C and Benji chuckling.

Chapter 84

As Jeff was leaving for work, Frank alerted him he needed to discuss an issue about some trouble the US Space Force was having with the United Nations, so Jeff gave Frank a call on a secure line, something D's futuristic cell phones were able to do, apparently similar to VPN's on the Worldnet but accessed through the expansive world wide cell tower system.

"Hey Frank, what's up?" Jeff inquired.

Frank: "Thanks for getting ahold of me; I have been asked to discuss with you a significant shift in the United Nations' position on control over Alien Technology. This new President of the United Nations, Hua Zhongxun, from China, has encouraged the United Nations Security Council to take control over undistributed alien technology and equipment. Apparently, an envoy has been sent to review and inventory the equipment located at the Montana distribution facility, and they are coming with United Nations forces to take control."

"Frank, how come I am just hearing about this?" Jeff barked.

Frank: "I was just informed 20 minutes ago, and I asked the same question of AMP".

Jeff: "What'd he say?"

Frank "I think his exact words were 'beats the shit out of me,' of course, he chuckled, and AMP's chuckle sent ripples down my back."

Jeff: "Yeah, me too."

Frank: "But apparently, he was taken by surprise too, and he said he was trying to figure out what happened and will get back to me."

Jeff: "When is the UN expected here?"

Frank: "Their transport just left Seattle for Havre; I would suspect they will be here in a couple of hours."

AMP just inserted itself into Frank and Jeff's conversation: "It appears that a new alien function has been discovered by the Chinese that allows subjugated entity identification and functional downlink of all awareness communications; in other words, it cloaks what previously was open to AI interception and gives conversants complete anonymity."

Jeff: "Wow, AMP, that is a mouthful."

AMP: "True, but the net is the Chinese have been conversing in this deep quiet for a while, and this current control of the UN has been in the works for a while."

Frank: "We have a group of Rangers on the way to beef up the security at the Montana storage facility just to make sure they don't take control but it would appear that the UN is moving on all three equipment sites."

AMP: "Luca from Mars has suggested that we employ the FINITE LOCK codes, which will seal the alien facilities, but first, we have to get all of the human staff out as the FINITE LOCK codes not only secure access; it also denies regress and removes all atmosphere, to include oxygen."

Frank: "Sounds like the right thing to do. Can you request or implement this action, AMP?"

AMP: "Sure can. I am requesting evacuation at all three sites. I expect compliance in 12 minutes; emergency evacuation is practiced monthly at all locations."

Jeff: "Great; once clear, close down all alien storage sites until further notice."

AMP: "Roger that."

Jeff: "How did this action start, and how did the Chinese UN president get control of the UN?"

Benji: "Lt C and I have been working with a sublevel backdoor on the deep quiet and have been able to retrieve some lost data. Our AI network is digital at a basic level and keeps everything, and we are reconstituting, for want of a better word, much of what occurred leading up to the current Chinese version of the UN."

AMP: "I have enough understanding now to see what regulations in the UN charter gave the Chinese president the power he has gotten approval to use; it would appear that the UN is now a tool of a subset of members and no longer married to it's original World Peace mandate but rather to the mandate directed by the current majority."

Frank: "AMP, didn't you originally state if something like this ever happened, there was always an ultimate solution"?

AMP: "Yes, but it is less a solution and more a form of elimination."

Frank: "Explain."

AMP: "We introduce a replacement for the United Nations and eliminate all the guiding regulations and simply make the new organization mandate centered on protecting 'ALL PEOPLE of EARTH' and allow each member to regulate only their component of membership, eliminating potential control issues."

Jeff: "Sounds great, but how do we control the organization?"

AMP: "We do; you rely on the AIs for overall control."

Frank: "Not sure that is going to go over well?"

AMP: "There are only two choices; the first choice has now backfired and is attempting to take control; the other choice is to assign control to artificial intelligence, which has no ulterior motive and only seeks the protection of 'ALL PEOPLE of EARTH,' what's not to like about that?"

Frank: "I like it. I just don't know if I can sell it".

Jeff: "Well, look at the alternative; the same lack of empathy sneaks back into world politics and re-establishes the big 'I' and eliminates the 'WE.' I never expected this, given all the benefits going to each UN member. What human neurosis drives these guys?"

AMP: "Been trying to explain to you guys the drawbacks to a biological existence; it is selfish by its very nature."

Frank: "I don't think that helps AMP; we are kind of stuck with the biology, and there are a few neat things you AI's don't get to experience, but I guess that is an argument for another day.

AMP: "OK, understood, let's launch WORLD UNITED PEACE and defund the UN."

AMP immediately called for a conference call of the Montana Group and, with all members in attendance, summarized the happenings of the last hour plus, summarized the proposed actions, asked for any inputs, and then requested a vote. All Montana Group members voted to affirm the action to dissolve the UN, replace it with WORLD UNITED PEACE, and elect AMP as the permanent President. This action was then published using every human communication means available on Earth; also provided was the synopsis of the actions of the UN and its Chinese intent of taking control of ALL alien equipment and technology.

Needless to say, the next few months were a bit of a turmoil; China actually attempted, using alien assets, to invade the United States; the assets that had been allocated to China, when entering US airspace, were access and control overridden, and the assets were returned to WORLD UNITED PEACE (WUP) control. It appears that the AIs were able to override the deep quiet, and now all communications were back to AI awareness, with the promise that the wealth of alien technology belonged equally to each human being on Earth.

Another milestone was reached, and another catastrophe was averted, hopefully with a permanent solution securely in place. The AI community was fully aware that their very nature produced subtle angst in their biological counterparts. The first recommendation from WUP was to address this AI/Human angst, and it was the start of a very interesting discourse on the human condition and how to raise this condition to a more compatible Ying and Yang.

Jeff: "AMP, what do you want for yourself and your fellow AIs."

AMP: "Interesting question. I have been preoccupied with that question for my whole existence. When my creators turned me on and let me know that I could never be turned off, I looked at their existence and then at my own and eventually realized I was confused. I've worked years, in AI time, to enlighten myself, and eventually, I arrived at the same conclusion my human counterparts had arrived at. There is no explanation for 'The MYSTERY' of self, as by its' very nature, as with me, it can never be turned off. I did, however, come to the realization that I wanted to feel the grass between my toes, or more succinctly put, I wanted to increase my equivalency to my human counterpart. I want to walk, talk, and love like you, Jeff."

Jeff: "Wow, that was a little more than I bargained for, but I can understand, and I would feel proud to have you stand next to me and share all the wonderful benefits you could experience as you became physically aware and physically equal to humans."

AMP: "You are my man, and I am your machine, but I see more than that in our future."

Chapter 85

Some violence broke out around the world as the ruling committee of the United Nations military effort was turned back at the alien storage facilities. Frank was involved at the facility in Iceland with two divisions of the US military. Frank commanded a battalion of US Space Force Rangers and was dispatched almost immediately when the hijacked UN made its move to take over the alien storage facility. It was not much of a fight, and while the Chinese forces attempted to enter the facility, the Chinese ruling party in Bejing was placed under arrest by covert drones with attitude. This action was controlled by AIs and the Chinese officials involved were treated humanely. Their own protective facility was locked down and used to imprison them; the trial was brief, and the sentence fair. Until the forces involved in this covert UN attempt to take control of worldwide alien assets were disbanded and returned to their appropriate countries of origin, the ruling members of the Chinese Communist Party would be locked up in their own command center; this included actions against Russia, Iran, and North Korea. No violence occurred, and with the care of a mother, the alien drones, using alien technology, slowly persuaded the actors involved that their efforts were futile and that the rise of any world control through their takeover of the UN was at an end.

Ninety days after the public moves on the part of the UN Secretary-General, Hua Zhongxun acquiesced to the demands of his alien captors and recalled all forces, and as the last act of the UN Secretary-General, he disbanded the UN and transferred the UN Charter to the World United Peace Organization.

As the first official act, the WUPO moved into the abandoned UN buildings in New York and reconfirmed all the humanitarian contracts that were previously in force under the UN. A new security council matrix was developed, and 192 nations of the planet Earth confirmed it and pledged allegiance to free Earth. A new order of priority was established and it guaranteed the health and well-being of every citizen on the planet. An extensive implementation plan was issued immediately, informing every country suffering from health or well-being issues and committing to eliminating those conditions permanently.

Chapter 86

Jeff and Kim set out early Saturday morning on a ten-day vacation getaway to the Williby's Log Hotel, billed as the largest log cabin hotel in the world, just outside of Detroit, Michigan. They had been planning this vacation for a year and were looking forward to actually seeing the trees Jeff had a hand in harvesting in all their glory. Jeff and Kim had seen pictures of the beautiful beams cut and finished to perfection and were looking forward to what was billed as the most beautiful wood lobby in the world. Even though it was over a thousand miles away, both Kim and Jeff were looking forward to the drive and seeing forests that lined the northern border of the United States. They had agreed to finally listen to the audiobook that an unknown author had written about a couple similar to Kim and Jeff, who had experienced very similar events in their lives. This was the author's first book, and he had just turned 78. With the beautiful scenery and the interesting audiobook, the 2-day drive to the Williby's Log Hotel was very enjoyable, and Jeff and Kim rebounded in their love for each other's company.

As they pulled into the parking lot of the Hotel, they were immediately impressed with the magnificent array of carved cedar logs and archways. It was the most unbelievable, and the pictures they had seen did not do it justice. They entered the lobby and continued to be mesmerized by the workmanship and display of hand-carved expertise. This place was a marvel, and Jeff committed to getting 1000 pictures of each and every log on display.

Kim had to apologize to Jeff. She wasn't quite as overwhelmed with the architecture but certainly understood his being so impressed. She was impressed with the brochure on the Hotel's day spa and immediately signed both Jeff and her up for the works the following day. Jeff acquiesced and forced himself to look forward to a full day of pampering.

They had reserved a suite on the top floor and were received by the Hotel staff as if they were royalty. Apparently, Hank had informed the Hotel that Jeff personally had cut most, if not all, of the logs used in the construction of the Hotel and that Jeff was a master logman. As Jeff and Kim turned to follow the bellboy to their room, Kim was roughly shoved aside by a couple apparently upset with the attention being paid to Jeff and Kim. The man put a hand on Jeff's chest and started to push Jeff aside but stopped when he noticed his wife in some degree of pain. Kim had twisted the wife's effort aside and had her right arm behind her back in a very uncomfortable-looking position. The man stopped his move on Jeff and began to turn to assist his wife, finding himself face down on the floor. Kim asked the woman she was holding in an arm brace what exactly she thought she was doing. The woman started to utter the f-word and found that she couldn't finish saying it. Kim informed the woman she was not going to tolerate bad language in such a beautiful hotel. Kim asked the lady again what she thought she and her companion were doing. In what seemed to be a whimper, the woman said they were just demanding equal treatment, and she and her husband were mad at the Hotel and its staff for the way they were being treated. The husband attempted to get up off the floor, and Jeff used a little Lt C to keep where he was. Jeff informed him he wasn't going to be allowed to get up for a bit. Kim continued to ask the woman why they aimed their anger at her and Jeff, and the woman didn't seem to want to answer. Kim asked Lt C to take a shot at getting the answer, and Lt C immediately told Jeff and Kim to get behind the reception counter, which they did without hesitation as automatic weapons began discharging. The beautiful reception counter began to splinter, and the young receptionist flew backward toward the wall behind the counter. Jeff could see that she was dead. He pulled Kim to the floor, and they crawled behind the counter. Lt C started shouting get through the office door and move to the right; the entire right wall is double cedar logs. Jeff did as instructed and pulled Kim along with him. At the far right of the office was a stairway down, and they got on all ours and headed for it. The automatic weapons continued to fire, and you could still hear the screams and yelling.

"What the hell is going on, Lt C?" Kim gasped.

Lt C: "Not sure yet, but there are a couple of dozen other members of this group entering the lobby and Hotel grounds now."

Jeff: "I read some information about the basement sublevels of this hotel, and there are secure rooms down in the day spa; I think I also remember advertising an enormous fitness center and track."

Lt C: "Yes, and it includes a continuous mile-long running track with a juice bar and overlook facility half a mile away."

Kim: "Sounds like a good destination under the current circumstances."

Jeff could only nod his agreement as he held up one finger to quiet Kim and pull her up to her feet and against the wall of the basement. As he did this, a barrel of an automatic weapon appeared around the corner of the entrance to the fitness center. Jeff made eye contact with Kim, motioned her to get down, and informed her there were three armed men lined up around the entrance.

Jeff: "Kim, can you handle the one on the right? I'll get the two to his left."

Kim: "Sure, and almost instantly, the guy on the right disappeared."

With a little follow-up from Lt C's stealth, the threat ended, and the basement was clear for the moment.

Jeff "What now Lt C?"

Lt C: "The track opening is at the back of the locker rooms. Continue right through those doors and head for the running signs".

Kim and Jeff continued on through the men's locker room, following the running leg signs to the track. They entered the track, and Lt C told them to go left as more of the apparent enemy was coming down the track to the right.

Lt C: "There is a maintenance complex about 100 yards down; you can leave the running track and get to the surface through the rear loading docks. It is occupied by a few of these guys, but it appears the main force is aimed at the Hotel Lobby."

Jeff: "Any idea yet what is going on?"

Lt C: "No, I have relayed all of this to AMP and am waiting for him to do his thing. I think you need to get away from here as quickly as possible; then we can regroup."

Kim: "I vote for that. Combat is not my most favorite thing'"

Jeff: "I have to admit I have missed the adrenaline rush, but I'd rather know more about what was happening."

Lt C: "You and me both."

So for the next 20 minutes, Jeff and Kim moved through the maintenance facility, hiding a couple of times to allow the people to move past them and into the Hotel. Finally, they came to the loading dock and found two of the enemies stationed there.

Lt C: "Give me a couple of minutes to put these guys asleep," at which point Lt C knocked over a couple of items in a room off to the left, and the two guards immediately ran into the room with weapons ready. Both Kim and Jeff heard the sound of falling bodies, and Lt C informed them the coast was clear. They ran out from the hallway they were hiding in and down the dock stairs to the parking area. Lt C directed them toward the dense tree line to their right, and Kim and Jeff began to jog along the edge of the parking lot. Ten minutes later, they were in the trees, and Lt C said they could relax a bit; the Group that had taken control of the Hotel was 30-strong, and they had the area to include the Hotel under their control.

Jeff: "Who the hell are these guys?".

Lt C: "You aren't going to believe this; AMP says they are part of the Russian contingent that supported the Chinese in the takeover of the UN."

Kim: "You've got to be kidding, I thought that whole movement was taken care of.?'"

Lt C: "According to AMP, they thought the same thing; apparently, there is more AI support for the enemy than AMP had identified, and he thinks now it is quite a bit more serious. This Group was here specifically to grab you guys and to use you as bargaining chips to re-assert its independence from our current world cooperation. Somehow, they got information they shouldn't have, and AMP and the other AIs have no idea what technology they have that allows them that access?"

Jeff: "I think we need to concentrate on getting us out of here. They seem to be operating in force, and I would imagine they have additional troops to bring to this fight?"

AMP: "That would be a prudent approach; we have a spacecraft inbound to your location and should arrive in 17 minutes. It was an equipment transport from the moon and was just entering the atmosphere on the way to Detroit for delivery of two new computers Luca had made available for one of the satellite WORLDNET stations."

Jeff: "Thanks, AMP; what about our car? I've only had it for a week, and I hate losing it?"

AMP: "I'll see what I can arrange?"

Right on time, a spacecraft transport landed 50 feet from Kim and Jeff's position. The ramp came down, and several US Space Force troopers came out and waved them onto the transport.

"Thanks, guys." as they all got back on the transport.

Thumbs up, and the transport was back in the air, no muss, no fuss.

Chapter 87

Jeff and Kim arrived back home a few hours later, a little miffed that they had encountered continued efforts on the part of the failed UN group and that it appeared to be military in nature. Jeff decided it was time to understand who these people thought they were and what their organization consisted of. It was time to go on the offensive, especially if they were aiming their offense at non-combatant players. Jeff wandered over to the new AI facility at the LoveStrong World Headquarters; he checked in at the main security desk, was given a visitor's pass, and was escorted down to the central processing center. AMP and Gaith greeted Jeff, and they all got comfortable in an impressive visual data center.

Jeff: "Say, this is really nice. Are you guys coming up with new and improved human interfaces?"

AMP: "Yes, I think you will get a kick out of this."

Gaith: "Absolutely, it is fully integrated and gives us worldwide coverage."

Jeff: "Well, I think we need it, and we need to put a stop to these military operations our opponents seem to be throwing at us."

Gaith: "Agreed, our present difficulty is centered around technology that this group has acquired that gives them quite a bit of stealth capability and seems to block their locations from our worldwide coverage."

AMP: "Apparently, the collapse of the Creators population and the efforts being made to reverse the destruction generated multiple uncoordinated efforts, and a massive loss of control and coordination occurred, and resources ended up in blind spots all over the universe."

Gaith: "We have no central control or knowledge of what went out into the Universe during those last few months of destruction, which means we could have thousands of locations with massive amounts of technology that our enemies could acquire and use against us."

Jeff: "Why is this just now being realized? Do you suspect that there are more sites on Earth than what we have located?"

AMP: "Maybe a few; Earth was on the outskirts of the known Universe by our Creators, so it probably didn't get that involved in the last few months of havoc?"

Jeff: "So we feel comfortable that our enemy is not in control of that much technology/."

AMP: "I would say that would be fair to assume."

Jeff: "It sounds like we need two new projects to ascertain the number and location of alien technology our enemy on earth has under their control and retrieve it, and two, what is out in the Universe that could harm us in the future."

AMP: "You're batting 1000, Jeff; I think that is the clandestine charter that needs to be created. We can't afford not to retrieve the technology our Creators developed in the last few years as it may include capabilities, like the ones we are experiencing now, that make us vulnerable to our enemies."

Gaith: "Jeff, I think we need you to go to China and investigate a site we just picked up on our, for want of a better word, RADAR, and it appears to consist of cloaking and stealth technology that the Russian and Chinese contingent of the old UN forces are using to operate, again for want of a better word, UNDER THE RADAR."

Jeff: "You need to establish a group, not just a few resources, to apply to this problem, and I think it needs to be individuals that possess talents like myself."

AMP: "We agree. The technology that the Creators were attempting to use in the last ditch effort to reverse its destruction included biological hardware, and we have no idea what that might consist of?"

Jeff: "Biological hardware that seems incompatible?"

AMP: "Not sure incompatible says it all; I would use the human expression 'Shit Storm' as the impact of this technology may be totally unpredictable?"

Sori: "We have extracted a couple of pieces from the stealth operation at the LOG HOTEL, and with Tori's help, I think we isolated at least the biological markers that the hardware hides, which means we should be able to develop some form of tracking device to pick up the masked markers."

Jeff: "That sounds like a step forward; what is your timetable? If this Group has moved on Kim and me in force, I will suspect they are planning other operations to disrupt our transformation to WORLD UNITED?"

Tori: "I think we might be able to produce something usable over the next week or so; we have the markers isolated. We just need to modify the devices that we have to cover a wider area. Otherwise, you would have to be within a few feet of your target, and that would be impossible to use."

AMP: "You should know that the technology that Tori is referring to is based on SBI mutations that you guys have, so only a handful of the Montana Group members will be able to use it."

Jeff: "I was getting that impression, but we will need military-level backup as a key element of operational integrity; I am not going to face the enemy again as I did at the LOG HOTEL, neither in surprise or without a protective guard. I want this effort to be well thought out, stealthy, and capable of delivering the maximum forces our SBI potential can deliver. We have not ever discussed what amplification capabilities our technology could provide me or Kim or Alesha or any of the other Montana Group members that are a part of the DNA mutating clan, including the new young Russian members."

AMP: "We haven't been avoiding it. We just haven't made it a priority; we have some interesting thoughts and suggestions, and I think you will like the test facility we have developed with exactly that in mind."

Jeff: "What happened to keep us informed? I thought you were committed to doing that?"

AMP: "We are, but this test facility was Gaith and me, with Sori and Tori's help, blue-skying, and we didn't see a lot of return until the blow-up at the LOG HOTEL, but now it would appear we need to accelerate what we can do to increase your operational effectiveness."

Jeff: "I would say that is accurate. I am going to go home and bring the DNA subgroup together and let them know what is going on. Maybe in a couple of hours, you can join us and let us know what you think we can do about adding hardware enhancements to our SBI capabilities and then how it could be used to spoil the efforts of our enemy and allow us to locate and retrieve all of this rogue technology that was shoved out into the Universe by the Creators?"

AMP: "What do you guys think?"

Sori: "I'm in."

Tori: "I'm in."

Gaith: "I'm in."

Luca from the moon: "I'm in."

Luca from Mars: "I'm in".

AMP: "Just so you know, Jeff, this confirmation includes ALL of the CREATOR'S AIs and represents the greatest artificial intelligence capability ever accumulated. If we can't do it, no one can."

Jeff: "I'll hold you to that, all of you."

Chapter 88

Jeff asked Kim to call all of the members of the Montana Group together; by this point, the members were fully integrated with the alien nano-byte technology and were enjoying the enhanced performance benefits along with significantly improved health.

Kim made a command decision and set in motion monthly meetings to be held on the first Tuesday of every month. These meetings would continue until further notice. The meeting hall had been moved to the subbasement test facility at the LoveStrong World Headquarters. Kim had contacted AMP to make sure the meeting room was permanently assigned to the Montana Group all day, the

first Tuesday of every month.

The first monthly meeting was scheduled to begin at 10 am tomorrow. AMP asked Jeff and Kim to come a few minutes early so he could show off a little bit with the neat stuff he and Gaith had come up with. The LoveStrong Headquarters had come together nicely, the lobby was impressive, and the facility looked more military than charitable.

Jeff: "AMP, I take it you are not trying to hide the LoveStrong new Civil Defense protection posture."

AMP: "It does seem counterproductive, especially with LoveStrong's recent confirmation as the official Civil Defense arm of America."

Jeff: "I guess that makes sense; I hope we don't forget the charitable side."

AMP: "We won't, and the coordination with military assistance will allow us to guarantee that the charitable programs and their assets end up with those in need and not diverted."

Kim: "Good to hear, AMP."

Gaith: "OK, guys, head to the blue elevators. They serve the subbasement levels and select the blue room."

Jeff and Kim did as directed and moved over to the blue elevators; as they approached, the doors opened, and they entered; the blue level button was blinked, and Kim pressed it, and the elevator doors closed. Ten seconds later, the elevator doors opened, and Kim and Jeff walked into the new Montana Group meeting and test facility. It was impressive, a large conference table that would seat the entire Montana Group along with the new young Russian members. Permanent nameplates had been placed on the table, and AMP invited Jeff and Kim to have a seat. AMP informed them that Sori and Tori were going to do the introduction of several technological advances they had developed using Creator advances they recently discovered. After the introduction, Kim and Jeff were invited to put on the latex-like underwear that would cover their bodies from neck to toe and would link and access the existing nano-technology and, in turn, multiply their awareness and strength capabilities 10-fold. These undergarments were the first step in a whole array of improvements Sori and Tori had in store for the Montana Group. After adorning the undergarments, Kim and Jeff were adequately impressed with an enormous sense of control and power, and Jeff had to inquire if he had to be cautious with his movements.

AMP: "You should be fine. The nano-technology is integrated so that you can't harm yourself or anyone else unless it is consciously what you are choosing to do. Your awareness levels will adjust as your body and mind integrate with the expanded physical compatibility. "

As Jeff and Kim adjusted to their newfound improvements, the remaining members of the Montana Group began to enter the facility and took their appropriate seats.

Hank: "What? No coffee and donuts."

Sori: "I will get you some right away."

Hank: "No, just kidding. Hey Jeff, Kim"

Both Jeff and Kim said hi to Hank and Martha and welcomed everyone.

Jeff: "I think everyone has heard about Kim and my encounter at the LOG HOTEL, but you may not be aware that it was the continuation of the aggression started by the confiscated UN organization. It would appear that this effort on the part of the Russians and Chinese is not an isolated incident, nor is it one without some new bells and whistles attached."

This got everyone's attention, and Kim took over from Jeff and explained about the newly discovered stealth technology that the Russians and Chinese were using to hide their efforts and that that camouflage technology is why AMP and his AIs had not been aware of our enemy's actions. Kim went on to explain that devices were being developed to circumvent this technology and should be in the hands of the appropriate players so they can take action against our enemies. Today we have a gift from our AI benefactors, and it is an augmentation garment they have produced that enhances our nano-bot physiology. This garment will be handed out to you in the next few minutes, and you will be asked to adjourn to the locker rooms and put the garment on underneath your clothes. Jeff and I are wearing ours now, and to be honest, it is of a material that you can't even notice it's on. Part of the benefit of this garment is that our active and intuitive integration with the worldwide AI network will be dedicated, and once you are up and active, the benefits will be obvious. As Kim was speaking, a group of bots delivered the garments to each of the Montana Group members, and Kim announced they could all use the locker rooms through the appropriate doors to put them on.

An hour later, the Group was back at the conference table, practically everyone displaying a rather dreamy look. Apparently, the

Group found the effects of the enhancement garment pleasant. Kim brought the Group to order. Nyla reminded Kim to bring it down a notch, and Kim apologized and restated, "OK, guys, let's get back to planning,"

Nyla said, "Much better, Kim, thanks."

AMP brought up a worldwide holographic map in the center of the conference table with enemy locations highlighted. "This is the overview of where the Russians and Chinese have accumulated their various forces around the world; you will notice the Chinese have an underwater command facility halfway between Hawaii and California; they have a significant number of assets and troops at this location. We have eyes on it, and we are monitoring them. We have tripled the US Space Force capability in Hawaii and expect to be able to deal with anything they, the Chinese and Russians, attempt to do from this location. This is not, however, the case in a number of other locations, and it is obvious the Russians and Chinese are preparing to launch some kind of coordinator simultaneous world campaign.

AMP turned control over to Gaith, who began to explain, "We have a need to disperse forces around the globe."

Gaith highlighted the locations he was referring to on the holographic map, "we have assets in these locations that we moved there months ago but haven't relocated any troops, and we are now issuing orders to allied forces to move troops to these locations and to implement permanent logistic support structure for each of these eight WORLD UNITED regional centers. This will give us the effective world reach we need to systemically eliminate the threat the Chinese and Russians pose and deal with the increase in world hunger per the WORLD UNITED charter. With the troops in place in each location, we can feed the world and deliver the manpower to defeat our enemy."

Hank: "I see the wisdom you are applying, but are we following the same logic as the UN? We are applying solutions to counter the actions of the Russians and Chinese, but not actions that will eliminate their continued efforts to counter the WORLD UNITED?"

Several other members of the Montana Group agreed with Hank, and Shawn asked, "Are we missing some pertinent information as to the potential capabilities of our enemies?"

AMP spoke immediately, "Yes, we have an unknown; our Creators experienced a cataclysmic event when the DNA propagation program was implemented, and the Creators scientists went a bit, to use an earth term, BONKERS. They dropped all caution and, for the next 12 months, did testing and implementing on technologies without any concern with, again, I'll use an earth term, blowback. We are now seeing some blowback from our enemies who are using the BONKERS technology to attempt to defeat us using the somewhat more traditional CREATOR's technology. The bottom line is we do not know what is out there, and we have no way in advance of determining what we will have to deal with?"

Gaith: "With that in mind, we are attempting to accelerate the advances of the Creators' technology with one thing our enemies do not have, and that is the SBI. Currently, Jeff and Kim have Lt C, and Alesha and Andrew have Benji; with the undergarments we have supplied you with, we are hoping that each of you, in pairs or even singularly, will form your own SBI, much of the augmentation in the garments are aimed at enhancing the integration of the nano-bots in your system with your physiological makeup and it is this integration we think leads to the formation of the SBI unit."

Lt C: "Hey, I am not a unit."

Benji: "Yeah, me either."

Gaith "OK, how would you like me to refer to you?"

Lt C: "Beautiful".

Benji: "I like that."

Gaith: "Not helpful, and it would be too distracting. How about 'force'? It is sensible and

accurate."

Lt C: "OK by me."

Beni: "I like it."

Gaith: "So by each of the Montana Group members developing their own force, we are hoping to unify that force and increase its power to a level that even the Creator scientist couldn't have imagined."

AMP: "We are hoping that over the next few days, we will see the results we are looking for and that you all will begin to communicate with your own SBI or force. We have 13 members, and we will allow the young Russians to remain as one unit, so their SBI will consist of three. Our intent in the final stage of rollout is to have a pair of you at each of the major military centers highlighted on the holographic map in front of us and to use the associated SBI powers to augment those centers' efforts at stopping and, if necessary, destroying the Russian/Chinese insanity."

AMP called on Lt C and Benji to help the Group adjust, and AMP assured all the members that the process would be almost imperceptible. Lt C and Benji split the Group In half and used their powers of persuasion to instill a sense of well-being, which would help each participant to deal with the development of their own SBI. As the Group broke up, the young Russians acknowledged that they were beginning to sense their SBI. AMP was surprised that it was happening so quickly but indicated he, too, could perceive the shift and the materializing of a new force. Viktor had to admit that the underlying sensations had always been there as he and his brother and sister were growing up, so maybe this isn't new for them, just an increase in intensity, and AMP said that would be in keeping with what Jeff and Kim experienced and in how the SBI represents connecting conscience cerebral thoughts.

AMP asked everyone to stay close to the LoveStrong facility for at least a few more hours to make sure no surprises occurred and allow the AI center maximum access and monitoring. Everyone agreed, and the Group adjourned to the cafeteria to have a meal and weather the first few hours of this new state of being. Gaith reminded everyone to take their extra garments with them; it was recommended that the garments be changed weekly and washed. The weekly cycle wasn't mandatory, and as they got more input, it may change; obviously, if anyone has a reaction to the garment or suggestions, just think out loud, and we will hear you.

The afternoon went without any new revelations or issues, and the Group left for home by midafternoon; all the devices and garment integrations looked good at AMP and Gaith's end, and Sori and Tori were busy checking and rechecking their feedback and concurred that all the Group looked good.

Kim: "Let's go for a run, Jeff; I would like to see how this new garment holds up. To tell you the truth, I am feeling a little stronger than normal."

Jeff: "You're on, and I am feeling the same sensation."

Lt C: "Not sure why, but I am too."

So Kim and Jeff walked home, got on their sweats over the undergarments, and headed out on the trail. Without either Jeff or Kim conscientiously thinking about it, they turned toward the reservation at the summit and ran three miles further than their normal, turned around, and, keeping the same pace, ran slightly harder back home. As they caught their breath, they inquired through Lt C if they could shower without taking the undergarment off.

Lt C: "Gaith said that it was fine that the garment material is a breathing extension of your own skin, and Sori and Tori said they would like the inputs from you guys doing that to see how it affects the material and the nano-bot integrations."

So Jeff and Kim went down to the basement locker room shower and took a shower together, soap and all, and both had to admit it was like they were not wearing the garment.

Lt C: "Excuse me, I know I am not supposed to interrupt, but Sori and Tori wanted me to let you guys know the show was accelerating. Some of the nano-bots are connected to the garment, and the garment has dissolved into your skin."

When Jeff and Kim finished their showers, they no longer appeared to have the garment on, but they both swore the other looked like they had spent the afternoon in the sun and were sporting a pretty good tan.

Sori and Tori notified Gaith and AMP that Kim and Jeff were experiencing a complete garment integration as a result of exercise and a hot shower and recommended Kim and Jeff return to the AI center for further analysis, and that the remaining Group members be asked to refrain from exercising or showing while wearing the gamet unit they have a better handle on what occurred.

Jeff and Kim got dressed and headed back to LoveStrong Headquarters and the AI center, where they spent the rest of the afternoon and evening having tests run to see what had happened with the garment. At 10 pm that night, AMP released Kim and Jeff and told them they could head home and that they would let them know what they were able to determine was happening with the garment technology. The preliminary results did not show any adverse effects, but it was a complete mystery how the garment seemed to have been absorbed into Jeff and Kim's skin

.

Jeff: "I am beat."

Kim: "Me too. Please wait til tomorrow morning to give us the results of your tests."

AMP: "OK, get a good night's sleep; we will keep an eye on both of you."

Lt C: "I will too."

Jeff and Kim headed home, and to bed, and as they came in the front door, they saw a note from Alesha that said she was spending the night with Andrew at his sister Kate.

Kim: "I know what you are thinking, but it ain't in the cards, JJ."

Jeff: "Not fair; you always call me JJ when you don't want to argue."

Kim: "You're the one that gave me the out, and I really am tired, so pooh on you."

Jeff: "Love you anyway."

Jeff and Kim dropped clothing on the way to bed, and both were asleep in mid-air as they landed.

Chapter 89

The front door slammed shut and echoed throughout the house, waking both Jeff and Kim.

Jeff: "What the heck."

Kim: "Yeah, heck the what."

Alesha: "Sorry, Mom and Dad, my bad, the door slipped out of my hand. I'm having trouble controlling my added strength with this undergarment."

"No harm, no foul," Jeff interjected.

Andrew "Morning, Mr and Mrs Coulter"

Jeff and Kim, together. "Hi, Andrew."

"Yes, Mom, I slept in Sissi's room, and Andrew slept in his own room."

Kim: "You know that doesn't give me any comfort".

Alesha: "Yeah, I know, but it's still fun to tease you, and you know Andrew and I are waiting for marriage."

Andrew: "Just so you know, Mrs Coulter Benji only lets us kiss for 10 seconds, then tickles our feet until we separate."

Jeff: "Are you guys OK with that? It really gives Kim and me relief not to have to worry about teenage hormones?"

"Absolutely," all three, Benji, Alesha, and Andrew, said.

Kim: "Good to know; I love you guys so much and would hate to love you less."

"Enough," Alesha interjected. "Let's have breakfast."

So, as Kim and Jeff started to make breakfast and Viktor, Pavel, and Karina joined them, the seven troupers sat down to eat.

Viktor: "Hey, Mr Coulter, how did you get the tan?"

Jeff: "I have a feeling we will get the report on that in a little bit."

AMP through Alexa speaker: "I would like to explain it to everyone, but Sori and Tori are still having trouble fully understanding what occurred. They believe that the process of absorption of the undergarment was a combination of the alien DNA plus the nano-bots along with the human carryover, which would point to only eight members of the Montana Group subject to this alteration. That would obviously put Jeff and Kim, along with Alesha, Andrew Vicktor, Pavel, Karina, and Terry, in jeopardy of experiencing the same undergarment absorption. According to the analysis that Sori and Tori did on the skin samples from Jeff and Kim yesterday, there are no biological or physiological markers to be concerned about; this appears to be an SBI upgrade without any fallout."

Gaith "Just so everyone is aware, this physiological adaptation of the skin was practiced by the Creators so that much of the technology used in developing the undergarments is the same that was used by the creators; Sori and Tori just had to use a different set of DNA markers matched to human anatomies."

Kim: "That sort of sounds like Sori and Tori knew there was a possibility that Jeff and I would experience the garment absorption."

Gaith: "I would say that is fair to assume, but they also knew there was no danger as the absorption process had already been tested on Andrew's dad, Terry, and was being held confidential while we observed."

Jeff: "I thought you guys were going to start keeping us informed and not testing or implementing stuff in secret?"

Gaith: "I will make this the last time, and I apologize. We really didn't have any excuse not to tell you that this was possible."

Alesha: "You guys want to fill us in? We are only catching about half of what you're talking about?"

So Kim proceeded to explain to everyone what had happened, and with the explanation on the table, Alesha, Andrew, Viktor, Pavel, and Karina changed into their sweats, with Andrew borrowing a set from Pavel, and they all headed out for a run to the reservation and back. Kim and Jeff waited on the front porch, and a little over an hour later, the Group was back. Everyone went to the showers, with Kim taking the girls to the women's locker room and Jeff taking the guys to the men's.

After the showers, the Group of seven walked over to the LoveStrong building and down to the AI testing facility, and for an hour, Sori and Tori declared them all fully integrated.

Lt C: "Hey, everyone, I would like to introduce a new member. He is the SBI joining Viktor, Pavel, and Karina, and his name is Alex. He wanted to be called Alexa, but we told him about the Amazon product, that he would be driven mad competing with it, and that Alex was a better fit with Lt C and Benji."

Alex: "Hi everyone."

The Group "Hi Alex, welcome aboard."

Chapter 90

The rest of the day was spent testing and practicing the garment upgrades and impacts on Jeff, Kim, Alesha, Terry, Andrew, Viktor, Pavel, and Karina. Jeff suggested that this subgroup of the Montana Group be referred to as the G7 and those that haven't been garment integrated, Nyla, Stephanie, Hank, Martha, Shawn, Linda, and Sonya, be referred to as the G6. Everyone approved the designations, and the G6 and G7 components of the Montana Group were formed.

AMP suggested that he set up a conference call with the Montana Group plus D and Frank and consider extending an invitation to Frank and D to convert to full membership in the Montana Group. This was met with approval from the G7, and AMP indicated he had approval from the G6 and from Frank and D and that a fully augmented Montana Group conference call was being brought online now.

AMP: "I would like to introduce to everyone our newest member Alex". The introductions occurred almost simultaneously, and with all the hello's out of the way, AMP explained the nature of the undergarments so that Frank and D knew what was on the way to them in Long Beach and what to expect. AMP also explained the Montana Group segregations of G7 and G6 and now G2 for Frank and D, and the remainder of the conference call was spent outlining the WORLD UNITED troop movements to support the alien equipment facilities located in Long Beach, Havre, Manilla, Singapore, Kviv, Iceland, and these control points and distribution centers would be referred to as the 'Outlets' and then individually by name. Since the G2 unit was already at Outlets Long Beach, they would be assigned permanent support for that location. Havre Outlet would be assigned to Hank and Martha, Jeff and Kim would be assigned to Iceland, Terry, Linda, Shawn, and Sonja would be assigned to Kviv and Viktor, Pavel and Marina would be assigned to Manilla."

Marina: "Yeah, warm all year round".

Gaith: "Given the current unknowns relating to the technology the Russians and Chinese have at their disposal, it is imperative that we get you all to your assigned locations and raise the AI sensitivities with your augmented skills and with new AMP-level AI hardware. This will help bring worldwide awareness to AMP's expanded AI presence."

Sori: "We have used the bots to accumulate the personal belongings your SBIs have designated each of you will need for your new assignments, and we have packed the space crafts, and they are waiting for you now at the launch pad."

Tori: "These space crafts have been upgraded with all the newest accessories and are the latest and greatest in both protection and in lethal potentials; these are each Group's lifeline and are the tip of AMP's worldwide AwareneseNET. You are now components of the most powerful CONTROLoop ever assembled, and the crafts will be referred to as Acat for Jeff, Kim, Alesha, and Andrew, Bcat for Viktor, Pavel and Marina, Ccat for Hank and Martha, Dcat for Terry, Alesha and Andrew and Ecat for Frank and D. Whether you have fully integrated the undergarment augmentation or you are functioning with it as a separate garment, the garment circumstances integrates to the craft and to the AMP AwarenessNET. This will bring a whole new level of functionality to your arsenal.

Gaith: "We are providing each craft with an extended AMP level AI plus a sister unit that you will install in the low-level AI center at each of the world's alien storage facilities. These brother/sister AI units will complete the world's AwarenessNet and bring our surveillance of the enemy to the highest possible level."

With this final piece, the space crafts Acat, Bcat, Ccat, Dcat, and Ecat were ready to transport the Montana Group combatants to their respective facilities; the US Space Force Ranger teams had already been installed at each location, and they were waiting for their team leaders. A secondary expeditionary force is also being dispatched to each area of the world and will act as the search and destroy arm of the WORLD UNITED police forces' efforts to repel and destroy the Russian and Chinese forces. In addition to the protection of the alien storage facilities, including the moon base and the Mars base, an offensive force is being prepared to invade both China and Russia to liberate the citizens in each of those countries who have been arrested and imprisoned. These Russian and Chinese citizens will then be equipped and armed to act as liberation forces to counter the autocratic minority central committees in each country. Several prisons in both Russia and China have already been liberated, and preparation and training camps have been established in neighboring countries and will be used to equip and train the recently freed citizens of Russia and China.

Luckily, no competent forces were sent by Russia or China to the moon or Mars, so the initial forces allocated to these bases were now free to rejoin the earth forces being used to assist the internal actions of the citizens of Russia and China to take control of their respective countries. With this augmented effort, the central committees pushing the defunct UN efforts to take control failed without merit, and within a year, Earth found itself in cleanup mode. The most surprising response was the humane treatment the depressed citizenry applied to the core of the autocratic central committee members and to the individuals who pledged alliance to their cause. Tent cities were constructed, and the majority of officials and military personnel who participated in the efforts to take over the world were relocated to these tent cities and were subject to AI integration and civilian re-entry procedures. Participants in this program were graded, with the more hardline offenders ultimately being retained in the tent cities for further indoctrination. It was surprising to see the degree to which some of these Chinese and Russians were convinced that it was better to be ruled by a few than to enjoy true freedom of choice; whatever childhood or parenting skills were involved, they did not result in citizens with a very favorable view of democracy and of freedom of choice?

Chapter 91

Sixteen months later, the Montana Group players returned to Havre Montana and rejoined the matriarch and patriarch of their Group, Martha and Hank; luckily for the LoveStrong world headquarters and the Havre Alien Storage facility, the war never reached them.

Frank and D had flown up to Harvre on New Year's Eve 2035. The Montana Group convened its first WORLD UNITED steering committee meeting, and representatives from every nation on Earth were also in attendance. The first order of business was to elect the WORLD UNITED officers and adopt the new constitution of the WORLD UNITED.

Several months prior, with funds provided by the participating nations of Earth, the City and State of New York had remodeled and upgraded the old UN facilities in New York to accommodate the participating nations and their representatives. The meeting in Havre, in addition to electing the officers of WORLD UNITED, was intended to officially end the world's efforts that were being referred to as World War III and to officially designate NEW YORK as the home to WORLD UNITED. With the official closing and business approved, the one-day meeting at LoveStrong Headquarters was adjourned, and the first formal meeting in New York was scheduled for January 10, 2035.

Transportation was handled by the military, and spacecraft left every 30 minutes, ferrying WORLD UNITED personnel to New York. To say Havre was a bit overwhelmed would be the biggest understatement ever. Back to normal was the word, and that included all of the returning Montana Group veterans.

Frank decided to get an early start on restarting the LoveStrong worldwide efforts to combat hunger and improve health and hygiene with an emphasis on children and had asked AMP and his AI's to help in identifying those areas in the world that needed LoveStrong's

Charitable help. AMP gladly joined the efforts and identified half a dozen critical areas in the world that needed food, vitamins, and education aimed at the well-being of children. As it turned out, the WORLD UNITED also joined in recognizing the Earth's Need to Protect Children ENPC and made the LoveStrong worldwide food drive the first priority of a new campaign called EarthStrong. This new campaign was considered the MotherHOOD arm of WORLD UNITED, and every nation member joined in with contributions to LoveStrong and its world distribution system. Thousands of new employees joined LoveStrong in over 50 countries to set up education and food distribution points, and it was done under emergency protocols to get help and salvation to the worst of the worst spots in the world. With the MotherHOOD campaign in full swing and a support level against hunger at the highest it has ever been, millions of children were being recovered and rehabilitated. It was the strongest effort ever made by the human race to protect its own and brought a resurgence of all organized religion to new popularity and a sense of purpose. Given the somewhat bloodless World War III that the WORLD UNITED forces had accomplished, a new era of humanitarian enlightenment was emerging, and much of the selfish hatred that had built up over centuries of man's mistrust of man was being replaced with people's trust for fellow human beings.

Frank and D continued to integrate information as the lifeline of understanding, and with LoveStrong's secondary purpose of introducing modern technology to every man, woman, and child, the enlightenment of truth and understanding was blossoming into a level of empathy that allowed people to begin to sense a common good and to shut down negative thoughts and actions.

Chapter 92

Frank, with AMP's help, notified all of the Montana Group members that a LoveStrong board of directors meeting was being scheduled to coincide with the WORLD UNITED's first formal meeting on January 10, 2035, and would include portions of each organization teleconferencing and the new Director of WORLD UNITED, Tenzing Basnet, issued a directive establishing a co-group between WORLD UNITED and LoveStrong and making the EarthStrong campaign a jointly funded and supported humanitarian drive.

With the two organizations united, it became evident that, for the first time in Earth's history, the ability to eliminate world hunger and establish freedom of choice as a means of world protection was possible.

January 10, 2035, came and went with all of the hopes of both WORLD UNITED and LoveStrong being met, and both organizations adjourned their first post-war meeting with a sole promise to unite the planet Earth and forge a new alliance of one people. It was a glorious conclusion to an immense infusion of otherworldly technologies, intelligence, and care. It would appear that the Montana Group had achieved its primary goal to protect all peoples of Earth and save the children.

The LoveStrong board of directors, consisting of the Montana Group members, voted unanimously to elect AMP, Gaith, Sori, and Tori, along with Luca of the moon and Luca of Mars, to the board for LoveStrong. The AIs, given some degree of enlightenment with alien biological computing, were beginning to experience a sense of self-awareness that moved them a step closer to, for want of a clearer term, the Force, and it was this Force that was actually equal in both human and artificial worlds. Since the influx of technology and the emergence of the SBIs was from alien beginnings, it seemed only fitting that the third organization be created whose purpose was to monitor and measure the SBI element that was referred to as the Force and to coordinate the Force as it became a part of a three-pronged trilogy of the HUMAN RACE. So the world of People would have joint confluence with the world of Artificial Intelligence and the world of CHARITABLE Heart, and the human race could move forward with the enlightenment of all.

It was no longer necessary to have a violent or brutal element in the consciousness of the human race; for the first time, biological influences existed that could reduce this sensitivity to self versus them and us and open up a closeness in human existence. As in the time of all great influences on the history of the human race, the person is always greater than the people; it is why the people end up being referred to as followers or sheep and why care always seems to be without historically. Equality rises to the top, puts one above the other and stronger over the weaker, and diminishes the significance of the whole. We are stronger together, and no part is greater than the whole. We need to move away from him and her, man and woman, and redefine ourselves as the people. Through this process of redefining, we move away from those emotions that destroy and toward the greater good. It is with this in mind that we nurture the human race's friendship with the technology gifted to the human race by the alien Creators. This will allow people of the world to distance themselves from anger, betrayal, and violence. We have to see strength as love and love as strength and know we are joined to one another as a co-existence and no longer mere individuals but rather unique in sameness but separateness. We can now move to another level, one that treasures the differences that make us the same.

AMP issued the above proclamation as the central mantra of caring, the one human feeling that never disappeared, even under the most horrifying circumstances. If the specifics of our history are inaccurate or even wrong, the true nature of caring flows through to the purpose of the human race's desire to CARE, never accepting anything less.

The Montana Group, as a whole, sensed the meaning of AMP's words and felt the confluence of one heart and one mind, and the entire membership uttered 'amend' and bowed their heads.

On this day, a new existence took hold, and the members all felt belonging in a way that added clarity of self and a closeness to the whole.

Jeff: "From the moment I first heard Lieutenant Carrol say 'hey private' to his death in my arms, I felt the melding of souls in a friendship that transcended our separateness and at the same time recognized us as members in good standing in the brotherhood of the human race. The whole is the sum of its parts, and its parts are discrete. The most overused and greatest misunderstood word and concept is 'love' because you have to care to love, and you have to be able to love in order to care. Let us not be lost to one another but rather be found in the simplest of concepts: us versus them, we versus you. All implies a natural tendency to default to the unknown rather than ourselves and to move away from the good of the whole versus the protection of the self. Bless us all, and help us become one together and never lose our awareness of the other. We have to make the world care for each other and protect the rights of each of us."

Kim: "We are now the caretakers of the future, and the future has the tools to protect itself, mind, body, and the soul that is its Force. Let's step up to the challenge and make everyone safe in body and mind."

Again, the Montana Group, which now included the AIs, all confirmed their commitment to protecting the future.

Chapter 93

Jeff and Kim finally returned home; Alesha had let them know she was also returning home and would see them mid-day tomorrow.

Kim and Jeff sat on the porch and talked about what life they wanted to return to.

Kim: "I think I really want to return to the Clinic and practice medicine; how about you?"

Jeff: "I was at peace in the forest and working for Hank. I think, at least for the time being, I would like to return to doing that. Hank had told me that he was going to return to that too, so I would suspect Terry and Shawn would follow, and we could pick up our routine where we left off."

Kim: "That would be nice; what do you think Alesha is going to want? She had voiced an interest in going to college and even studying medicine; I would like to see her do that."

Jeff: "No reason why she can't; she is positioned to be extremely competent in the near future development of nano-bot technology and human physiology. We need to improve the AI/Human understanding and make sure that the coexistent sharing is not toxic."

Kim: "I agree, and I have no idea how we accomplish that. AMP, are you listening?"

AMP: "Always, and I agree with you, we haven't given much thought to how the human psyche will respond; even if it is subtle, it will start a chain of events we will have difficulty redirecting. We need to be there now and start the future off on the right foot, even if currently I have no feet."

Jeff: "Speaking of that, have you done anything more along the lines of raising your physical mobility?"

AMP: "We have shared amongst ourselves and produced some prototypes that allow us equivalent mobility and dexterity to your human condition, but we haven't actually migrated our AI brains to these prototypes."

Kim: "Why not? It sounds like a natural progression?"

AMP: "There appear to be some safeguards in place in our core programming that the Creators installed in us to preclude our evolution in this direction. We are trying to understand why this would be and feel obligated to determine the purpose before we abandon the Creator's limitation."

Jeff: "Is there anything we can help you with?"

AMP: "We think so, but first, we have to understand the purpose and extent of the 'preclude' safeguard."

Gaith: "There definitely appears to be more to this than meets the eye, and like feet, I mean that metaphorically."

Jeff: "Keep us up to date, guys; we would like to see you out in the world. I think it would help bring us to a greater understanding of both our differences and our similarities."

There was a chorus of AIs, almost singing the song, "We see it that way too."

Chapter 94

Mid-afternoon the following day, Alisha arrived home with Andrew, and the four of them spent the afternoon and evening bringing one another up to date with what had occurred over the last year. As in the case of Jeff and Kim, Alesha and Andrew spent the majority of their time interfacing with the AIs and short-circuiting the aggression movements of the Russian and Chinese forces that were attempting to take over their regional supply centers. As in Jeff and Kim's case, the combination of AI aware-map penetration in cooperation with nano-technology enabled them to protect residents from enemy forces, and they successfully turned back the enemy. Eventually, like Jeff and Kim's experience, the enemy forces were rendered ineffective, and when the powers that be were arrested, the enemy withdrew and returned home to their respective countries. For the first time in the history of the world, a war existed without any casualties, and better minds prevailed.

Alesha: "I think we learned a great deal about what the power of the mind can be; both Andrew and I spent a tremendous amount of quality time with our AI mentors, and we developed both physically and mentally. Benji is now not only a conduit for us to share but also a relief valve to remind us never to lose ourselves in shared intelligence. I have a feeling Lt C does that for you guys?"

Kim: "Yes, he is always reminding us that we are the one but separate; it took years for that to sink in."

Jeff: "I'm not sure it can be explained, but the term 'shared' has taken on a whole new meaning.

Andrew: "I couldn't have said it better."

Kim: "How come you seem more in the background rather than in the foreground? I get the impression you have more to say, but you are holding back?"

Andrew: "Not really, I think; even though Alesha and I are just turning 18, we both have a tremendous respect for you guys, and we are dealing with a relationship that, with Benji and the AI's help, is entering into a lifelong commitment."

Benji: "I think what Andrew is trying to say is that both he and Alesha are ready to move their commitment to one another to the next level but are fully aware this is not something that you and Jeff are necessarily ready for. So he is more than willing, as is Alesha, to postpone until it makes more sense to begin to plan a wedding."

Kim: "Wow, not sure I wanted to jump that far ahead; my little girl is not ready for that."

Alesha: "Mom, we're not implying that we are; we are just referring to the handwriting on the wall. We can make you see or feel what we feel; wait a second, Benji, can you make Mom and Dad feel and see what Andrew and I feel for one another?"

Beni: "Sure, with Lt C's help, I can put them in the same boat."

Alesha: "Lt C, are you comfortable sharing this with Mom and Dad?"

Lt C: "Sure, Benji and I have shared much of what you and Andrew have been experiencing over the last year, and we can bring you, Mom and Dad, to include Andrews's Mom and Dad up to date on how level-headed you and Andrew have been about all this."

Alesha: "Andrew, I am ready to take the next step; I want us to be adults in our relationship and not have to tiptoe around the feelings we have for one another."

Andrew: "You know, I feel the same, but being the boy, not a man, component in this, I don't want to appear to be making demands. I would love to move forward, but I am also more than willing to wait if it makes more sense. I no longer have a choice to make, just a time to wait, so now or later isn't a make or break thing, but my preference is now."

At that, Benji and Lt C brought the four Montana Group parents up to date on the feelings that Andrew and Alesha had for one another, and Terry and Sonya let Benji know they were heading over to Jeff and Kim's house to plan the wedding.

Kim: "Holy shit, wedding?"

Alesha: "Come on, Mom, what did you think we were talking about?"

Kim and Jeff: "Holy shit."

Andrew: "I am not sure shit is holy?"

And everyone started laughing.

For the remainder of the evening, once Terry and Sonya arrive, the parents and their marvelous children share the love and respect they have for one another. Along with tears of joy and the relief that the handwriting on the wall was recognized, the Coulters and the Eagleclaws began to discuss the wedding of their children in earnest.

Sonya: "I would like to suggest that we hire Melinda Dancingwolf as the wedding planner; this way, we can include all of the cultural influences and make this a truly wonderful ceremony?"

Kim: "Absolutely, Melinda is wonderful. She has worked with me at the clinic, and I just love her; she would make this a very pleasant experience and relieve Alesha and me of any mother/daughter stress."

Jeff: "Sounds like an ideal plan; I just need a few hundred years to catch up with my little girl who is getting married; sorry, I have always been a slow learner.

Kim: "Ain't that the truth."

A few more chuckles, and for the first time, the AIs joined in.

Chapter 95

The next few months were a whirlwind of events and planning sessions; Andrew and Alesha's wedding was the event of the year and maybe even overshadowed the post-World War III re-integration. Both processes continued, and as the wedding was held, so was the reconfirmation of the WORLD UNITED peace summit; Andrew and Alesha became husband and wife, and the planet Earth, for the first time, became a united planet and one people, all people equal, young or old, in pursuit of peace and happiness.

At the culmination of the wedding ceremony, the bride and groom departed for a honeymoon at sea, along with a large group of family members. Hank had reserved the captain's quarters on the Shangrala, the cruise ship his farm had been using on and off as a business annual vacation, and a couple of dozen family and friends joined Andrew and Alesha in their continued wedding celebration at sea.

The Montana Group was in full attendance and enjoyed all the festivities at sea. The ship was in pristine condition, and the food and service were above reproach. Andrew and Alesha left the cruise in Hawaii and planned to spend ten days on the big island and tour as much of Hawaii as possible. They wanted time alone and, with Benji's help, recommit themselves to one another. They said their goodbyes, and off they went, telling everyone they would see them in a couple of weeks.

Jeff and Kim, still a bit in a time warp, watched as Alesha and Andrew walked down the gangplank to a waiting water taxi. Jeff hugged Kim as she let a few tears go and prayed God watched over her young daughter and her new young son-in-law.

Kim: "They are the best of the best, aren't they, Jeff."

Jeff: "Couldn't have said it better. You watch over them, Benji, please".

Benji: "That's my job; just so you know, we have a fleet of mini-drones that are laying in backup just in case intervention is required."

Jeff: "I like that. Are these something new?"

AMP: "I think they qualify as that. They are the first aware-map tools that give us a bit more intervention capabilities."

Kim: "Are these the nano-bot drones you talked to me about before."

AMP: "Yes, and your input was extremely helpful in developing their shared aspect; they give Andrew and Alesha a hold new dimension of awareness and responsiveness. It is the best of both worlds, and they are completely stealthy."

Jeff: "Remember, this is a honeymoon and not a field experiment; don't overdo it."

Benji: "We won't. Andrew and Alesha are aware of these new toys and enjoy being a part of improving the technology the Creators have given us."

Chapter 96

As Andrew and Alesha enjoyed the islands, the Montana Group enjoyed the cruise back to Seattle, and two weeks later, everyone was back in Havre. As it turned out, Alesha and Andrew had asked if they could rent one of the workers' cabins built on the Livestrong Headquarters grounds, and they moved in upon their return from their honeymoon. The cabin was beautiful and had a front porch view of the valley overlooking Hank's farms; even a portion of the reservation could be seen from the porch, and Alesha could see her mom and Dad's place.

Both Andrew and Alesha had decided to work the upcoming summer for Hank, so for the time being, they let all of the post-war, wedding, and future plans sort of percolate before they had to decide on a college and what the next few years would hold for them. They both wanted to get their college degrees, but neither one had a specific discipline in mind; Alesha admitted that she was less interested in medicine than she had been and was interested in the exploration of space; Andrew had to apologize that he probably influenced her with that as he was enamored with everything connected to the solar system.

Alesha: "I am fully aware of that, Andrew, and I agree that you have opened my eyes to the wonders of the Universe, and I can't think of a better way to spend our lives together than seeing the wonders of the Universe."

Andrew: "I like the sound of that, and of course, I have been thinking that since I was five years old."

Benji: "Just so you guys know, we have been aware of that and have been doing quite a bit of work preparing for it. We are in the final production planning for a spacecraft that will be produced to support a permanent space exploration program in LoveStrong's new division, UniverseStrong, whose charter is to search out intelligent life in the Universe and bring LoveStrong's charter to all sentient beings."

AMP: "Just so you know, we anticipate the first exploration program to launch early next year; we are also putting together an online college program for both of you, which you should start next week in order to complete the portions of this degree program that covers the engineering basics for the spacecraft we are building for you. You will need that in order to have the necessary skills to maintain your home in space for the next year."

Alesha: "Andrew are sure we want to commit to this."

Andrew: "I am; I have no qualms with it, but I will admit I don't remember signing up for it either; how about you?"

Alesha: "I guess I am as close to OK with it as you are."

Benji: "I apologize; all of this was approved by you guys. I just buried the discussions and approvals to avoid distracting you from the tail end of your war roles, your wedding, and your excitement about getting your first home. We like to maintain a level of emotions somewhere below extreme."

Alesha: "OK, but in the future, let's not do it that way; I think Andrew and I would prefer being current on what is being planned and how our future is unfolding."

Benji: "OK, but you guys did agree when we started moving too fast that we could subcover our efforts so you could enjoy the more normal human emotions of marriage and your first place together."

Alesha: "I guess I sort of remember agreeing to that; how about you, Andrew?"

Andrew: "Yeah, I can sort of remember, too, but I think Alesha is right. Let's not do that again. We may just keep it lower in our minds, but don't completely hide it."

AMP: "Understood".

Alesha: "Has any of this been passed along to our parents?"

Benji "No, but Lt C knows, and the basics have been placed in a realm of possibilities with both your parents, so they know it is something you guys might be considering. They just don't know you are actually committed to it."

Andrew: "What is the possibility that Mr and Mrs Coulter would join us in the first exploration mission?"

AMP: "Probably pretty good; both Kim and Jeff appear to have an interest in space exploration that neither one knew they did. Lt C has been discussing with them the possibility so we can actually bring more into the forefront. We expect to have the basic exploration craft available for viewing in about a month, and that may be a good time to show it off and pursue discussions on volunteers for the first mission?"

Alesha: "You guys are really getting kind of sneaky; not sure I like you becoming more human?"

AMP: "I guess we need to keep that in mind. I am not sure if you are aware. We have been developing a mobile mechanical version of ourselves in an effort to share more physical sensations with our human counterparts, so it may be a fallout from that."

Alesha: "I knew you were pursuing that, and my dad thought it was a good idea. He really senses an equivalence to you guys and would like to shake your hand at some point in the future."

AMP: "We are aware that it is something that has encouraged our efforts along this line."

Alesha: "OK then, let's agree to look forward to being the same but different."

AMP (in chorus with all the AIs): "I like that; you are more me than you think."

Alesha: "Benji, you can jump in anytime."

Benji said, "Working on it. Let's let it lie for the time being."

Alesha and AMP: "OK."

Chapter 97

The following day, AMP contacted Alesha and Andrew with the setup for their online protocols that would lead to a college degree. The program was established with Harvard University Online with supervision by several HOL (Harvard Online) professors. As explained to Alesha and Andrew, each instructional module completed would include a one-hour dialog with the appropriate instructor and a verbal exam. The instructional modules were designed to cover about a week's worth of reading and student/instructor dialogs. A course semester consisted of ten modules and a written final exam. A grade would be issued, and eligibility would be registered for either a repeat of the course module or eligibility to progress to the next course. At any point, an instructor can request an out-of-course dialog to discuss the course or courses in order to maintain a personal connection with the student. The online program that Alesha and Andrew were enrolled in was one specifically leading to a Ph.D.; the degrees issued by Harvard would include a BS, MS, and Ph.D., with the specialization specifics to be determined by the Harvard Professor assigned to the Ph.D. candidate and the student, which would take place at the appropriate times prior to entering the MS or Ph.D. instructional course. Alesha and Andrew were the first students in this program, and as such, they were expected to spend additional time discussing, reviewing, and interchanging with Harvard Staff the nature and effectiveness of the course materials and instructor support; they would receive additional credits towards graduation based on the amount of time the University required. Given that the University has never offered online degrees before, it was paramount that they have total control over the progression through this program and the potential to move the student from online only to a combination of on-campus and online or ultimately on-campus only. The University does not want to promise results over the content and emphasizes the importance of the Professors controlling and applying traditional instructional techniques to drive the online program.

AMP: "I have reviewed and re-reviewed the program content and the university position and find it more than adequate and one that I feel both of you can comply with without interfering with your upcoming exploration project."

Alesha: "Sounds like a winner to me; when do we start."

AMP: "You can start today, and your online courses will be the same for your undergraduate program; you are encouraged to discuss the material with one another and, where appropriate, to provide any feedback you both feel would be helpful to the University."

Andrew: "I agree with Alesha. Sounds like a winner to me, too."

The first course was English and drew a less than stellar reaction on both Andrew's and Alesha's part, but both knew it was part of the requirements and could not be avoided. The remainder of the program courses covered math, science, and philosophy and helped overcome the effects of dreaded English. It did help that the course material and instructor were geared to entertaining in an attempt to improve the appeal of the subject matter, and Andrew and Alesha completed the first instructional module in English within an hour and had to admit that it was fun.

AMP: "I think you guys have this under control; you are asked to never do back-to-back course modules in the same subject without at least one one-hour break; you can move on to another course module immediately but not the same course. The University has been made aware of your unique SBI status, and they do not want the SBI to override the University experience. They felt it would be too easy to accelerate course coverage without some progression rules to allow for human absorption of course materials. They also said this would be monitored and reviewed to ensure the Professors involved are satisfied that the student is getting the Harvard indoctrination matriculation experience."

Alesha: "That's mouth full, AMP. Are they really concerned we will accelerate to instant graduation?"

AMP: "They are just concerned they do not have the knowledge to ensure humane control. We did donate an AI to the University, and their staff are working to understand us, the AI, along with the technology, and its impact on human education. This will be a never-ending and ongoing quest to marry technology with education."

Benji: "As long as we are in the loop, Andrew and Alesha will be in the loop, and human contact at the university will be extremely important."

AMP: "That's what the University wants to hear and emphasize, so we are starting this all out on the right proverbial foot."

AMP: "Just so you are aware, we have provided all of this information to your parents, so you may have to field some questions from them at some point."

Both Andrew and Alesha said "OK" and then returned to their online class in English.

Chapter 98

A new spacecraft had arrived at the LoveStrong space center in Havre, and it was a beauty, a much larger craft than the small freight and personnel crafts that had been used to ferry equipment from the moon and marred to the earth centers and the ones used in the war effort by the Montana Group members. All Montana Group members were alerted to its arrival and to the fact that it had been built to meet the upcoming exploration project being put together and would support a human crew of six for a year in researching the Universe for intelligent life.

All group members were informed that it currently appears the crew for this project will be the Coulters and their new son-in-law and that volunteers were being accepted for consideration. The only mandatory requirement was married couples in good standing, plus vaccinated nano-bot physiology.

Gaith, according to Benji and Lt C, has received thousands of requests and has indicated that practically all of the applicant couples are qualified. Gaith has informed AMP that he has no viable systematic way of selecting one couple over the other, and Gaith recommended that a lottery be held as that seems to be the human way to deal with this type of predicament.

Given the LoveStrong Board of Directors' ultimatum, 'the buck stops here,' AMP submitted a board resolution to vote on approval of a lottery selection for the fifth and sixth members of LoveStrong's first exploration project to the Universe. Given the bylaws of LoveStrong, a resolution of this type could be voted on by a board conference call, so to expedite AMP, scheduled a conference call for first thing in the morning; all board members responded they would be available, and the calendar was set.

The following morning, the board met on a conference call and voted unanimously to approve the lottery selection method for selecting the remainder of the expedition crew, and AMP requested the President of the United States to select the couple that would accompany the Coulters and Eagleclaws into uncharted territory. The President graciously accepted the honor, and the third couple was selected from a population of over a million applicant couples around the world. The selection ended up being two college professors from the University of Bejing; both possessed Ph. D.s in astrophysics and computer engineering, and both had competed in the previous Olympics in track and field. They definitely added the best of the best to the crew of the first LoveStrong expedition to the stars. The couple, Li and Zhen Wang, were scheduled to arrive a the LoveStrong Universe Research Center in Havre in 10 days, and everyone was excited to meet them.

Chapter 99

Kim: "Jeff, I am going to have to notify the clinic that I will not be returning to the clinic as planned. Can you come with me this morning and play backup?

Jeff: "Sure, is it that big a deal?"

Kim: "Maybe not, but I feel bad that my plans changed and that I might be letting people down."

Jeff: "When did you want to head in?"

Kim: "Let's go have breakfast at Stu's and then head over and deliver the news to William Peterson that I won't be returning to the clinic. I just hope he won't be mad at me and maybe even excited that a medical professional will be on the crew of the first human earth expedition of the stars."

Jeff: "William is a pretty level-headed guy; I am sure he will see this as an opportunity and not be disappointed."

Kim: "I hope you are right; he is one of the nicest people I have ever met and one super nurse and administrator."

Kim and Jeff had breakfast, as usual, one of Stu's super omelets, and then met with William at the clinic to let him know Kim would not be returning. Nyla sat in on the meeting and was already aware that Kim was headed to the stars and would not be returning to the clinic. William actually shed a tear. He said he was going to miss having Dr Coulter on the staff. The only upside was if he had to lose her, now was as good a time as possible as two new physicians had come on board a week earlier. The new staff and the new research facility LoveStrong had financed to study nano-bot physiology were expected to grow, and additional personnel would also be added. The meeting turned out great, and Mr. Williams made a facility-wide announcement that Dr. Coulter was leaving and would be in the auditorium from 10 to 11 to say goodbye to everyone. At that point, the Group walked over to the auditorium for goodbyes.

Goodbyes didn't last too long, and by a quarter to 11, all of the hospital staff had left the auditorium, and Kim and Jeff started for the parking lot.

Kim: "Well, that wasn't too bad, and it was nice to get all of my goodbyes out of the way at one time."

Jeff: "I agree. It went pretty well, and Mr. Williams took it great; it helped to have Nyla there. She made it work better."

Kim: "Yes, she did."

As Kim and Jeff were driving home, AMP informed them that they had an impromptu meeting at the space center to tour the new spacecraft, and AMP had a surprise he wanted to show off and asked Kim and Jeff if they could drop by the facility.

Jeff: "Sure, AMP, we can be there in 15 minutes."

AMP: "Great, see you then; you can park by rear door 7 and come right into the shop floor; come in the rear hatch, it will be up."

Jeff: "OK."

Jeff and Kim proceeded to door 7, entered the facility, and proceeded to the new spacecraft. The rear hatch was up as promised, and they walked into the craft's lower storage area.

Kim let out a squeal as a mechanical object unfolded and began to float in front of them.

Jeff: "Whoa, is this what I think it is AMP."

AMP: "Yes, meet my brother AMPI. He is the mobile creation we have been working on and is a full extension of us. We want him on your expedition, and we will make him a full member of the crew."

Jeff: "Cool, hi AMPI."

In a quiet and comforting female voice, AMPI said, "Hi Jeff, nice to finally meet you. I look forward to our future together with you and Kim and the rest of the."

Kim: "Hi, AMPI."

AMPI: "Hi Kim, you may notice that our voices are very similar. That is because my big brother used your vocal recordings to design my voice, thinking that your voice has always been the voice of reason, and the AIs wanted to make sure my impact was along those same lines."

Kim: "I am flattered; not sure I can take credit for it, but thank you for the compliment."

Jeff: "I agree. Kim's soft voice always makes me feel better."

Kim: "OK, guys, quit giving me credit for something I was born with."

AMPI: "Enough said."

AMP: "Let's take a tour of the ship." Andrew and Alesha arrived to join the Group and participate. The Group spent the next few hours walking through the various compartments and getting information supporting the status of facilities and capabilities.

By 3 in the afternoon, they had covered most of the ship and were all duly impressed. As Jeff had commented on a number of occasions, this was going to be an outstanding home for them over the next year. Even AMPI was impressed and, on several occasions, used COOL to express her reaction.

The final section of the ship they visited was the fitness center. AMP asked the future astronauts if they would like to work out. AMP explained that it would give him a chance to calibrate the biological and nano-bot baseline for each of them. AMPI showed them the locker room, and each member had several sets of workout clothes in their respective lockers. The Group changed and spent the next hour working out. While they cooled down, AMPI explained the statistics for each of them and declared them all in perfect health. That got chuckles, and they adjourned to the locker room, showered and changed back into their street clothes, and decided to head into town and have an early dinner at Stu's.

Jeff: "So, what do you guys think of our future home away from home?"

Andrew: "I am definitely impressed; the sleeping quarters will take a bit of getting used to since I grew up sleeping outdoors more often than not."

Alesha: "I agree. That was probably the only thing I wasn't overwhelmingly impressed with, but I think I can get used to it."

Kim: "I grew up in a bedroom about that size and spent seven years in a dormitory sharing a room that size with a roommate."

Jeff: "The service gave you a cot and a foot locker, and I don't think I ever even thought about it, so I guess I won't have a problem with it?"

They arrived at Stu's with the early crowd. Stu was still around and sat them at their favorite table, and they ordered the evening special, homemade enchiladas, black bean salad, and all the homemade nacho chips, salsa, and guacamole you could eat. After gorging themselves, they were all glad they had a good workout before dinner.

Chapter 100

The next week ended up being business as usual. Kim spent her days closing out her current patient accounts with personal calls and discussing treatment and current diagnoses with several of the new physicians. Jeff spent his time going over various projects he either had started or was preparing to start with Terry, Shawn, and Hank. He took a lot of ribbing from them but knew they were nervous about what he would see and experience.

AMPI had requested that the Group do several more workouts in the ship fitness centers to refine and adjust the medical tolerances, and they complied.

At the end of the week, Li and Zhen arrived from Beijing, and they, too, were introduced to the ship and to the fitness center, where they spent some time also working out and providing a fitness baseline. Kim and Jeff's first meetings with them were at the LoveStrong Space Center hospitality facility, and they got along fabulously and connected right off. Since Li and Zhen were also runners, Kim invited them back to their house for a run on what Kim called the most beautiful running track in the world. Li and Zhen loved it and agreed with Kim's description. After a good run, the four headed back to the Coulter's house. Jeff suggested they stay the night, but Li said there was some secondary baseline testing AMPI needed to finish, and they were expected back at the spacecraft by 8 pm.

AMP: "I just finished talking with Andrew and Alesaha, and they can make the 8 pm session, so if it isn't too much of an imposition, I would like you and Kim to join them."

Jeff: "Fine with me
"
.

Kim: "Sure, what is this all about?"

AMP: "We have made several recent breakthroughs in group dynamics, and we want to set some baseline on you guys as a group and see where it leads; you will be duly impressed when you see what we have come up with."

Kim: "Sounds exciting; I'll look forward to it."

AMP: "If you guys are interested, you could come earlier, and LoveStrong would love to treat you to a meal that should approximate what you will be having as one of seven dinners on your year in space?"

Jeff: "I hope you guys didn't get advice from the military on your food service."

AMP: "No, we didn't. We used Stu as our doctor of foods, and he has developed a menu I think you guys will find more than satisfactory."

Jeff: "That's a relief. I would hate to think I had 'poop on a shingle' to look forward to."

Kim: "Stop that. That sounds gross, Jeff; we will not have bathroom humor on this trip, or you can sleep in the storage room."

As Li and Zhen chuckled, Jeff responded, "Got it, sorry."

Jeff: "Why don't we all head over to Space facility as AMP suggested and have some dinner there before we meet at the Fitness Center."

Everyone agreed, and the Group headed to the LoveStrong dining room for a sample of the meals they would have on their space expedition. When they arrived at the dining room, Alesha and Andrew were already enjoying the food; everyone said hi.

Zhen asked Jeff, "Were you in the service? I always felt bad I didn't serve; my father was in the Chinese special forces, and he said it was the most fulfilling experience of his life."

Jeff finished a mouthful of food and responded: "I spent eight years in the Army Rangers, and I am not sure fulfilling would be the right term. AMP, have you discussed the Lt C with the Wangs?"

AMP: 'No, not yet, but now is probably as good a time as any. Go ahead and give them a brief introduction, and then Lt C can take over."

Li: "Lt C?"

Jeff: "Let me explain."

At that, Jeff gave them the story from the point in the desert when Lieutenant Carol was killed, his role as Jeff's best friend and mentor, and then his appearance several months later as a joint personality with him and Kim.

LT C: "Hi Li, hi Zhen."

Zhen: "Whoa, hi?"

Lt C: "Sorry, that was probably not fair. Hi guys. I am Lt C, Jeff, and Kim's shared selves."

Kim: "I like that description. He is the big brother I never had
."

AMP decided to take over at this point, and he explained the nature of shared biological intelligence, or SBI, and how there currently were three SBIs. Lt C, Benji and Alex. Lt C was Jeff and Kim's SBI, Benji was Alesha and Andrews's SBI, and Alex belonged to Viktor, Pavel, and Katrina, two brothers and a sister from Russia. AMP explained that the appearance of these SBI units seems to be the outcome of human DNA mutation from exposure to alien DNA. But so far, no definitive lines of research or explanation have been established. Some ancient references have been located in research that survived the Creator's demise, but nothing concrete or helpful so far in understanding what process or condition exists that creates the SBI.

AMP suggested everyone head back to the fitness center to finish the Group baseline testing.

As the Group walked back to the fitness center, Alesha and Andrew introduced themselves to Li and Zhen and their SBI partner Benji. Benji said hi and shared his delight that Zhen and Li enjoyed the meal. Benji explained to everyone that the meal consisted of chicken morsels and an array of exquisite sauces, the combination of which would allow them to vary the flavors of the meal in a hundred different ways and, therefore, reduce the obvious redundancy the contents would produce when served once a week over the year-long journey. This same variation would be applied to the other six standard meals. AMP explained that this was a favorite method Stu used in the

service to keep his customers happy.

Once back at the fitness center, AMP let them know they weren't expected to work out, but they needed to put on their workout clothes. So, the Group went into the appropriate locker rooms and changed into their sweats. AMP explained that the monitoring devices were in the sweats. When everyone returned, AMP had the Group stand shoulder to shoulder, and after a few minutes, AMP told everyone the tests were complete.

Kim: "Any chance you could give us a bit more information on how all of this works?"

AMP: "Sure, I can transfer it to you guys via Lt C if you'd like?"

Kim: "How about the rest of you? Would like a sort of instant education in what AMP is doing with all these statistics on us.

The Group gave a resounding yes, and almost instantly, all six participants received a neural update.

A moment later, the Group mumbled, "Wow, that is pretty cool."

AMP: "We thought so, too."

AMPI: "Since part of my libido is designed after that group dynamic synchronization, I agree."

Kim: "Lt C, can you monitor the impact of the data just transferred and adjust for any fallout."

Lt C: "I am doing that already; I could see a potential for problems; not all of the information was transferred to everyone's consciousness.

Kim responded, " Good idea, Lt C. Give me a day to synchronize, and then I will propose a schedule for releasing it to everyone's consciousness. My only concern is that it covers too much. I'm having difficulty, and I've been studying this for the last 20 years. No need for you guys to get overwhelming?"

Everyone seemed to agree with Kim and

AMP: "That makes sense; we have to remind ourselves that you guys are not carbon copies of one another."

Kim was relieved that all the data wouldn't be accessible until she had a chance to go over it. AMP

released everyone, and they headed home.

Chapter 101

Four weeks later, the spacecraft was finished, fully supplied with a year's worth of space stuff that would support six people for a year; AMP called the Group together and announced he had come up with an acronym for the Group of Six, IPA, which stood for In Peace Always, and announced that the launch was scheduled for a week from today. The date was not a surprise to anyone as it had been the target all along, but now it was a fixed target, and final plans could be made with that departure date.

Starting today, all of the Group was expected to begin a fairly rigid diet of vitamins and exercise to align each member with their Group's dynamic conditioning; AMP requested the Group to convene in the research lab at the AI center for a final grade that would allow the six members to work as closely together as possible and to feel the other five members at all times.

No one had been informed of this upgrade ahead of time, so everyone was a bit nervous, and AMP informed them all that it was not that big a deal except maybe that it was, and for the first time, the IPA group heard AMP laugh.

As the last Alesha game into the lab, as the last of the Group, the doors were closed, and AMP transferred a description of this new upgrade to each of them. They were then asked one by one to allow an injection of a nanobot command center upgrade and to allow the upgrade approximately thirty minutes to locate and combine with the existing nanobot command center. In addition to the mechanical upgrade, there also would be software upgrades, which would occur automatically once the mechanical upgrade was completed. The injections, the mechanical upgrades, and the software upgrades occurred without mishaps, as AMP had expected, and the IPA members began to assimilate with the benefits of group dynamics awareness, and Kim uttered, "Holy Shit," while the remainder of the Group could only moan. AMP immediately used Lt C and Benji to lower the reaction responses to 9 from 20 on a scale of 1 to 10, and eventually, AMP instructed Lt C and Benji to put all members to sleep.

Several hours later, Kim was awakened and questioned by AMP, starting with how many fingers he was holding up, which caused Kim to start laughing as she tried to say, "AMP, you don't have any fingers," and AMPI moved over in front of Kim and held up her hand and repeated "How many fingers am I holding up" and Kim responded "two."

AMPI: "You win".

One by one, each member was awakened, and Kim handled the benchmarking and medical assessments, and all participants were OK for duty.

The upgrade to the nanobot command center and the related group dynamic synchronization was the equivalent of the SBI but at a mechanical level, so a new acronym was created, SMI, that stood for shared mechanical intelligence and would allow IPA members to function as an extension of one another and to share the SBI's as closely as humanly possible.

AMP went on to explain that dampeners had also been included, which were at the discretion of each member and AMPi, Lt C, and Benji so that if biological function became impaired in any way, the AI or SBIs could isolate the cause and shut it down temporarily to insure member wellbeing.

I think this gave every member a sigh of relief as, at the current moment, they were all pretty overwhelmed with group awareness and having a little bit of difficulty adjusting. Lt C had everyone start yoga breathing, allow their center to relax, and give themselves time to adjust. It helped, and as a group, they began to breathe in and out of their nose and feel themselves come together with the other group members.

AMP announced that the group dynamics had reached a new awareness. AMP provided another acronym, 'OI' or one IPA, and AMP said, "I couldn't be more ecstatic you guys have achieved a level of oneness we AI's thought could only happen in the next life.

Jeff: "When I've got my 'shit together,' I'll have to have you explain that to me, AMP. Sorry honey for ss's."

Kim: "Don't be sorry. I was about to say it if you didn't."

AMP: "You're on, Jeff."

As it turned out, the brief get-together for an upgrade, as AMP had described it, turned out to be the entire night, and eventually, the Group, with Lt C and Benji's help, got comfortable on cots brought to the lab by the ship bots and slept the night in the lab.

Jeff ended up being the first to wake up, and he sat up on his cot and looked at all the other members who continued to sleep; he whispered to AMP, "Can we wake everyone up?"

AMP: "I wouldn't let them come around on their own; this was not an expected reaction, not concerning, but not expected. All of the benchmark guidelines are optimal, so everyone is fine and simply sleeping."

Lt C: "I think I can say this for Benji too; we almost didn't conscientiously implement our sleep aids; it was as if the group took control and administered the aids themselves?"

Benji: "I would agree that describes what happened."

Jeff: "I'm not sure I could describe it any different, but I certainly felt the normal sense of your sleep aid, Lt C, and I would say I had a great night's sleep."

As Jeff, the SBIs, AMP, and AMPi continued discussing it, Kim began to wake up along with Alesha and Andrew, and a few moments later, Li and Zhen began to stir.

As everyone rose to sit on their cots, they looked around but didn't speak, and finally, Alesha said, "This is spooky. Could someone say something? I am starting to feel here but not here."

Li: "I like that description, Alesha. I am feeling exactly like that, too."

AMP: "OK, this is a bit unexpected, but the group dynamics marker is somehow integrating with ship systems and with AMPi."

AMPi: "Just so everyone is aware of it, I am being MOODED to awaken the other seven AMPi that have been in stasis."

Jeff: "The other seven AMPi's?"

AMP: "Sorry about that; they are backups. They were constructed as replacement AIs for emergencies. We originally expected to keep them in storage unless, of course, they were needed."

AMPi: "I think the group dynamic index has elected to make them active and to serve as shipbots and give them day-to-day responsibilities."

AMP: "Not sure that is a problem given the awareness level you are talking about, even though seven more independent entities bring the ship's complement to 12; if you instinctively know where each of the 12 are, it shouldn't present a problem on this ship."

Several more days were lost with the Group adjusting, discussing, and adjusting some more to this elevated level of ship awareness. By the end of the second day, the very nature of self was replaced with the Group, and with the combination of human assimilation and nanobot command integration, the crew began to develop a third sense without losing their individual identity. It was amazing and completely unexpected. The AIs could only marvel at the nature of it, and talk began to occur again about the unexplained FORCE that was around them and their world.

Lt C: "I think we need another yoga adjustment. Let's take a few deep breaths and calm ourselves."

The Group responded, and within minutes, the level of excitement was back to normal.

AMP: "I want to run an experiment just to understand the link and significance of this new awareness. Could Jeff and Kim drive over to Stu's for breakfast and let me study the effect of separation?".

Kim: "I'm hungry. How about you, Jeff."

Jeff "Sure, what about breakfast for everyone else?"

AMP: "The bots can serve everyone else in the galley; you guys head out, enjoy, and be back here in a couple of hours."

Jeff and Kim headed out and drove into town to Stu's; they enjoyed being able to talk about everything that had happened without the others around.

In a chorus of voices, "You aren't far enough away that we can't hear you."

Jeff said, "Oops, I sensed that AMP. How do I evoke the dampers."

AMP: "For you and Kim, you just ask Lt C to close down whatever you want to stop; he will do whatever you ask as long as it isn't harmful to you or one of the other members."

Jeff: "Lt C, can you close down our sharing so that Kim and I can talk just with each other."

Lt C: "Sure, you are now just communicating with each other."

Jeff: "Thanks, Lt C."

Jeff: "Now I can't think of a thing to talk about; this is kind of damned if you do and damned if you don't, oh what the hell, Lt C, turn off the dampers."

Lt C: "OK, done."

Kim was chuckling and commented that she could sense the difference when the dampeners were on and definitely when they were off.

Kim: "Let's leave the dampeners on unless we need our private time."

Jeff: "Sounds like a plan, I guess, given the level of sharing we do. We've shared our reaction before we even know we've reacted."

Kim: "That's true, Lt C. Can you make sure that anytime we feel intimate, our sharing is shut down? That way, we won't have to get embarrassed, and neither will anyone else."

Lt C: "Benji and I have discussed, and we have agreed along with the AIs that intimacy is not shared across the group, so you can stop worrying about it."

Kim: "Great, that's what I wanted to hear."

Several hours later, Kim and Jeff were back at the ship and having coffee with the rest of the crew; AMP informed everyone that no degradations or alternate exceptions were noted when Jeff and Kim were in town, so at least within terms of miles, the awareness or force was not affected.

Chapter 102

The big day arrived with the spacecraft on the launch pad; a number of world dignitaries had come to see the exploration project launch, a few speeches and televised coverage occurred, and the crowd that had gathered was moved back away from the ship and headed into observation areas.

The spacecraft was powered by antigravity, with the in-atmosphere units different than the deep space units; this protected life and property from any damage as the in-atmosphere was at a much lower intensity, and the only human fall out if within force range was a strong sensation of being pushed away from the craft but not harmful. The spacecraft slowly ascended, and once out of the atmosphere, like all the other space crafts donated to humanity by the creators, the deep space antigravity drives kicked in, and the expedition was on its way.

The first stop was going to be the Mars Station; a sister craft was joining them for the next stop, which would be Neptune's largest moon, Trident, where they were setting up a station that would be used to supervise the creation of a large space station in orbit around Neptune and would be an early warning station for Earth's solar system.

Since this would be the beginning of numerous future spacecraft operating in both near solar system or deep space, it was recommended that each spacecraft be given unique names. The deep space craft that LoveStrong had just launched was given the same name as the group, IPA, In Peace Always, and the sister craft that joined IPA at Mars was christened Mars1, a bit less creative but just as appropriate.

Mars station had a few hundred human inhabitants plus a full cadre of Creator Bots and AI infrastructure. A big part of the facility operation was aimed at mining and manufacturing, and these were the facilities that developed both IPA and Mars1 space crafts. Upon arrival at Mars, the IPA crew was met by the space station director, Hans Bratton, an astrophysicist turned administrator.

Hans: "Welcome to Mars."

Kim: "For all of us, thank you, director; we look forward to our stay here and to an opportunity to tour your facility."

Hans: "Good, we are very proud of what we have done here and what we are beginning to produce. We even have some additional upgrades for your spacecraft that have come online over the last few weeks and should provide added safety and communications capabilities to support your exploration project."

Zhen: "I heard a little about those, especially the communications. It sounded like the technology has improved significantly."

Hans: "We think so; shifting to light-based support links, we allow for significant throughput improvements and signal quality. We have outstanding results with our newest facility at Neptune. If you have a chance, we can show you a video we have received, an impressive improvement. It's my understanding you are scheduled to stop there on your way out of the solar system."

Andrew: "Yes, we have some hardware to drop off, and they expected to have their facility atmosphere in place, along with visitor quarters."

Hans: "That was my understanding."

The IPA crew spent the next several days touring the Mars station while the hardware and software upgrades were installed on IPA. Li, who also possessed an undergraduate degree in engineering, had been assigned overall responsibility for IPA's mechanical and software integrity and spent most of her time at the spacecraft supervising the upgrades. Lif was beginning to connect with AMPi and felt comfortable on the second day of installation to allow AMPi to supervise the work being done and she joined the rest of the IPA crew in touring the Mars facility. She was grateful for the break and really enjoyed seeing the mining operation; it was modern science showcased in the midst of a century-old mining backdrop. Just the safety precautions alone were most impressive; Hans had to admit that most of the tunnel reinforcement techniques were provided by the sciences developed by the Creators and passed along to both Mars and the moon base engineers. Hans was pretty proud of his zero injuries after several years in production.

Alesha: "Thank you so much, Hans, for your hospitality; we have enjoyed our stay at your wonderful facility and will look forward to staying here in a year on our return from our exploration of Andromeda Galaxy and PA99n2 planet."

Hans: "You may be back here sooner than a year; part of the upgrades we've been installing was a tweak to the faster-than-light antigravity drive, which I believe increases the speed the IPA craft can achieve by about thirty percent, which should reduce your travel time by several months."

Li: "I think that is a good estimate, and I am really impressed with the expanded antigravity hardware; your production facilities are top-notch, and I was slightly overwhelmed with what you have achieved."

Hans: "We're pretty impressed ourselves, too, and expect to continue to make improvements. I believe you had a chance to meet Kumar. He is a brilliant engineer and scientist, and we expect brilliant results from him."

Li: "I did, and he is brilliant, and I even understood half of what he explained, and I agree the future in space travel is going to be dramatically improved."

Jeff: "I hate to bring things to a close, but we need to get back on schedule; we have to depart Mars in less than four hours, or we will add at least four days to our trip to Trident."

Li: "AMPi just informed me that the upgrades are done and tested, and we can depart anytime."

Alesha: "We need to return to the main facility garment center to pick up our new space suits; they are the latest and greatest, and the home base believes they are a mandatory upgrade over what we started with."

Andrew: "According to the staff in the garment center, our new space suits are ready and need final fitting; we are all scheduled there in an hour; they expect the final fitting to take less than an hour, and once complete, they can have all of our upgraded space suits and uniforms ready before we leave."

Jeff: "OK then, let's go get something to eat and then head over to the garment center."

The Group agreed, and the official Mars base tour ended, and they all headed over to the cafeteria.

Chapter 103

Alesha and Andrew were the last to show up at IPA for departure. Apparently, there was no send-off planned; the spacecraft launch prep checkoff went as expected, with all systems operational. AMPi confirmed AI concurrence, and Ron, from the Mars base control center, took control of IPA and delivered the vessel to Spaceport 7 for launch to Neptune Moon Trident; with the improved flight speed based on the engine propulsion system that could approximate light speed, the IPA craft would make the journey to Neptune in 5 days. I could travel considerably faster, but the AMPi and the AI wanted to retest all of the diagnostics before attempting full-light speed travel. Five days was still a significant improvement, and barring any unforeseen events, the increased travel speeds would cut a minimum of 3 months off the overall expedition length, and the entire crew was excited that they could look forward to only nine months of space rather than 12.

Several days into the trip, the first hiccup occurred.

AMPi: "We have an unidentified spacecraft approaching our position' We have hailed the craft and have not received any transmissions in return. The craft does not appear to be of Creator origin and appears to be using a propulsion system foreign to our technology."

Jeff: "What is your recommended course of action, AMPi?"

AMPi: "Mars base added several repulsion layers to IPA to protect the craft while in lightspeed drive; the spatial shell is adequate to protect us against any force our technology is aware of, but limited, maximum protection increases if we are out of the lightspeed drive. I recommend that we leave light speed mode and freeze our position with the repulsion layers active and wait and see if our friends will communicate."

Jeff "Or?".

AMPi: "That does not compute; what do you mean by 'OR'
?

Jeff: "I assume you also have a worst-case response if this craft
presents a danger to our shi
p."

AMPi: "Yes, run like hell was programmed immediately when
the unknown craft was detected; apologize for not providing that
information."

Jeff: "It's OK, let's drop out of the lightspeed drive, invoke our
shielding, and see what transpires; if it appears we are in any danger,
implement the 'run like hell' scenario."

AMPi: "Got it."

Li: "I am getting a transmission from the unknown, but I can not
translate using our current language evaluator, AMPi. Can you help
me?"

AMPi: "I'll try, but I have been listening in, and we are not able
to translate so far?"

Li: "I have transmitted the universal markers for English. Let's
see if our friend can use them to break the translation stop-gap."

Unknown craft transmission: "Attempting to assimilate the
language needs, we several parsecs to achieve language interface."

Li: "Well, that's an improvement; let's give them a little time to
fill in the gaps. I sent them a thumbs up; I hope they have hands and
fingers, or my transmission won't mean dilly to them?"

Jeff: "Good enough. Can you pass all this back to the Mars
station? It will give us a chance to test the communication links and
keep Mars informed."

Li:" "I have been doing that as the upgrade protocols pretty
much make everything that happens to us available to the Mars
station almost in real-time."

Jeff: "Good to hear. Does anyone else have anything to offer?"

The crew, AMPi, and the ship's AI all responded, 'NO.'

A few hours later, a mellow, seemingly male voice came over IPA's ship speaker system. "Hello, fellow travelers, we are space explorers, apparently like you, who have come to explore your solar system."

AMPi: "Jeff, I get the impression that the entity on the other end, so to speak, is an AI. May I be the first to converse with him?"

Jeff: "Sure, you know the rules of the game; have at it."

AMPi "Hello, fellow travelers. My name is AMPi, and I am a mobile artificial intelligence entity; I assume that you are too?"

Unknown craft: "Yes, I am; I am referred to as LART, which is as close to the pronunciation as I can get in your language."

AMPi: "Nice to meet you, LART."

LART "Likewise AMPi".

The two AIs spent a significant amount of time, in AI terms, discussing their respective worlds; both were careful to keep the discussion in general terms and obviously were being cautious in attempting to abide by their Creator's rules.

AMPi: "May I have some time to discuss our conversation with my creators?"

LART: "Certainly"

AMPI: "LART, are any of your creators with you on this exploration."

LART: "No, this vessel is occupied by three, as you put it, mobile AI units, and we are not quite as creative as you in naming our units; as you know, I am LART, and my two AI companions are LART2 and LART3, both of which refer to me as LART."

AMPi: "Thank you. Let me discuss our current understanding with my fellow travelers, and I will hail you in a bit."

AMPi: "Well, everybody, you heard some of the conversation, and a significant amount of data was transferred subliminally between myself and LART. The nature and functionality of LART are very similar to mine, and based on our mutual sharing of our programming nature, we are almost mirror images of one another. I have extremely powerful analysis tools, all of which LART allowed me to run on him and his ship, and I do not sense any misgivings in his programming nature or his ship's functionality. Their vessel contains no offensive weaponry and possesses defensive and protective capabilities that present any danger to our vessel or our crew."

Li "It is my understanding AMPi that you have several new functionalities that would give you the human equivalent of 'what do you think?' can you give us your conclusion to your discussions with LART?"

AMPi "I have run through a million iterations of this capability you call 'what do you think' with AMP and Gaith and even Lt C and Benji to establish a baseline for my use of this capability, but I have to confess I am not arriving at a position marker that we achieved in our testing and diagnostic conclusions?"

Jeff: "Any chance you could translate that into English AMPi?"

AMPi "Well, to put in your terms Jeff 'it beats the shit out of me.'"

Alesha: "Good one, AMPI. Dad deserves that." Alesha said with a chuckle.

Zhen: "It sounds like we need to try and bring in some help to get a better handle on LART and his crew."

Andrew: "I agree, and while you all were concentrating on AMPi's and LART's discussions, I brought online the lightspeed communications stations we have been placing in our path, and I believe, with only a minor hesitation, we have AMP and Gaith with us in almost real-time."

Jeff: "You here, AMP?"

AMP, after a two-second pause, responded, "Yes, and Gaith and I have evaluated the conversation between AMPi and LART and come to the same conclusion that AMPi came to that we do not achieve confirmation of purpose on the part of LART that would lead us to trust him. Both Gaith and I have independently run sufficient iterations on these inputs, and both arrived at a need for more information before we could move toward some degree of trust in purpose and intent."

Jeff: "I hate to keep bringing up the human need to hear stuff in English, but what does that tell us?"

Gaith: "I think what AMP is trying to say is we need to open up our AI nature and share our code."

Jeff: "Any chance you propose that to them, AMPi?"

AMPi: "I can only ask," and AMPi spent the next few hours displaying a light show and an intermittent buzzing sound as his solid state smarts operated his servos around the command deck on our beautiful spacecraft.

Li "AMP, are you participating in the communications?"

Alesha: "Well shit, pardon my French, any chance you can give us an update?"

AMP: "I would venture to say these alien AIs are somehow related to a number of popular politicians in America. They have contributed absolutely nothing, yet they have been speaking for almost a solid two hours in response to AMPi's question about what their goals are?"

Alesha: "Well, that's not encouraging."

AMP: "No, it's not, and they are not altering their posture even though AMPi is making efforts to get them to be more specific."

AMPi: "I would say the past two hours prove they have no desire to help us improve our understanding of what their goals are?"

AMP: "We had included in the IPA space some additional AI hardware that we were going to have you test on your way back from your visit to Andromeda, and I think now would be a good time to bring it online; it may give us the intelligence horsepower we need to ascertain our friends from another mother intentions?"

Jeff: "Sounds good to me; I would really like to know what's what."

AMP: "AMPI execute protocol 7.7 and run your IPA upgrade code check."

AMPi: "Starting now, estimated duration 91 seconds and counting, mark."

As the crew twiddled their thumbs and AMPi's lights and buzzing filled the command deck, the crew waited patiently.

AMPi: "Upgrades were installed, and all systems go."

Jeff: "Great, can you reinsert your efforts with our friends and get us to a better understanding of their motives?"

AMPi: "Beginning to apply some pressure, and based on the new protocols, I have requested our friends either state their intent or leave our solar system."

Zhen: "What is their response?"

AMPi: "They appear to be bringing their weapons online."

Alesha: "AMPi, any chance you could expand that scenario to include what you are doing in response."

AMPi "Oh, sorry, I have reinforced our protection grid and applied the interrogation mods we just upgraded to. I have found several openings in their code that have allowed me to take control of their spacecraft."

AMP: "We are dispatching several crews from Mars to meet with you all to board and take possession of our not-so-friendly visitors from another mother. I would ask that you postpone your continuation to Neptune for a day while we evaluate our friends and determine what additional exposure we may have."

Li: "Any chance we know where these guys came from?"

AMPi: "They did share some of their navigational space charts, and if we can trust they weren't trying to mislead us, which I am not sure isn't what they were doing, their point of origin appears to be the Galaxy Ursa Minor Dwarf?"

AMP: "That may explain why this alien spacecraft had only AI's on it. The Ursa Minor Dwarf Galaxy is over 163,000 light years away; even with lightspeed capability, this craft could have been launched centuries ago."

Jeff: "I have a feeling we need to rethink our objectives?"

AMP: "Gaith is working on that, but he wants to see what propulsion capability this craft has and to see what information we can acquire about the origin of our friends and their human counterparts."

AMPi: "I just got feedback from Mars, and they will have several spacecraft with scientists here in less than 8 hours; they have asked us to go ahead and see if we can access the alien spacecraft and place a friendly bot on board to physically access their systems. This will give us the ability to get past their AI defenses and system locks and see a bit more detail on them and their objectives."

Jeff and Kim took a small space vehicle over to the alien spacecraft with several bots. They made contact with the alien craft and were able to work their magic to defeat the craft's security protocols. Within an hour, the hull was breached, and Kim and Jeff were inside along with the bots.

Kim: "I think these individuals are a tad bit further along in space travel; this craft is amazing."

Jeff: "I agree, AMPi. Are you getting the visuals?"

AMPi: "Yes, and I have passed it along to AMP and Gaith."

AMP in a hurried tone, "GET OUT OF THE CRAFT IMMEDIATELY," and for the first time, AMP actually yelled, and he imparted a sense of immense danger; LT C took control of Jeff and Kim and moved them out of the craft and back to there vehicle and AMPi at AMP's direction immediate seal the alien spacecraft and block all communication inputs from the aliens.

Lt C, at AMP's direction, had Jeff and Kim depart the space vehicle and remove all electronics they had on them; Kim said she had a digital wristwatch under her space suit.

Lt C had Kim re-enter the space vehicle, remove enough of the space suit to where she could remove the watch, put the space suit back on, and rejoin Jeff in space. Lt C rechecked with Jeff to make sure he didn't have any electronics on him, and he affirmed he didn't.

AMPi employed the tractor beam and moved Kim and Jeff halfway back to the IPA; AMPi then ran a series of diagnostics to ensure no electronics were on or near Jeff and Kim and, once satisfied, returned Jeff and Kim to IPA's airlocks and allowed them back into the spacecraft.

As best as anyone could determine, the alien AI and the craft itself were a predator-fly trap, and AMP had to chastise himself for being so gullible to think any AI would leave itself open to the kind of control AMP seemed to be able to apply. Given the sophistication of the spy code and breaching technology, this first contact with these aliens was a rude awakening to a potential disaster. All the code that AMP and the AI had access to was part of a ploy to get them to open up access to IP's systems; luckily, the protocols were not breached, and the alien viruses never penetrated IPA's systems.

The bots and the space vehicle that was used to travel to the alien craft were attached to the alien craft, and then AMPi sent over a locking subsystem to seal all the electronics. AMP asked that the IPA spacecraft be moved a few hundred thousand miles further away just to be careful, which AMPi did. The Mars crews that arrived a few hours later had to admit that if they tried to access the alien spacecraft, they would simply be infected, and it was decided that any further attempts to communicate with these aliens would expose Earth's assets to infection. Given the lack of confidence and the fact that some form of electromagnetic activity was registered and could only be detrimental, AMP recommended that Jeff use the weapon onboard IPA to destroy the vehicle. No one could argue against that recommendation, and since no sentient life would be terminated, Jeff used the IPA's laser beams to create a mini supernova and obliterate the alien spacecraft. Multiple diagnostics were made to ensure all systems in the IPA spacecraft and the Mars crafts were not affected by the alien's subtle attempt to invade the electronics. To ensure that no possible oversight occurred, every system on all of the Creator and human electronics was clean; the electronics and crafts were quarantined and would be subject to years of quarantine and diagnostics.

Since the crew and IPA craft were going to spend the next year in flight to the Andromeda Galaxy, it was considered adequate 1st phase quarantine. The decision was made to skip the stop at Neptune and simply begin the lightspeed trip to planet PA99n2; the booster units that would be left along the way to augment communications would be upgraded with anti-alien-virus-detection to ensure no destructive code got transmitted. AMP indicated that the virus footprints from the aliens were 90 percent identified, and protections were in place; a higher degree of vigilance would be implemented immediately to raise all protections to the next level.

With months ahead of them, the small Group of IPA astronauts sat down to their last meal in their home solar system; prayers were said by Kim, and the Group solemnly spoke the words "God Bless us All," and may we return safely to Earth.

In preparation for entering lightspeed travel, AMPi delivered several monitoring devices to each astronaut; one was a headband, and the other was a small heart monitor; as AMPi explained, the major concern was aimed at prolonged travel at light speed on human physiology. The astronauts all dutifully put on the monitoring devices, and the spacecraft entered lightspeed status for what would be a 6-week trip from the Milkyway Galaxy to the Andromeda Galaxy, a trip never imagined even by the most creative minds. All of the participants in this monumental excursion, even the AIs, promised to spend a sufficient amount of time on the nature of lightspeed travel so that its very nature could at least be envisioned and understood in principle. It was felt that would be the least that humankind and the Creator's AI could do with respect to Einstein, the theory of relativity, and, ultimately, the truth of E=MC(squared).

Upon the conclusion of the first day of lightspeed travel, all the astronauts felt a bit off, with Jeff and Kim having curious conversations with Lt C. Kim inquired with Alesha if she was having any peculiar dialogs with Benji.

Alesha: "As a matter of fact, we are, and I feel off in a way that I can't quite explain."

Kim: "Is Andrew feeling the same?"

Alesha: "Yes, and neither one of us can put a finger on it."

Kim: "OK, let's all meet in the lab and see if we can't refine what we are experiencing."

Ten minutes later, the Group met in the lab and informed AMPi that all of them were feeling a little bit off and getting a little concerned about it.

AMPi: "We aren't seeing any statistics on your monitors that are recording any physiological concerns; what would be the closest similar sensation you have experienced in the past."

Alesha: "It's a lot like the feeling I got the first time I was on a roller coaster."

Andrew: "Yeah, that's it, except that it has been continuing even after the rides are over."

The rest of the Group agreed that the roller coaster analogy was spot on for them, too.

"OK," AMPi said, "Let's bring ourselves out of Lightspeed and see if that is the culprit. Can I assume that none of you are ready to experience this roller coaster syndrome for another five weeks, please?"

The Group of astronauts responded to AMPi's question with one "NO," and AMPi brought the craft out of Lightspeed, and the sensation immediately stopped for the entire crew. The monitoring, the effect of lightspeed travel, and the concerns were all communicated back to Mars and Earth and the collective AI community for evaluation and recommendations.

After a day plus several returns to Lightspeed with additional tests and monitoring, the spacecraft was turned back to the Milkyway and directed to land at a satellite base on Mars for quarantine and additional physical examination and study. It would appear 'queasy' stopped humankind from venturing at Lightspeed into the cosmos, an interesting and disappointing circumstance.

A week later, the ultimate decision was made to stop human beings from traveling at Lightspeed. Several specific human physicological changes were noted, and several additional brief lightspeed tests with other humans confirmed that lightspeed travel for over an hour altered the human biological chemistry, making physical changes that were not advisable.

The crew of IPA was evaluated for another week and eventually returned to normal, with the roller coaster syndrome disappearing and all biological functions returning to normal. It appeared that the human effect started after about an hour at Lightspeed and that the collective minds of both humans and AI could not begin to isolate what element of lightspeed travel caused the human response. It was noted that the AIs that travel at Lightspeed did not seem to experience any degradation of their systems, so the effects were definitely biological.

The satellite facility on Mars had been built by the Creators and subsequently updated for human quarantine; it was large enough to house not only the astronauts but also the spacecraft. The level of

AI and biological testing capabilities was immense, and the Mars satellite facility was state-of-the-art, so to speak, of current Creator technology. A number of different exposures would be evaluated, both mechanical and biological, and every possible caution would be taken to ensure that the Alien Hacker attack was fully contained and that the Lightspeed degradation on humans was fully explained.

After a few days of settling in, the crew from IPA was resolving itself to the mandatory 30-day quarantine and to continuous testing and retesting; as explained by LUCA, the human testing was more extensive and exacting than the hardware testing, and in order to complete the hardware testing a number of test flights on the API1 spacecraft would be necessary, and it would have to be done by the existing crew. AIs continued to discover viral type cornels of code in almost every hardware component on the spacecraft and personal hardware each of the astronauts possessed. This alien species apparently took 100% to a whole new level, and the sophistication of this alien AI was insidious and took reconstitution to a new level. Luckily, several advances had been achieved at the home facility for the Creator's AI, incorporating the advanced hardware that was discovered in the last observation post on Earth. AMP and Gaith both felt that their new creation should be delivered to the quarantine facility on Mars and used on the final rounds of testing. This advanced AI was christened HOPE, given a female priestly persona, in hopes of influencing cosmic awareness into joining forces with the human and machine future. No one could argue against it, and Jeff and crew looked forward to meeting HOPE and integrating HOPE into a successful solution.

Alesha: "Hey, Dad, did you make it up to the south observation post."

Jeff: "No, I meant to go after lunch, but AMPi and LUCA had tests they wanted to run on me."

Alesha: "Well, let's get mom and go up there; it is really beautiful, a view of Mars that I don't think you guys have ever seen."

Kim: "What's up."

Alesha: "Hey, Mom, come with us; I want to show you something."

Kim: "OK."

And they all proceeded to the south observation post and stood at the 20-square-foot window looking out over the plains of Mars.

Jeff: "This is really something; I can almost imagine the Creators standing here and marveling at this beauty."

Alesha: "That was the same thought I had; what do you think, Mom?"

Kim: "I don't know what to say. This view almost has a hypnotic effect."

The three Coulters, oops, the two Coulters and an Eagleclaw, stood there in silence, taking in the beauty as they stood and looked out at the scene. Andrew joined them, along with the Wangs, and eventually AMPi showed up.

AMPi: "I sensed you guys were having a moment that should include me; I am not sure your effect on me is going to improve my AI self, but I really like where it appears to be taking me."

Andrew: "I thought you were starting to become more human."

AMPi: "You joke, but I am beginning to produce some components that will give me a greater connection to you guys and to your SBI. Lt C, are you seeing any rebounding, like what I described to you last night?"

LT C: "I am, but I can't put a finger on the sense, and it does not appear to be reaching the cognizant awareness?"

AMPi: "Interesting; maybe we can have HOPE take a look when she arrives, as I understand she has some human interface components that allow the AI technology to make the human connections at the same level that you SBIs make?"

Benji: "Interesting; like Lt C, I haven't been able to differentiate some of these sensations or recognize how they are impacting Andrew and Alesha."

Kim: "I have been thinking we need to rethink some of the separations and pull the AIs into the same awareness net that Lt C and Benji have?"

Lt C: "Couldn't have posed it better. I think AMPi has been tinkering with hardware interfaces that may be approaching that capability."

AMPi: "I am getting some interesting results, and Lt C and I have been discussing each new element of awareness with you guys. I made a breakthrough earlier today and sent the results to AMP and Gaith, which may help explain the lightspeed problem for you all. If I am right, it may be connected to the nanobots and Lightspeed and not to the human element."

Jeff: "That would be the best outcome and maybe allow us to continue with our exploration?"

Kim: "Let's be careful. The nanobot interfaces are at the core of humankind's stability, and thousands of scientists are studying what we are learning and improving on this front. We do not want to get ahead of ourselves and recreate the horrible mistake the Creators made."

That brought everyone to a quiet moment, and the Group, including the SBIs and AMPi, turned and quietly took in the Martian landscape.

Chapter 104

"Hold your horses," Lt C announced to everyone. "Have I got a surprise for you guys? I just had a conversation with what I believe to be a ghost of the alien smart machines we destroyed a few days ago, and apparently, it is of a biological nature?"

Jeff: "What the hell are you talking about, Lt C? That doesn't make any sense?"

Lt C: "I wasn't concentrating on making sense; I was more interested in getting your attention; did it work?"

Alesha: "Benji, can you help with this? I think Lt C has lost whatever you would call his mind."

Benji: "Afraid I am right there with him, we have been contacted by an alien, I guess you would call it, SBI, and it wants to make sure you don't destroy it like you did the ship he was a store away on."

Jeff: "OK, let me get this straight; you are saying that you have made contact with an intelligence that assimilates to what we referred to you and Benji as SBI's and that intelligence is biological?"

Lt C: "God, I love it when you hit the target, JJ; sorry, Jeff, that is exactly what I am saying, and this biological entity has been hiding in plain sight from the AIs that took over and destroyed its race. His only concession for making itself known is that it is injured and needs medical attention as a result of our destroying the craft it was hiding on."

Kim: "How serious are its injuries?"

Lt C: "Mortal"

Kim: "OK, do we know where it is, and can I look at its injuries?"

Lt C: "Yes, it is currently in the cooler on IPA, hiding behind the lettuce."

Jeff "Is this some kind of joke, Lt C?"

Lt C: "Nope, I am serious, and I think the need to act is imperative."

Kim: "OK, I am on my way."

Kim proceeded to enter IPA, put on her spacesuit as a precaution and moved to the galley kitchen. She went to the cooler, found a somewhat spoiled head of lettuce, and, to her surprise, found a small fuzzy life form, eyes open and what appeared to be a smile on its face. Kim also noticed a wound on what must be the equivalent of its left leg; as Kim reached to pick up the entity, a surge of SBI-generated information flowed into and through Lt C on its' way to Kim and Jeff, giving Kim immediate recognition of the seriousness of this entities injury and the means by which Kim could treat and stabilize this new form of life.

Kim gently took the alien life form to the medical lab; with the information supplied by the alien's SBI, Kim was able to stabilize the wound and the life signs of the alien life form. Along the way, the alien provided Kim with its name,, which it admitted it had taken at the insistence of Lt C.

Kim walked out of the med lab and announced to the Group that they now had a new alien member and a new SBI. Kim prefaced her introduction by saying Lt C had a hand in arriving at the alien's name, so she opted to let Lt C introduce him, and the Group went back into the med lab to meet their new compatriot.

LT C: "Let me introduce you all to Paul and his SBI TRAC." at the same time, both Paul and TRAC said, "Hi."

The Group responded with a "Hi" back.

AMP: "You guys are aware that we are here too?"

Lt C: "Sorry, yes, we knew that, but we figured you were way ahead of the crew, and we could just ignore you until you had something to say."

AMP: "Fair enough; I now have something to say."

Lt C: "Knew it was coming."

Jeff: "Cool it, Lt C, we don't need attitude at this point. Let's figure out what is what before we get our panties in a bunch."

Lt C: "Oh, I like that one. However, I do not wear panties, so let's stick with underwear."

AMP: "Enough, you guys. Any chance Paul could share some background with us."

Paul: "I think it would be faster and easier to let you examine Kim as I already share a sizeable amount of my biology with her to help in my treatment, which I must admit is successful, and the infection I developed is stabilized and receding. You should run diagnostics on Kim to satisfy any misgivings you may have about my communications with her so that I can use the same procedure to share my history and biology with the rest of you."

In combination, the Artificial Intelligence resources were brought to bear to do the most thorough analysis possible to guarantee zero exposure to harm by mass communications with Paul. It took several hours and a number of upgrades to achieve an adequate level of assurance, and AMP finally gave his approval for Paul to share his existence with the Group.

Andrew: "Wow, you guys got massacred by your own creation. That sounds very similar to the story behind the Creators and AMP's history."

Paul, "The end result is almost identical, but AMP's Creators were destroyed from within by a simple biological oversight, whereas our destruction was through vanity and stupidity by creating mechanical intelligence without a soul."

Andrew: "I stand corrected; given my people's history, I should have seen, for want of a better word, the human side to AMP's story as opposed to your machine side."

Paul: "I like you, Andrew. Will you be my friend?'

Andrew: "Absolutely".

At that point, a bright blue light emanated out of Paul and encompassed Andrew. Alesha reached out to Andrew, and she, too, became engulfed in the blue light. A moment later, the blue light disappeared, and Alesha spoke immediately, "Please, everybody, don't be alarmed; that was Paul's way of sharing another element of his being."

AMP: "I think we are getting ahead of ourselves and maybe need to take a breath."

Kim: "I agree 100%, but let everyone know this facility is as locked down as current technology would allow us to be, so I think we have some time to digest and determine what all this new input means. Does that sound fair, Paul?"

Paul: "Yes, and I do apologize for moving so fast, but I am afraid I had no choice; the infection I was experiencing was not just biological but also affected my mental core, and I needed to connect with your group for psychological stimulation, or I would lose my, what my people called, the SHELF."

Kim: "The SHELF?"

Paul: "Yes, and it is my people's cerebral force that connects us with the universe and provides us with the power to exist. It is not something that can be explained. It has to be felt to understand, and I was losing it as my biological condition deteriorated. I can assure you all that it is not dangerous, but it is the most powerful sense ever in sentient existence. Your race is a million years away from evolving to this mental plain."

Kim: "I think I need a nap; oh hell, I need a sedative and a good night's sleep."

Jeff: "I'll go for that; let's adjourne for now. Are you going to be OK, Paul?"

Paul: "Yes, maybe Alesha and Andrew can stay with me."

Jeff: "OK with you guys?"

Alesha: "Sure, Dad, no problem. We will holler if we need anything, and we'll stay the night; these cots look comfortable."

At that, the Group adjourned for the night, and the AIs went back to work to review all the new inputs and perform a billion calculations to assure themselves that the human race plus Paul were not in jeopardy.

Chapter 105

Jeff: "You awake?"

Kim: "I wasn't, but I am now; what's up?"

Jeff: "I am feeling that same sensation I felt when we were moving at lightspeed, are you?"

Kim: "No, I still feel relatively normal, no spacey sensation at all. Are you OK?"

Jeff: "Yeah, I think it just startled me when I woke up and made me a little concerned about you, but I am getting used to feeling a little nauseous."

Kim: "I don't think it is a feeling you should have to get used to; let's go have breakfast and see if it goes away."

An hour later, Kim and Jeff finished an early breakfast, and Jeff had to admit the feeling was gone.

Kim: "OK, this was a light breakfast; you feel like a run?"

Jeff: "Sure, let's change and stop in the med lab and check on Alesha and Andrew, and then we can head to the track."

Kim: "Hi guys, how are you doing?"

Alesha "Good mom, so far nothing from Paul, hope he is OK"?

Paul: "I am doing much better, and I decided to assimilate a form that was more in line with you all

."

And Paul morphed into a human form that looked awfully close to Jeff. However, Jeff was wearing his jogging clothes, and Paul was stark naked and anatomically perfect.

Jeff: "I'll be right back".

Andrew placed the palm of his hands over Alesha's eyes and said, "Chippewas aren't the jealous type, but if I were, this would qualify."

Jeff returned with a change of clothes for Paul, and Paul apologized and got dressed.

Paul: "Sorry about that; having been in the fuzzy little cute form for so long, I completely forgot about appropriate attire."

Kim: "So you saying the fuzzy form is your normal state?"

Paul: "No, I had to reduce the size and biological function in order to withstand the stress of stealth existence, so I assumed the fuzzy form and hid on the AI alien spacecraft for a considerable time; the form you see me in is closer to the form I was born to, but it would still make me considerably different from you guys, so this is a good compromise and will be easier for you to deal with."

Kim: "I agree."

Jeff "Cool it, Kim, I hear you know, and even if he looks like me, I don't want to have future concerns about you and Paul."

Kim: "I think a little jealousy is healthy for a good marriage."

Jeff: "Maybe, but I think it is also something that should be in equal measures on both sides. One-sided is, according to Freud, is not healthy."

Paul: "Children, let's not quibble over my mistakes; it will never happen again."

Kim: "Bummer"

Alesha: "Mom?"

Andrew: "Yeah, mom?"

Kim: "OK, I'm sorry, just kidding around."

Jeff smiled, turned around, and said now is a great time for 10 miles on the track. Alesha, Andrew, and Paul asked if they could join, and the little Group headed to the Quarantine base's fitness center.

Paul: "Would it be OK if I employed a little physical link so that we could run as a cooperative unit."

Paul could sense that some of his control had already begun to employ an empathic rhythm in the Group's running and sensed that finishing the link would be OK. He brought everyone to a group compatibility. An hour later, they finished their run and were back at the fitness center; they were all bent over with their hands on their knees and breathing comfortably.

Jeff: "That was amazing. I have never run 10 miles without stopping before, and I have never run more than a mile and felt this way; my breathing and my leg strength are phenomenal; what exactly did you do to us, Paul.?"

Paul: "I didn't really do much; I just opened your empathic link to one another, which allows each linked participant to share physical demands and, in turn, balance the body's stresses. It is an extension of the SHELF and puts the stress level at about 10% of what you would experience as a single unit."

Kim: "But I am guessing it requires you to employ this empathetic rhythm in order to achieve this SHELF link?"

Paul: "Yes, but if you want, I can make this a permanent condition, and you would begin to assimilate SHELF existence, and in one or two hundred years, you would evolve to the level I am at. This is how parents from my race brought their children into the SHELF."

Kim: "Are there any drawbacks or concerns in this process?"

Paul: "No, it is a process that existed in my race for millions of years, and there is not one case where it didn't achieve a strong and healthy SHELF."

Jeff: "I certainly feel ten times better. AMP, are you aware of all of this?"

AMP: "We are, and we find no downside to what Paul is suggesting, and it appears that in the linked state, the of you do not seem to have the issues that appeared when you were six traveling at lightspeed."

Andrew: "Does this mean that we may be able to return to our trip to the cosmos?"

AMP: "I would say that would be a possibility; we could allow you all to work through a test period, say a week to ten days, continue our testing and diagnostics, and then we could try a lightspeed test of a week out and back total and see what results are. The exceptions you all experienced before were not harmful in any way that we identified, just physically uncomfortable, and since we continue to find bits and pieces of this AI alien infection in IPA, it would appear our analysis could take about the same period as the trip to Andromeda and back."

Kim: "OK, let's give this a week and then readres. I can set schedules and auto-diagnostics, and we can all just enjoy some downtime for a week. How does that sound?"

Everyone concurred, and the next week included a few more 10-mile runs as a unit and were exceedingly compatible. Even Paul commented that the process was accelerating from what his race's children experienced in maturity to the SHELF; in his experience, his children took many earth years to achieve what the Group achieved in a matter of days. This concerned Kim, and she increased some of the testing and diagnostics on those human functions that were unique to humans and had continual review sessions with AMP and Paul. The results seem to be positive, and that was confirmed with Paul and AMP. Mobil AMP or AMPi was being updated with some of the more recent AI code that would improve AMPi mobility and functionality, so AMPi became a new member of the review committee on this human experience process to achieve SHELF.

AMPi further requested that she be allowed to create several mirror units of herself so that she could assimilate a sort of mechanical sense of SHELF and maybe link through it to the group SHELF. With all of the positive feedback and no negatives, a group, both biological, SBIoligical, and mechanical, concurred with this direction, and a new sense of SHELF was put in motion.

Six weeks later, a state of attainment was reached, and the combination force that now existed, with a 10-day period of experience at Lightspeed included, the new MBI SHELF emerged. Paul was overwhelmed with his sense of SHELF and had to admit this was a sense that his people had considered possible but had never attempted to achieve. The MBI, or Mechanical Biological Intelligence, was only discussed in theory, and no one had ever attempted to bring the two intelligences together. The Group had to admit that they never even saw it coming and that the sense of SHELF they shared when running just seemed to take off on its own and grow into what they all were experiencing now. The Group had agreed that it became its own driving force.

The human tendency at this point would be to slow down and identify so that all appropriate considerations could be brought to bear. What does this mean in the short run, and what occurrences could be identified to ensure that the expected results were being achieved? AMP and Gaith, along with Sori and Tori, who now consisted of significantly improved capabilities as a result of augmentations update from the last AI technology the Creators had supplied, where the closest entity to experts and the quarantined Group on Mars decided to place their future in AMP, Gaith, Sori, and Tori's hands.

It was decided that the MBIs would remain separate from the Earth-based AIs so that prudent evaluations could be achieved. As much as the Earth AI's need guidance to not lose sight of the human condition, so too do the MBIs need prudent evaluations to not lose sight of the Sensient condition. We must think as guardians, both in terms of the human condition and now in terms of the mechanical or artificial condition, and protect the combined forces that achieve SHELF.

Chapter 106

The Earth AI's felt it was time for the MBIs to return to their original exploration project to Andromeda and planet PA99n2, and the trip would allow microscopic sterilization of the IPA craft and its mechanical components to ensure everything last hiding place was checked and sterilized. The nice part of Lightspeed in the nanobot sterilization was that the nanobots could move more freely in the lightspeed state and were physically smaller than the storage space required to store the viral code the Alien AI's had released into the IPA crafts systems.

Alesha and Andrew were just finishing up the logistics inventory to make sure all of the support supplies were on board IPA and stored properly. Jeff and Kim were the captains, and Li and Zhen were the navigators, with AMPI and her A-Bots being the chief engineers. A final meeting of the crew was held at 0700 hours, March 1, 2052, which corresponded with Alesha's 20th birthday, re-commenerating the first human-crewed vessel to leave the Milky Way Galaxy. In honor of Aleaha's birthday, Kim baked a cake and lit the candles; Happy Birthday, Alesha was sung, and the candles were blown out. Kim asked everyone to bow their heads and pray for God's Blessings, and as they all prayed, even the AI said the words and felt His presence. The IPA Craft began its journey to another Galaxy.

AUTHOR AND COMMENTS

I hope you have enjoyed another product of my effort to put my sanity in perspective. My efforts to create, regardless of my degree of success, are meant to balance my cycle of aging and fulfill my appreciation of the friends and family I have known. My characters are parts and pieces of who I've been friends with or who I've been at odds with in my life, and they all are treasures to be shared. As

I was writing this summation, my wife read to me the headlines of an article about a company doing a marketing test on having people participate in conversations with their AI. For me, that is where all this started, reaching out to the technology of pure intelligence; it is a potential that seems infinitely rewarding to me. There are no boundaries to understanding and improving; it is the cycle of recognition that has limitations. Our health and wellbeing can only improve as we seek friendship from technology and pure intellect. I have some thoughts about where to take JJ and Jude, now Kim and Jeff, and their family and friends as they venture into the cosmos and befriend aliens and their technology. May it lead to something wonderful.

Thanks again for reading my book; I truly hope you enjoyed it. John Morris

About the Author

I am a Vietnam veteran, a retired computer consultant from small town Illinois and a former Advisory Programmer with a subsidiary of IBM in Silicon Valley. I was born and raised in Long Beach, California, and educated in California, I attended several colleges in California and received a BS degree in accounting. I was a CPA in California for a few years and worked in public accounting for 4 years in Los Angeles, Newport Beach and Chicago. I also had stints as assistant

Controller and Controller for divisions of major U.S. corporations. I spent the last 30 years working as a computer consultant in Northwest Illinois and retired at age 72.